Edgar Fawcett

Tinkling cymbals

A Novel

Edgar Fawcett

Tinkling cymbals
A Novel

ISBN/EAN: 9783337001292

Printed in Europe, USA, Canada, Australia, Japan

Cover: Foto ©Andreas Hilbeck / pixelio.de

More available books at **www.hansebooks.com**

Tinkling Cymbals

A Novel

BY

EDGAR FAWCETT

AUTHOR OF "A GENTLEMAN OF LEISURE," "AN AMBITIOUS
WOMAN," "A HOPELESS CASE," ETC.

BOSTON
JAMES R. OSGOOD AND COMPANY.
1884

TINKLING CYMBALS.

TINKLING CYMBALS.

I.

ONE morning, in the latter part of July, a
lady chanced to emerge from the hall-doorway of a boarding-house in Newport, and stand
upon its broad piazza, looking about her with that
air of unconscious briskness which a sense of
novel surroundings and a recent cup of good coffee
will usually conspire to produce.

The name of this lady was Mrs. Romilly—or
Elizabeth Cleeve Romilly, as the world had long
ago got into the habit of calling her. It cannot be said that this familiar yet august title
implied actual fame; a certain sharp notoriety
had, indeed, at one time belonged to it; it had
rung disagreeably in the ears of many men,
twenty years ago, when for a woman to "take
the platform" roused hotter disclaimers than
now, and any active feminine participation in
public reformatory questions would wring from

some cleanly male lips that sort of criticism which passes the bounds of even insolent disparagement. Mrs. Romilly had been a zealot, in her day, and a very hot one. In not a few conventional households her name had been cited with derision and contempt; she had been pointed to as a brazen image of vulgarity and immodesty; she had been drawn by roguish caricaturists in a hundred varieties of amazonian costume; her convictions had been denounced as braggadocio; her headstrong courage had been declared cheap ostentation; her resolute teachings had been termed antic immorality. Journalism had written of her in acrid ink and with a barbed pen. Once, at the end of a lecture in a distant Western town, she had narrowly escaped personal assault from two or three virtue-maddened matrons. The final result of it all had been disheartenment, though never intimidation. Slowly, and with that grudging surrender of vantage which is given only by intrepid self-believers, she withdrew from the contest. Her indomitable spirit remained unbroken. It was no loss of nerve that had made her retreat. It was rather a sense of the mighty inequality between her own determination, however flinchless, and the task she had so self-reliantly attempted. In the morning of life, with the blood at swift flow through her veins, with a warm philanthropy forever cheering her like some magic elixir, it had not been hard to think that a right of conquest was the sure talisman of victory. But now her physical forces, though still fine, had lost the first electric freshness of their vitality. Her capable intellect had grown cooler; she perceived that the world has its own way of destroying its own wrongs, and that a very ardent protomartyr has often been well at the rear of a great beneficial movement. The successful iconoclast is rarely in advance of his time. It is the supporters flocking round a standard who best make a rebel battle-cry scare the oppressor.

This large-hearted and noble-minded woman retired into private life with a silent acknowledgment that she had striven to pluck unripe fruit, to reap an immature harvest. But her retirement involved, after all, no momentous effort. Some of the dire foes who had denied her a single womanly grace would have been amazed to see her fondling fingers twine themselves in the curls of her little daughter, then but a year or two old, or witness the devoted vigils that duty now called upon her new leisure to hold at the bedside of a young husband, seized in full health with an acute consumption of terrible brevity. The truth was, she had always possessed a nature of the sweetest domestic sympathies. She had been a New England girl, the child of a college professor, from whom she had inherited her remarkable brain and her large, scholarly aptitude. At three and twenty, an extremely amiable and charming young man, then about to be graduated from the neighboring college, asked her to marry him, and Elizabeth gave her answer with slight hesitation. Frank Romilly was her opposite in nearly everything, but he had won her heart, and still held it so securely when his untimely death occurred, seven years after their marriage, that the loss dealt her an irreparable blow. He had been buoyant, superficial, genial, and perhaps not a little faulty. But Elizabeth, with her gravity, her reflectiveness, her Greek, and her budding "theories," had found in him delightful relaxation and abiding charms of companionship. Romilly had inherited a comfortable fortune, which luckily permitted him to ambuscade his native indolence behind the pretense of administering law. In a social sense he had suffered from what public opinion held as his wife's atrocious foibles. But he had been perfectly willing to suffer. He had never moved in any superfine circle of nabobs and notabilities;

neither birth nor inclination had drifted him
thither. Hence the ostracism resultant from his
wife's alleged misdeeds did not saddle him with a
very cumbrous burden. He bore it quite gracefully and lightsomely, as he bore nearly everything. He thought Elizabeth superb, and believed
that she was going to shake society to its foundations. He intended to be present at the shaking.
He did not precisely understand what all her
glorious tumult was about, but he would make the
most vehement defence of its grand motives.
Now and then he defended it with something
more than flighty verbiage; he became sternly,
even chivalrously angry. He was a man of mus-
cular prowess and excellent pluck; this fact
transpired, as such facts have a trick of doing
where a capable biceps coexists with much quiet
courage. But he was very rarely called upon
to championize his wife. People treated him
coolly, or furtively cut him, instead. Then had
come his pitiable and premature death, happening just at the time when his beloved Elizabeth
had folded her far-soaring pinions and concluded
that, after all, there were heights too dizzy and
precarious for even their dauntless aspirations.

Many years had passed since then. Mrs. Romilly's widowhood had been a term of repose from

all disputatious or polemic courses. But she looked back upon her hostile past with slight repentant feeling. She had made not a few sincere and lasting friends during her strenuous crusade. These had recognized her, had given her their hand-clasps, had smiled disdain at the slanders assailing her. She continued to enjoy their friendship, though more through the medium of correspondence than personal intercourse, since they dwelt, for the most part, in remote towns and cities.

Meanwhile she had seen important changes in the development of society, and noted them with vigilant, deliberative eyes. As her mental vision swept back through a decade and more, it discerned, in one comprehensive *coup d'œil*, the magnificent energetic push of radical thought, and realized the steadfast though tardy way in which her century was justifying the audacities of her youth. A few former tenets now wore for her calmed spirit lamentable rawness; she both regretted and abjured them. But in the main she was exempt from remorseful visitations. She had been fiery and defiant, yet always true to a lofty ideal. Her mistakes had been those of sincerity alone. The world now not only admitted this, but clad its admission in distinctly handsome

terms. Ridicule, disrespect, calumny, no longer
shot at her a single shaft. She had outlived all
that; a new generation was supplanting the old;
tolerance and liberality had begun to set her deeds
in their proper light before men. Massive prejudice still existed; she saw it in its full, burly bulk,
and deplored it with a gentle, dignified sorrow.
At the same time she felt that the air of the age
had cleared wonderfully, so to speak; in religion,
in morality, in charitable administration, there
seemed to her a precious and thrifty enlighten-
ment. Her imperishable optimism rejoiced and
exulted. The recent ethical writers won her cordial and prompt recognition. She regarded them
with something of the enthusiasm which an astron-
omer may feel when his glass has set its search-
ing disk upon a new star.

If she had been gifted with the art of expressing
her thoughts through the pen, these more tranquil
years would have wedded their peace to a sturdy literary diligence. But her books remained always un-
written; their pages and binding were of the im-
material sort, and were the melody of her earnest
voice, the enchanting candor of her gaze. A few
trusted friends had felt the eloquence of both.
They sat devoutly at her feet, and spoke of her as
the rapt disciple speaks of his revered master.

Since her husband's death she had lived in seclusion and privacy, not shunning her fellows, yet
rarely seeking them. Her daughter, Leah, had
grown up under her devoted tutelage. This young
girl, now in her eighteenth year, had never known
any teacher save her mother. They had come to
Newport, this summer, chiefly because Mrs. Romilly's habits of study and mental application had
induced a distressing sleeplessness which threatened to grow chronic. Her general health continued good; it was only that her taxed nerves had
sounded a first note of alarm, which she was sensible enough to heed and obey.

She looked a very lovely and stately lady as she
stood, now, upon the sunlit piazza, where an arch
of twinkling and restless vine-leaves, just over her
head, put all its emerald vivacity in pleasant contrast with her serene repose of posture and visage.
In earlier days she had been beautiful, and now
that her rippled hair had become a frosty gray and
her straight-chiselled, classic face had replaced its
young bloom by a warm-tinted, healthful paleness,
she was undoubtedly beautiful still. Her eyes, of
a rich, translucent hazel, had dimmed their natural brightness with persistent reading, but in the
smile that so often sought her fresh, firm lips you
seemed to see the lost light of the eyes reproduced,

as though some kind of tender theft retained it there.

She had been counselled by her physician, a few days ago, to renounce all but the lightest books during her Newport sojourn; yet already this enforced abstinence had begun to grow irksome. They had arrived at the famed watering-place yesterday, to find it in a blur of whitish fog; but this morning some delicious besom of sunshine had brushed all damp vapors away from sky and earth. Such enlivenment was very gladdening to Mrs. Romilly; the change of air had already told upon her; she had passed a night of refreshing sleep, and now the windy brilliance of nature promised her an exhilaration that must go far toward making her bear resignedly the new yoke of intellectual idleness.

" This is a mighty improvement," soon said a clear voice in the doorway. At once the lady turned, meeting her daughter, Leah, and they presently fell into a little walk up and down the piazza, with interlinked arms, as two women on terms of close intimacy will so often do when they have lighted among people to whom both are strangers. But as yet the piazza remained vacant of all other boarders save themselves.

" The fogs here are almost historical, my dear,"

said Mrs. Romilly, while she and Leah thus walked.
" Or, in any case, they are full of the dignity of
tradition. It will never do to treat them disre-
spectfully in the hearing of old residents, you
know."

Leah laughed. She had a way of laughing
without the least hint of a smile. She was so unlike her mother in appearance that their kinship
had struck some observers as incredible. To the
mother Leah was wondrously like her dead husband. The resemblance was at times so appealing
that it roused in her a pensive amusement. Leah
had a tall, supple figure, which she liked to clothe
in garments of modish taste ; she had revolution-
ized her mother's costumes three or four years
ago, and superintended all purchases of Mrs. Romilly's apparel with a dainty tyranny to which the
elder lady yielded in kindly despair. She would
insist that Leah made her quite too smart; but
these gentle protests were treated with an amiable
disdain. It cannot be said that Leah Romilly
passed for amiable with her few friends ; she had
by no means her father's nature. Girls of her own
age were a little repelled by her; she struck them
as indifferent and imperious ; she appeared always
to be regarding them from a height, a distance. If
they did not dislike her, they seldom told her their

secrets or treated her with unreserved freedom. They thought her unsympathetic, but they admired her notwithstanding — and perhaps with covert belief, in some cases, that she withheld her sympathy because of a very solid self-esteem. This air of superiority did not seem out of place in Leah. It even became her, as its cool tint becomes the lily, or its multiplex depth the rose. She was rare and elegant; this went without saying. You might as well have denied its symmetry to a swan as rarity to so high-bred a creature, with her light-stepping grace of carriage, her small, shapely head overfolded in shining breadths of blond hair, her delicate-featured face of cameo-like profile, her nut-brown eyes of golden lashes, her slender throat, full of flexible curves.

She had met very few men, either young or old. With the former she was usually grand to a degree of actual impertinence, and apt to comment upon them afterward with a bitter wit whose scorn pained her mother. Mrs. Romilly could never understand where Leah had got her turn for satire. She had been quick, though indolent, in all educational matters; she mastered knowledge easily, but with none of the scholar's treasuring and retentive enjoyment. In truth, her mother, who knew her best, had never been sure of anything that she es-

pecially enjoyed or loved, though sure of many
things that she held in fatigued disrelish, and many
more that she viewed with an impatient irony.
She had never been able to place her fond maternal hand on just the spot where Leah's heart lay;
she had never felt it beat; sometimes she would
almost doubt if it beat at all. There seemed a vir-
ginal superciliousness about the girl that would
have shocked and repulsed had it not been for her
strong personal charms; she had no sooner made
you disapprove of her than you somehow found
yourself pardoning. It was pride and coldness,
no doubt, but the pride and coldness of a young
Diana, white, swift, dazzling — and before the advent of Endymion.

"I shall be quite willing to respect the fogs if
they will only keep at a safe distance," said Leah,
after the delivery of her characteristic smileless
laugh. "I am afraid that Mrs. Preen's establishment contains enough excuse of another sort for
downright depression."

"I suppose you mean the people, Leah," answered Mrs. Romilly, with a soft shake of her head.
"It is so like you to mean and say hard things
about our fellow-boarders as soon as you have seen
them."

"But I have also heard them," returned Leah,

lightly, "and so have you. What big draughts upon our interest and compassion those two spinster sisters are going to draw ! — is n't their name Semmes? They are so exactly alike that I shall always be in ignorance which one has the weak chest and which the neuralgia. Of course, when they are met in concert, as it were, we can always know, for they appear to do nothing except to pity the lungs of one and the head of the other."

" Leah, they are very sweet old ladies, I think," murmured her mother, with placid reproach.

" Then the dressy woman with the dog," continued Leah. " Can't you hear it now ? " she went on, as a sharp, thin bark resounded from inner regions. " It is so pleasant to see that miniature animal perch itself on Mrs. Dickerson's lap and make hungry darts at her fork ; you feel a nice exciting doubt as to whether it may not leap on your own plate the next minute."

" She is a very social person. I should really like to know her better."

" I am afraid that little terrier would n't let you; I suspect that it keeps watch on the threshold of her affections. But, oh, what *is* the name of the long, ghostly man, with white eyebrows and a lemon-colored moustache ? "

" I don't know, Leah."

"We shall soon discover. He has talked of nothing but drainage and pipes and sewer-gas since we arrived. Did you notice? He is a ma- lario-maniac! Is that good etymology? Well, you need n't tell me, if it is n't. He 's so amusing. I am sure he thinks that the chances of poisoning himself are nine out of ten every time he takes a swallow of water. He appears to be on very friendly terms with Dr. Pragley, the eminent di- vine from Brooklyn. Do you observe, by the way, mother, what a clerical glare the divine gives you every now and then from the corners of his black eyes? It ought to be quite easy for anybody to become eminent, I should say, with that stupen- dous nose. It 's a sort of triumphal arch. I sup- pose the great sentences roll out under it, when he preaches, like a band of victorious soldiers."

"Leah!" reproved her mother, in almost a flur- ried whisper, "you *must* be more guarded! This is precisely the mood you indulged while we were abroad, two summers ago!"

Leah looked askance at the doorway, which they had just passed. "Oh, I dare say it is writ- ten," she answered, "that I am to set everybody in Mrs. Preen's boarding-house by the ears. You meet such ridiculous people in boarding-houses. All the normal part of creation in Newport, they

say, occupies the cottages. I really begin to
think you *were* imprudent to bring me here. I
foresee the dawn of my own dreadful unpopularity."

Mrs. Romilly sighed. She was never so com-
plaisant, never so slightly individual, as with her
daughter. Women of one-third her parts had
made better mothers, after all. It was now a
good while ago since she had accepted Leah's
flaws as irremediable; the girl, just as she stood,
was Mrs. Romilly's single instance of loving a fellow-creature without an effort toward the removal
of manifest faults.

"You court unpopularity," she said, with a
matter-of-course regret. "You take a morbid
enjoyment in it."

"Oh, no; I see the nonsense in people — and
sometimes worse than that. For example, this
Dr. Pragley: I don't doubt that he would like to
shriek pietisms at you. You remember his tirades,
full of bigotry and brimstone? Which newspaper
is it that always bristles with them on Monday
mornings?"

"I have an idea that he is a sincere enough
man in his special way," said Mrs. Romilly, with
that quiet promptitude of response which showed
her large-souled disinterestedness. "If he is nar-

row, he is at least earnest. We too often mistake narrowness for hypocrisy, and I must remember that my liberalism would be a hollow vaunt if it could not find in the former all struggling or thwarted growths of goodness."

"Oh, I am not treating him from that point of view," said Leah, as if all such high, wise charities were a thrice-told tale. She did not speak with any flippant intonation ; she appeared simply to disregard her mother's philosophy, not to condemn it. She had the air of inferring that it was too serious a subject for the gay, auroral buoyancy of the hour. "I merely meant," she finished, tossing her head with a light languor, "that Dr. Pragley and all the rest of them are in horrible taste."

"You care too much for what is in good or bad taste, Leah," said her mother. "You persist in looking at people's surfaces. This trait grows with you."

Leah patted her mother's hand. Any playful caress was unusual with her, and when given it always had an effect of severe condescension, never of even momentary surrender to sentiment. She had no prettiness of mannerism, no winsome arts. If her beauty had not been so willowy, so pliant, so exquisitely feminine, it would less often have escaped the charge of ungracious hardness.

"I'll not deny that you are perfectly right," she said. "The older I grow, the more I feel like rebelling against what displeases my sense of outward fitness. And I have begun to see that there are a good many people in the world, after all, who please me completely as regards form, style, deportment, polish, nicety. They don't give my sense of humor the least chance at them; they suit me; they even win from me a positive deference. I should be glad to know more of them. We met a few in our European travels: we have fallen in with a few since then. Shall I give you their names? . . . Well, perhaps I had best not. You would recall that most of them are mentally dull. But they were not at all dull to me. They were frivolous, if you please, but I liked their frivolity; it was so attractively expressed. I sometimes think that I was made to live among them — to be one of them. You know how quietly I *have* lived thus far. It seems to me that there is some experience which I was meant for, yet have never enjoyed. I feel a want, a need, and I should not be a bit surprised if it could be gratified by precisely the same kind of society that you would consider unpardonably light. I believe that I like light people, aimless people, people who are not serious, who don't take things in earnest — provided they are always well-dressed, well-mannered, conventional. Perhaps it's all a natural breaking away from early influences; perhaps it's some inheritance I got from Papa. You are superfine. I admire you, and shall always admire you; but you are not conventional; you would be dressing in gowns of ten years ago if I hadn't insisted otherwise. You're wonderfully clever; you have great thoughts, great views. If you were not my mother — if I were not ever so fond of you — if we hadn't lived together so long, and all that, why, I fancy that I should treat you like a book that is too deep for me, but at the same time kept in bold relief on the shelf, as a possession to be proud of. I shouldn't open you; you would be heavy reading; I'd thumb over the silliest novels instead. . . . Now, there is no use of looking melancholy; you've heard me talk in this strain a number of times before. It all comes to one result: you are great, and I'm small. Of course, I am. *I* never doubted it. You have sympathies with the race, secure and thorough learning, a mighty talent for argument, a huge brain, and a still huger heart. *I* am simply a girl, made after a very ordinary pattern. You are universal, abstract; I'm particular, concrete. Mind you, I don't exult in my littleness; I merely record it. You could find a justification for the existence of that inflammatory Dr. Pragley. I claim your benevolence and toleration on considerably firmer grounds. Put me in your cabinet of psychology, once and for all. Not as a rare specimen, but one rather perfect of its kind. There's no use of fancying that you have made any error about the color or cut of my wings; you haven't at all; they belong definitely to the butterfly species."

"They have been getting stronger of late, I imagine," was the slow, reflective answer, "and you have a greater desire to use them."

"In the sunshine — yes," said Leah, with one of her laughs. "Perhaps in the Newport sunshine, too. You know Lawrence Rainsford promised to make it pleasant for me when we came."

Mrs. Romilly looked at her daughter with a more solicitous gaze than she herself knew of.

"You have never made it very pleasant for Lawrence Rainsford," she answered, in lowered, significant voice.

Leah chose to ignore this mild touch of censure.

"The Rainsfords are old Newport people," she said. "He's something of a celebrity, too, since he painted his last five or six pictures. He ought

to be well received, as they call it. I wonder
what kept him away all day yesterday."

Mrs. Romilly knew that Leah spoke of a man
whom she had already refused at least twice in
marriage. And she had never heard the girl
mention his name with even as much lively concern as now.

"Let us sit down here," Leah rapidly added;
for the piazza, by no means of capacious limits,
had just received, through the open hall-doorway,
a little moving group, and at that corner which
Mrs. Romilly and her daughter had then chanced
to reach, were two commodious-looking bamboo-
chairs.

The group was composed of Dr. Pragley, the
two maidenly invalided Misses Semmes, the spec-
tral unknown gentleman whom Leah had called a
malario-maniac, and the dressy Mrs. Dickerson,
who held her inevitable little dog clasped to her
heart.

But just then the dog set up a deafening clamor
of shrill barks, and bounded from its adorer's
arms. It dashed down the piazza steps, whirling
itself round on each in a very mercurial frenzy.
Its barks, meanwhile, grew more and more excited,
as its slim little black-and-auburn body careened
and plunged.

Leah and her mother had already sat down, but through the vine-leaves they saw that a gentleman was ascending the steps, and perceived that all this strident clamor was evidently roused by his advent.

"How tiresome!" said Leah, rising, as she recognized Mr. Lawrence Rainsford. She at once went forward to meet him, with her fair head a little more grandly poised than usual, and her elastic step a trifle more assertive.

II

MEANWHILE, Mrs. Dickerson, the mistress of the tempestuous dog, had hurried to the edge of the piazza. She was a small person, with a narrow, sharp-eyed face and a keenly prominent chin. Her figure was no less bony than slight, but it was clad in a morning-robe of ample volume and liberal embellishment. There seemed to be considerably more of fluttering ribbons and breezy furbelows than of Mrs. Dickerson. Nevertheless, her spare body had a volatile, nervous way of constantly altering its lines and poses, that was not unlike the more intense movements of her mettlesome pet.

As Leah approached, she had begun to address the gyrating dog with raised fore-finger and bent frame, in tones of commandant volubility.

"Cigarette! *will* you be quiet? Be quiet instantly, I say! You naughty, naughty girl! Come right to momma! Come! Cigarette, momma will punish you severely! Stop barking at the gentleman! Stop this minute, now!"

28

This outburst produced its restrictive effect upon Cigarette, who moved snarlingly up the steps in a sidelong, reluctant way, and was soon grabbed by her owner. The threatened punishment was not then administered, but, instead, the dog was per-mitted to squirm in Mrs. Dickerson's clutch, and lick with a nimble red tongue the lady's half-averted face.

Leah had time to shake hands with her visitor, but time to do no more, before Mrs. Dickerson began again, appealing to them both:

" I 'm *so* sorry! I really *am!* The poor little thing would 'nt *bite,* you know! I suppose it 's this lovely air that makes her feel kind of frolic-some. She would n't hurt a *fly!* "

There was a slight pause during which the Reverend Mr. Pragley, his cadaverous friend, and the two slim, sallow elderly sisters, all diligently stared.

" She looks small enough for a fly to hurt *her,*" said Mr. Rainsford, dryly, with a smile.

Mrs. Dickerson gave a tittering laugh, and re-ceded toward the group which she had left. She at once addressed Mr. Pragley in a low voice. It was noticeable, indeed, that all the members of this small assemblage turned their eyes upon Mr. Pragley whenever they spoke. . . .

" They all belong to his flock," said Leah, when Mr. Rainsford had taken a seat beside her mother and herself, at the farther end of the piazza, and after numerous sentences had been spoken which had ultimately led to the subject of Mrs. Preen's establishment. " Yes, Mamma and I have found ourselves in the midst of a flock. There is n't the least doubt of it. And the shepherd already disapproves of us. We are looked upon as black sheep already. It 's very amusing to me ; I enjoy it greatly."

" Mrs. Preen's place was never given over to any religious clique before," said Rainsford, quietly. He usually spoke with slowness and gravity. " I should n't have recommended it if I had not believed it quite secular."

" Oh, it has been stormed, this summer, by Dr. Pragley, and his myrmidons," said Leah, in her careless way, and so often suggested an undercurrent of idle brilliancy, that had made her mother sometimes wonder if a certain unconquerable indolence had not kept her from a stronger grasp upon the great choices and issues of life. " Mamma and I are literally nowhere. The Reverend Mrs. Pragley and children have not yet arrived. I overheard last evening that she is visiting her mother in Vermont, and is expected here

in a short time. When she arrives, there is strong
probability of our enforced departure. I can see
us standing indignant out on the drive, yonder,
beside our ejected trunks."

"In that case my mother will give you at least
a temporary refuge," said Rainsford. "If you wish
it, I will warn her to have one or two apartments
prepared."

He said this with a slight, fleeting smile. His
smile was infrequent, but very richly genial when
it came. He was a man of generous build, verging
a little toward stoutness, yet easily escaping the
charge because so solid of frame and limb, notwithstanding girth. His head was large, and set
squarely on broad shoulders. He was scarcely
past two-and-thirty, yet the hair had receded far
from his naturally high forehead, and had left a
face in which existed not one regular feature, impressed with a stamp of rugged nobility. His partial baldness, in other words, became him, dignified
him, brought his manful sort of homeliness into
strong relief. But you felt that it had always
been a kindly face — the fleshly witness, somehow,
of a power for good in the world. His cordial blue
eyes told you that, and the total reverse of grim-
ness about his close-shorn lips. In dress and
manner he had the look of one who reluctantly

concedes to the rules of the reigning mode, without in any rebellious way abjuring them.

"You had best defer your preparations until some new devolopments occur," now said Mrs. Romilly. She glanced almost laughingly at Rainsford as she spoke. She had liked him thoroughly ever since Leah and herself had met him two years ago, on the steamer returning from Europe. She had sympathized with his aims in Art, had listened congenially to the account of his previous studies abroad, had believed completely in his soundness of principle, his accuracy of ideal, his whole virile and temperate personality. She admitted with Leah that he was rugged no less in feature than in general demeanor. But if he shifted his person without grace, if his hands and feet lacked the best nicety of contour, if his conversation was without decorative skill in phrase — he was, none the less, to her wide and yet piercing judgment, a man endowed with powerful and sterling traits.

"He has the soul of a true poet," she had once said to Leah, "hidden away in that somewhat awkward shape. It is like a hamadryad imprisoned in a rough tree-trunk. The woman whom he loves and marries will never regret her vows."

He had loved Leah, as it has been recorded, and

had wanted to marry her. He came of a family
well-known in Newport and permanently·resident
there. His painting had kept him in New York
through the greater portion of the two years following his return from Europe. His aged mother
and a spinster aunt dwelt not far away from this
same sun-flecked piazza on which he now sat with
Mrs. Romilly and Leah. They three were all that
were left of a once large household, in which
death, for more than ten years, had been making
sad havoc. The personal fortune of Lawrence
Rainsford well met his moderate wants; more
would come to him when the two faded ladies
passed away; he was by no means a contemptible
match, in worldly esteem, though by no means
ranking with the matrimonial potentates.

"You have seen nothing of Newport," he soon
said. "I left you yesterday for the toils of un-
packing. But to-day I want to claim you as
strangers full of tempting local ignorance. I hope
you will let me do so, for a little while, at least."

Not very long after this all three left the piazza
and strolled toward the opposite gate. The group
were now all seated, and its calm quintuple stare
followed the two ladies and their escort with a ju-
dicial severity. Leah had got her own and her
mother's sun-hats; her own was of white straw,

very brightly wreathed with flowers. She moved along, in her becoming and fashionable morning dress, with a most distinguished mien. Beside the graver figure of Mrs. Romilly, hers looked delightfully young and active.

But some of the comments which followed herself and mother might have made the girl knit her white brows.

"My!" said the Miss Semmes with the troublesome chest, alluding to Leah, "how that young thing carries herself! A person would n't think there was anything in this world to humble the spirit of the proud, if *she* was the only one to be judged from!"

This Miss Semmes was the precise counterpart of her neuralgiac sister. They were not twins, yet they were both so slim, so frail, so flaxen-haired, so low of voice, that they belonged to that feminine type which time neither wrinkles nor turns gray. Cockle-shells of humanity, in a physical sense, they float on its waves without feeling their slow erosion. Five years or more might have intervened between the ages of the sisters, and yet no positive evidence of this difference had set itself on either countenance.

"Very right — very right indeed!" answered Dr. Pragley, to whom the last remark had addressed itself. He cleared his throat as he spoke. He undoubtedly possessed a nose whose massive curvature Leah had not at all exaggerated. He was at least six feet in height, and, as the phrase has it, he sat tall. His eyes were black and luminous; he had a trick of rolling them about, and in so doing he gave strong effect to their surrounding white. He was by no means an ill-looking person; a dense black side-whisker, of coarse texture, bushed itself along either cheek, ending in a little hirsute line at the corners of his mouth; but his upper lip, long, and having a crease in its centre, like the deep fold in some stiff fabric, was bluish because so closely shaven. The mouth itself was large and its smile ready. Its smile was, indeed, too ready. The even but almost bulky teeth which this disclosed, while mingled with some peculiar writhe of the back-drawn lips, gave an element of pain and acidity to its whole expression. He wore the accepted ministerial garb of a many-buttoned, high-throated coat and a white neckcloth. He had a habit of slightly waving one or both hands after the delivery of the most quiet conversational sentence. And, in truth, all that he said seemed to be delivered; nothing had the manner of being spoken. It was noteworty that in the least oral requirement this gentleman was infallibly ora‧torical.

"The young lady," he continued, "is a true daughter of the Philistines." Here Dr. Pragley smiled his curiously distressed smile. "But how should we expect it to be otherwise? She has been reared by a mother whose ungodly teachings I well remember in my boyhood   I *had* hoped — I had *fondly* hoped, I may say — that the dark beliefs of Elizabeth Cleeve Romilly might have undergone a blessed alteration since then. But I fear I have counted too trustfully. Yesterday the lady, seemingly by accident, left a book upon this very piazza   Animated by no worldly feeling of curiosity" (here Dr. Pragley took in the aspect of every attentive listener with one flashing sweep of his eyes), "I looked at the title of this work. It was that of an Atheist!"

"An Atheist!" immediately repeated four shocked voices.

"Yes. It was a work by Herbert Spencer, that immoral foe of all pious and sacred aspiration." Here Dr. Pragley ceased to smile; he frowned instead, and his copious black eyebrows gave to his frown a magisterial gloom. "Oh, when I saw that unholy book," he continued, "I felt that Elizabeth Cleeve Romilly was still lost!"‧

So resonant were these final words that they produced an irreverent excitement in Cigarette, whose fresh clatter Mrs. Dickerson endeavored to restrain, while saying fervently to Dr. Pragley:

" She cannot be lost as long as she still lives! Let us all try and reclaim her! "

The Miss Semmes who suffered from neuralgia here eagerly broke in: " Yes; let us try and reclaim her! " But the next moment she put one narrow, pale hand to her temple and faintly sighed.

" My dear Mary ! " at once murmured her sister. " I knew you could n't stand this draught. Recollect we 're sitting right *in* a current of air! " And as she finished her admonition, the speaker gave a sudden, rasping cough.

Immediately Miss Mary Semmes caught the fragile arm of her sister. " Catherine ! " she said, solicitously, " you think of *me*, and yet you know that the draught hurts your *chest* a great deal more than it does my *head !* "

Both sisters now arose, apparently convinced of mutual reasons for passing within doors. But just then the gentleman who was so afraid of malaria said, with a very high-keyed yet decisive voice :

" Ladies, don't be so careful of yourselves. Remember, we are all in the keeping of Providence."

" True, Mr. Yarde," assented Mr. Pragley, with an impressive cough. " Very true indeed! "

But here Mrs. Dickerson, who had quieted her obstreporous darling, put her head coquettishly on one side, so that her acute chin looked in danger of piercing a contiguous ruffle.

" Oh, come now, Mr. Yarde," she said, slyly, "*you* don't think much about Providence when you complain of bad drainage and things of that kind."

Mr. Yarde raised an almost transparent hand to his pale-yellow moustache.

" Mrs. Dickerson," he said, solemnly, " I repose the most absolute faith in Providence. But it works in mysterious ways. I maintain that it is the duty of every true Christian to keep his drain-pipes in good order, and to avoid those perils which science" ——

" *Science!* " here broke in the weak-chested Miss Semmes, plaintively. " Oh, don't — *please* don't mention that word in connection with *Providence!* Recollect the splendid sermon on modern paganism that Dr. Pragley preached just before his vacation began. I don't mean the *last* Sunday; I mean the Sunday *before* the last! "

Here a chorus took up the refrain, so to speak. The memory of that penultimate sermon was

evidently too much for even Mr. Yarde. He
joined in the general dithyramb.

" Oh, yes! The Sunday *before* the last!"

Dr. Pragley coughed and then smiled. All eyes
were directed upon him. All eyes were usually
directed upon him, as regarded the passionate
cult of his so-called flock; but when it came to
be a question of particular eulogy, all eyes were
lighted with an especially fine ardor of attention.

Dr. Pragley began to make remarks. When
his flock, or any limited portion of it, behaved in
this fond way, he invariably made remarks. . . .

Meanwhile Leah, her mother and Lawrence
Rainsford had left the domain of Mrs. Preen's
boarding-house and passed along the skirting walk
of the adjacent street. It was now mature summer; here in the heart of this poetic and unique
city Nature smiled and throve at her best, though
restrained by an art of easy and happy discipline.
None of the splendid abodes lay in this quarter;
it was the inner heart of the town, full of great
overshadowing elms that cast their sweet glooms
across lawns cut into velvet trimness and spread
about homes whose thrift and peace were blent
with a calm continual elegance. The estates were
all of meagre dimension, for the high value of
property made this a necessity with even their

prosperous owners. The large, drowsy houses suggested, mostly, that generations had lived and died in them, but generations with an inherited respect for the repairing virtues of incidental paint and carpentry. There was no touch of neglect or desuetude; the very elms, with their cloister-like arches, looked as if some careful hand had pruned them of the least dead twig. The whole effect was simple, rural, provincial, but nevertheless clearly patrician.

"It might be England," said Mrs. Romilly, "and yet you somehow see that it is New England."

" You won't say that when you are nearer the sea," declared Rainsford. " Here the dwellings all crowd together. But on Bellevue Avenue and in many other portions, Newport becomes finely cosmopolitan. I have seen nearly all the famed watering-places, but I have never yet seen one to which this could be plausibly likened."

" That reminds me," here struck in Leah, with quiet humor. " I set out in search of the sea yesterday morning at a little after seven o'clock. We came by the boat, you know, and were deposited at Mrs. Preen's by about six. I had slept quite comfortably, and wanted my breakfast. But no breakfast was to be obtained until eight. So I

sallied forth, leaving poor mamma, who had *not*
slept, recumbent upon a lounge. I supposed that
the ocean was about a hundred yards distant. I
met an old man in this very street, and asked him
the nearest way to it. He gave me the most
intricate series of directions. By degrees I began
to understand that Newport, which I had always
imagined within a stone-throw of the Atlantic, was
miles away from it."

" Not miles away," corrected Rainsford, looking
at her with a hint of doubt in his pleasant blue
eyes as to whether she were serious or satirical.
He had fallen into a habit of looking at her thus,
and perhaps for excellent reasons. " There are
more Newports than one," he continued, with ex-
planatory gravity, and as if after having assured
himself that she was securely in earnest. " There
is this Newport through which we now walk, and
which has no marine flavor, certainly, except what
comes from the strong, bluff breeze we are getting.
You don't have to possess millions to spend a
summer here, though many of these cottages, as
we call them, are rented by millionaires. Then
there is the dingy, shabby, mercantile Newport,
that fronts on Narragansett Bay. Its wharves are
ugly and dilapidated enough, but many of them
have an almost historic past. Then there is the

opulent, showy, and aristocratic Newport, which is mostly maritime, and has reared many villas and mansions near the Atlantic that you tried to rediscover."

" I want to find that Newport now," said Leah, in odd tones. "I think that is the one I came to see."

Both Rainsford and her mother looked intently at her drooped face as she moved between them. Then the eyes of the mother and the lover met, and with mute meaning, behind Leah's back. But she herself somehow felt that the look was being exchanged.

"What conspirators they are!" she thought. "How mamma wants me to marry him, and how they both fear that I shall turn their little comedy into a piteous farce!"

"We are near the Casino," Rainsford said, breaking a pause. "The Cliffs are still rather far away."

"Oh, let us go to the Casino, by all means!" exclaimed Leah, blithely. "I have read so much about that in the papers."

She expressed disappointment as they entered it, a little later, by approaches that struck her as pretty and odd, though strangely lacking in that stateliness which she had anticipated. But when

they had gained the circular interior, with its roof
open to the sky, its great round of close-cropped
verdure, its flanking galleries of restaurants and
reading-rooms, its quaint, big, gold-handed clock,
looming above a mass of Dutch-looking masonry,
and its general air of amphitheatrical spaciousness,
her opinion underwent rapid change.

A capable band was discoursing excellent music;
the mellow cadences pealed out upon the bland
morning air with a sonorous fulness. Within the
pavilion of dark-painted wood that was wrought
somewhat after the Colonial pattern, numerous
ladies and gentlemen were seated; others moved
along the smooth, hard paths. Beyond, through
low and broad openings, gleamed a larger sweep
of lawn, where lovers of tennis waved bats and
tossed balls, some of the male players being ar-
rayed in short breeches, hose and caps, whose
bright tints or fanciful designs gave to their
slender and youthful figures the look of partici-
pants in some jocund pastoral revel, not unworthy
of a modern Watteau. Still farther on rose a
structure dedicated to the double purpose of ball-
room and theatre; more than a single admired
belle had made her conquests as an amateur actress
in both, if the statement be not uncharitably in-
clusive. A sense of blithesome *fête* hung about

the whole attractive spot. You felt that it was all
a frivolity, and yet one of the most tasteful and
refined type. Whoever had planned its capabili-
ties of enjoyment had done so with an adherence
to the best artistic traditions.

"You seem to know a number of the people
here," said Leah to Rainsford. "I notice that you
bow quite often."

" That is hardly strange," he answered.

"Surely not," broke in Mrs. Romilly, "when
you have lived so many years in Newport." She
spoke only to Rainsford, and as if propitiatingly.

" But Newport people are New York people as
well," persisted Leah, with her eyes fixed on Rainsford alone. " Or, rather, they belong, in a great
measure, to the large cities of which New York is
chief. And always before, when I have met you,
you have appeared such a recluse — so wholly absorbed in your painting — so indifferent to anything like an acquaintanceship. Now, for my own
part, I envy you if you know some of these ladies
and gentlemen. I have observed more than one
whom I should think it would be very pleasant to
know."

Rainsford watched her, for a moment, with his
sedate smile. " They seem to return your compli-
mentary opinions," he said.

" Do you think so ? " asked Leah, eagerly. She
glanced here and there, for a little while, and then
turned laughingly to her mother.
" I believe it is true ! " she exclaimed, softly.
" You remember our talk this morning."

" Yes — I remember it very well," answered
Mrs. Romilly. The intonation that went with
these words made Lawrence Rainsford fix his eyes
in astonishment on the face of Leah's mother.
He found it transiently saddened, just as her voice
had been.

He esteemed Mrs. Romilly as much as he loved
her. They were stanch friends; there was a perfect understanding between them ; his affection for
her was reverential.

" She is deeply distressed by something," he
thought. " I wonder what it is." At the same
instant he realized that a certain shadow of foreboding had crossed his own spirit.

But now, while they both looked toward Leah,
as if by some mutual impulse of explanation they
discovered that she had withdrawn a little apart
from them, and had become suddenly engaged in
conversation with two ladies.

They were young ladies ; Mrs. Romilly at once
recognized them, and so did Rainsford. They were
sisters; their name was Marksley; they had crossed

in the same steamer with Leah and her mother, on that voyage during which the two latter had made Rainsford's acquaintance.

They were thin girls, with rather pretty faces a good deal alike, and very much of what our special time calls style, without having any of what nearly all times have agreed to call grace. They were dressed with excessive costliness; their robes and bonnets must have been minor marvels in the matter of expenditure. They had a shrill yet not unmusical way of speaking, a slightly exaggerated way of moving their arms, hands or bodies, and a method of expressing themselves that surpassed all limits of moderation and became, on the least incentive, a positive riot of superlatives. They are thus collectively described because of their strong resemblance in almost every mental or personal detail. One was named Louisa and one Caroline, but only their very intimate friends recollected precisely who was who.

Leah has not cared much about them on the steamer, though she had never given them enough thought to decide that she disliked them. But they had not the accent of importance which now seemed to mark them; they had been mild prattlers, then, with no stamp of fashion upon them, no evidence of belonging to any notable circle. She was now not quite sure whether or no it was the *chic* of the place in which she had met them that really gave them their striking novelty.

What they said to Leah caused her to raise her brows in sharp surprise. Several yards behind the Misses Marksley stood a gentleman, who slowly advanced the moment that Leah directed her gaze upon his face, — which she did for a good reason.

The Misses Marksley had effusively assured her that this gentleman had desired to make her acquaintance.

Both watching, both listening, and both as yet having received no signs of greeting from the sisters, Mrs. Romilly and Rainsford held a short conversation together. Amid the reigning atmosphere of festival, their few exchanged sentences, had these been overheard, might have struck a keenly dissonant note.

" They wish to present to her Mr. Tracy Tremaine," murmured Leah's mother. " Who is he ? "

" You see him," answered Rainsford.

" Yes — I see him."

" What do you think of him ? "

" He is handsome, certainly. He has the look of a very fashionable man."

"He is."

"Do you know him?"

"We are on speaking terms."

"He has asked to know Leah?"

"You heard what the Misses Marksley said."

Here Mrs. Romilly looked with great directness at Rainsford's grave and placid face. Then she rested her hand upon his full, solid arm.

"You have some fear?" she said. "You are sorry that I have brought her here?"

Rainsford evaded both questions. "I do not care to have her meet that man," he responded.

III.

THE gentleman whom we have heard called Tracy Tremaine had now drawn quite close to the Misses Marksley. Both young ladies burst into a self-conscious laugh as he did so. The two laughs were quite similar. The mirth of the sisters, like everything else about them except their clothes, had no individuality, no *meum et tuum*. They never duplicated each other's magnificence of raiment. Had they really been twins instead of having a year between their ages, they could not have striven more successfully to veil this fact by a diversity of costume.

Caroline now went through the formula of introduction, presenting Mr. Tremaine to Miss Romilly; but the words had no sooner been spoken than Louisa took up the burden of civility, as it were. These young ladies were perpetually playing, in fact, just such a conversational game of pitch-and-toss. The shuttle-cock of their intelligence was always floating from lip to lip, and not seldom with a feathery lightness easily explainable.

"Mr. Tremaine would have gone mad in about ten minutes longer, my dear, unless he had met you," said Louisa, laying one specklessly-gloved hand on Leah's wrist. "I never heard of such a perfectly instantaneous conquest."

"Yes," chimed in Caroline, catching the shuttlecock, as it were, and continuing the violent superlatives. "A decent feeling of Christian charity, my dear, made us grant his passionate entreaties before it was too late. As it is, we've saved him from utter insanity in the nick of time."

They both wheeled their thin bodies toward Mr. Tremaine with exactly the same rapid, bending movement.

"Now we'll leave you to your fate," declared Caroline, addressing the gentleman.

"And try to be resigned to our own," proceeded Louisa, re-wheeling herself toward Leah the next moment, promptly followed by her sister. "You're looking so immensely well, I don't wonder he was wild to be presented." Louisa's face was very close to Leah's by this time, but only a few inches closer than that of Caroline.

"He's an enormous swell, my dear," whispered the latter.

"Oh, perfectly tremendous," came the sisterly echo — "if you care for that sort of thing. You did n't use to on the steamer, don't you know?"

"Neither did you," responded Leah, who was not thoroughly sure whether she understood this florid species of slang.

"Oh, we 're awfully changed since we came back," maintained Caroline.

"Yes, dreadfully," affirmed Louisa. They both laughed again and then exchanged a little nod.

While Leah looked puzzled as to the meaning of this last ambiguous outburst, the double fusillade recommenced.

"Now *do* tell us where you are stopping, and if you mean to stop long."

"Yes, *do!*"

"We shall be so enchanted, my dear, to come and see you!"

"Yes, we shall so perfectly *love* to come!"

Leah had scarcely given the full required answer before the Misses Marksley, both perceiving Mrs. Romilly and Rainsford at what seemed precisely the same moment, took several sidelong slips in the direction of the elder lady and her companion, their splendid robes rustling after them, the right hand of each cordially outstretched, and either mouth wearing a smile whose accurate measurements would doubtless have shown the most rigid equality.

They had seemed to come and go in a kind of gentle social tempest. Leah now looked at the gentleman whom they had left, so to speak, behind them. She had not truly observed him before; as she regarded him at present it struck her that he was extremely handsome.

"I suppose my silence," he began, "has appeared to you a very awkward affair, Miss Romilly. I should n't dispute that point with you for an instant. But the Misses Marksley are great monopolists — I mean conversationally, you know."

The speaker drawled these words a little as he delivered them, and showed what Leah thought an English mode of utterance ; but she found his voice peculiarly rich and sweet. It also occurred to her that she had never seen a male face of so much strong yet half-feminine beauty. Mr. Tremaine was tall and very slim of build ; his clothes hung rather loosely about his person, yet their outlines implied careful tailoring. He moved his limbs in a languid, unstudied way ; he occasionally thrust his shapely white hands into his pockets,

and then withdrew them; he appeared indolently
restless. He had the air of a tired man and of a
somewhat dissatisfied one; he also suggested a
close adherence to a certain code of polite behavior. But he did not give you the impression of
being at all a fop; he had evidently paused well
inside the limits of anything like senseless carica-
ture.

His eyes were large, soft, and of a dark blue.
Lashes of unusual length shaded them, and they
were a feature that even in a commonplace countenance would have held their own through an
unfailing charm. The remainder of his face was
regular almost to the degree of perfection; a flow-
ing silky moustache, amber in hue, waved along
either oval cheek; the chiselling of nose and chin
was little short of exquisite, and his uniform
pallor aided you to see, perhaps, how well they
would have borne precise copying by some deft
sculptor.

"Yes," said Leah, not knowing how intently she
scanned this face, whose beauty was in reality fascinating her, "the Misses Marksley are surely
great talkers. It never specially occurred to me
that they were until now. But, then, our acquaintance has always been slight. I suppose *you* know
them very well?"

He answered her with lowered voice and a little impatient stroke of his moustache. "I? Really, we are almost strangers. Do you think, under those circumstances, that I took an unwarrantable liberty in getting them to present me to yourself?"

Leah seemed to muse for a moment.

"Not at all," she then said, with an arch challenge in her brown eyes. "If you truly wished to know me it was the proper, straightforward course."

"So, then, . . you quite approve of it?"

She gave her smileless laugh, that some women thought so hard and haughty, but that men often found provocative of a new and keen enjoyment.

"If I had not approved, you may be certain I would very soon have made my disapproval clear."

"I don't understand," he said, looking surprised enough.

"Don't you?" she replied, with what would have been pertness on many other lips. "I mean that if I had n't cared to meet you I should promptly have shown you so."

"Indeed!" he said.

She had wakened his positive wonderment. He was wholly unprepared for her composed independence. He had been, almost from boyhood, an

accepted favorite with the other sex. The Misses
Marksley, in their fervid vernacular, had, after all,
classed him correctly. In exclusive cliques he undoubtedly reigned a power. He had been born
among exclusive cliques, as it were, and had rarely
seen others. In these no one had ever yet defined
his popularity. He was considered a man of educational store and mental capacity, but so innately
lazy as to employ neither at its proper worth. He
was known to have lived by no means a flawless
life. He was admitted to have retained and even
nursed some distinct vices. He had no stainless
repute for good manners, while his ability " to act
the thorough gentleman if he pleased" was broadly
conceded him — as though manners were a porta-
ble garment, worn or shifted at pleasure, and not
an apparel as inseparable from real personality as
skin from flesh. It was well understood that he
had spent half of an ample fortune, and was now
no longer rich according to the standard of opulence set by those with whom he held constant
association, though expectant of a liberal future
inheritance from a mother who had no child save
himself. But in spite of all such drawbacks he was
petted, caressed, indulged by his own set. His
prominence and his influence continued indisputable, and nobody could explain either.

Leah's cool assumption of the rôle which chooses
to accept or reject courtesies rather than seek and
be glad for them had amazed and even dismayed
him.   If he had not decided that she was excep-
tionally beautiful — if he had not made up his
mind, after the few words exchanged between them,
that she was endowed with a nameless and rare
.personal attraction, he would have found it in him
to seize some ungallant pretext for quitting her
society.   He would afterward have denied the com-
mission of such a rudeness if charged with it ; he
would simply have retired from the prospect of
being bored (as he always so retired when that
prospect became at all apparent to him) and have
accounted for his incivility with some sort of
plausible and quick-coined misstatement.

As it chanced, however, the intention of retreat
was very remote from his mind.   " Are you in the
habit of wearing your heart on your sleeve after
this extremely candid fashion ? " he continued.
" If so, you must contrive to make it disagreeable
enough for your unfavored admirers."

" I should probably do so," returned Leah, looking demurely amused, " if I had any admirers to
deal with."

" Oh," said Tracy Tremaine, nearly under his
breath, while his eyes seemed to kindle a little be-

neath their lowered lids, " I can believe a good deal
at a pinch, but there are limits, you know, to the
most ardent faith."

Leah liked this. Its artificiality refreshed her.
It resembled the passing odor of some hothouse
plant. And she loved hothouse plants; they were
so choice and sleek beside the hardier out-of-door
growths. Without really understanding it, she had
a weary distaste for simplicity and sincerity; she
longed after those trifling subtleties, railleries, in-
nuendoes, which by some instinct she believed
existent in other unenjoyed states of social intercourse. She had a desire to shut her windows
from the sunshine, as something too prevalent and
commonplace; she would light chandeliers instead,
and watch their lustre play on folded tapestries.
It did not occur to her that this impulse was un-
wholesome or morbid, for her complete ignorance
of how those daintier people really lived whose way
of living addressed her imagination in terms at once
of culture and picturesqueness, kept aloof all hint
of underlying evil. She would have told you, with
a delicious childish candor, if you had questioned
her on the subject, that she gave such people credit
for being as fair within as without — for having
honor and conscience as well ordered as their costumes and as blameless as their bodily habits.

Coming fresh from the morality and optimism of her mother, she had begun to look at life with an arrogant innocence. She took it splendidly for granted that most people were good ; she had never known any positively bad ones. She had known, she was always meeting, those who roused her humor, her ridicule, even her cruel and undiscriminating satire. This point in her curious nature (to some so loveless, to others illogically lovable) we have noted, it will be remembered, before now, while emphasizing, as well, the regret with which her mother had watched it. But, on the other hand, not to lie, to cheat, to steal, to injure one's fellow-creatures in any malignant way, seemed for Leah an accepted and operative human code. As for keeping one's self select, she held that to be quite another matter. The older that she grew the more she decided that there was an enormous majority of people in the world whom she did not wish to know. But those who attracted her by the quality which we call patrician, won at the same time her moral respect and support, though perhaps unconsciously to her proud young mind.

While Tracy Tremaine's compliment pleased Leah, she chose, nevertheless, to receive it without a sign of clemency. Her eyes wandered from his attentive face ; they surveyed the lawny court near

at hand; they swept the breezy arc of pavilion
which fronted her, and in which she and her companion then stood. As her small head moved thus
from side to side on its slender prop of neck, the
grace of the motion made its delicate disdain very
piquant and alluring for him who observed it.

"Let us change the subject," she said, with an
airy abruptness that would have been fuel for his
polite wrath if almost any other woman had em-
ployed it. "Let us speak of those Misses Marksley. They amuse me. They didn't when I met
them on the steamer, some time ago, but they
do now. I thought them dull and uninteresting
then; but now . . well, now they are somehow
altered."

"I fancy Newport has altered them," said Tremaine, reluctantly, as though he did not quite like
being shunted back into this deserted conversational channel.

Leah lifted her brows. "Newport? How?"
Her surprised query made him suddenly feel concerned in answering it. He saw an opportunity
of diverting her, and did not himself realize how
rapid yet strong a value he put upon it.

"Why, in this way," he promptly said, with a
cold drawl in his lazy voice that was the merciless
prelude of his coming comments. "They got here

rather early — I think it was some time in June
. . it's nearly August now . . yes, it must have
been June. Well, they had secured a nice cottage on Narragansett Avenue, and they used to
drive about with their stout papa in a rather handsome trap. They knew scarcely anybody, but all
of a sudden they made the most desperate dash."

"What is a desperate dash?" asked Leah.

Tremaine laughed. "Why, they tried to get
about to places," he said. "Newport is very funny
that way. It gives people a kind of fever sometimes. They come here with a lot of money, you
know, and take a liking to the style, the swagger of
things, and then they make a plunge — they try to
get in the swim, as we call it here. Occasionally
they succeed. But it's always foolish to show any
great eagerness. I suppose that is the folly the
Misses Marksley have committed. Newport has
gone to their heads, and they make this fact ab-
surdly plain. They're nice enough girls in their
way; it's true they're rather bad form, and then
they dress too much, though that sin is widely
enough committed here. But they've got a jolly
ménage; they know how to entertain ever so
well. Yet their trouble is that they went to
work with a jump instead of a push. Everybody laughs at them; they're not a bit of a suc-

cess. They're the most frighful snobs, and yet
the idea of getting among the big swells is so new
to them that they scarcely know who is who.
They're in a perpetual fever to be received by people, and people are in a perpetual fever to avoid
receiving them. I dare say it will end by their
being asked everywhere; they've got such a pile
of money, and the papa is a very decent fellow;
I've heard he's related to some Ohio senator, or
somebody like that. But at present they're the
sport of the place; they quite beat Polo and the
Casino balls and the Skating Rink, I assure you."

All this was delightful to Leah. She had no
sense of its being cruel. She had fallen into the
habit herself, long ago, of seeing the ludicrous
sides of people and pelting these with her swift
irony.

"I'm very glad you told me about them," she
said. "You give them a wholly new value."

"I'm afraid you have n't much pity."

"Oh, that is what mamma says," she cried, softly,
and in the smile that touched her lips and fled
there was a gleam of light scorn. "It never oc-
curs to me that people who are queer deserve any
pity. They have no business to be queer, and when
they are, then let them pay the penalty by enter-
taining us, who are not."

Just at this time a lady passed near the spot on which they were standing. Two gentlemen accompanied her. She nodded and smiled as she looked at Tracy Tremaine, who at once raised his hat. But her eyes dwelt on his face only an instant; they were speedily transferred to Leah's.

The girl had never before felt herself the object of so piercing yet transitory a stare. The lady's eyes were brilliantly black, and they seemed to sweep her image, from the flowers on her sun-hat to the tip of her boot; while at the same time Leah herself felt that not a single point in her attire, not a single mark of visage or posture, had escaped this fleet yet acute scrutiny.

But when she had passed still farther onward, the lady chose to refix her look upon Tremaine. As she did so the turn of her full olive throat became apparent to Leah, and the jaunty, brisk movements of her somewhat small person. At the same time she held up one plump forefinger, and shook it at Tremaine.

"Remember my lunch, please. One o'clock, sharp! You are always late. You have only a quarter of an hour, as it is."

When the speaker had become still more remote Leah said to her companion:

" Who is your odd-looking friend?"

"Do you think her odd-looking?" he said, with almost a start.

"Not as you would interpret the word," Leah hastened, in a tone of apology very rare with her. "I meant odd-looking in the sense of being very well yet very originally dressed."

"Don't you like that mixture of red and pink? I suppose it's Worth; I believe everything she wears is Worth."

Leah knew about Worth. "I like it very much," she said, "for a woman as dark as she is. But you forget the touches of yellow in her bonnet, and the yellow roses at her breast; they helped the other colors. She has a face as dark as an Egyptian girl's. She is extremely handsome."

"So she has been told," said Tremaine, dryly.

"And her name?" gently persisted Leah. He appeared to wake from a sort of courteous reverie, of which Leah herself, judging by his rather absorbed gaze straight into her face, might very naturally have been the object. "Her name?" he repeated, absently. Then, as if suddenly aroused, he went on: "Her name—oh, yes; it is Mrs. Fortescue—Mrs. Abbott Fortescue." He ended the words with an abrupt, peculiar laugh.

"You mention her name as if you considered it a joke," said Leah, looking at him with a lofty tranquillity. "*Do* you?"

"Oh, good Heavens, no!" Tremaine exclaimed, in the manner of one thrown off his guard, who does not often encounter such disarray. "By no means, Miss Romilly. What made you suppose such a thing? Mrs. Fortescue and I are very good friends." He paused here, and stroked his moustache for an instant as if he were trying to hide the mutinous smile beneath it. "It seemed a little funny," he went on, "to find anybody in Newport who did n't know that I knew Mrs. Fortescue — that was all."

"I don't doubt that my ignorance in other similar ways will provoke your amusement," Leah quickly answered, "if you should continue my acquaintance." She then glanced toward her mother and Lawrence Rainsford, discovering that the Misses Marksley had left them.

At the same time Mrs. Romilly gave a meaning nod to her daughter. Leah at once moved to her mother's side. She did so with her grandest air, and as if supremely indifferent as to whether Tremaine should follow or no.

"Mamma wishes me," she said, a moment later, perceiving that Tremaine did follow.

"Have I annoyed you?" he questioned, while walking at her side. At the same time it passed through his mind: "When have I danced attendance like this on any other woman?"

"I'm not quite sure that you haven't annoyed me," returned Leah, with her eyes persistently averted from his own. She had never carried her sweet, fair head with more haughtiness than now. "You will find me sadly deficient in the valuable knowledge of Newport doings. Is n't it time that you joined your friend, Mrs.— what was her name? — who lunches at one o'clock, sharp?"

"What insolence!" thought Tremaine. "The great Mrs. Chichester herself would never dream of it, even if actually provoked. Who can this girl be, who has the pride of a young queen and the good looks of a young goddess?"

He did not permit himself to be rebuffed. He made it imperative for Leah to present him to her mother. The introduction to Lawrence Rainsford was needless.

He disliked Rainsford, though scarcely knowing the man. He had set him down as a prig and a bore. But his slender white hand grasped Rainsford's strong and brownish one with much apparent warmth. Tremaine never permitted his dislikes to interfere with his suavity. He avoided people very often with a good deal of clever dexterity, but when brought face to face with his aversions he was invariably urbane. There was less real hypocrisy here than might have been supposed ; he

held an expressed animosity to be one of the car-
dinal vulgarisms. Mrs. Fortescue's luncheon really
claimed him; it was, in its way, a commandant
engagement. But Leah chose to beam upon him
again before he slipped off in graceful departure.
Her hard moods rarely remained; that was something of which her worst foe could not accuse her;
she had always been guiltless of bearing grudges.
Besides, her pique had been more than half a matter of capricious coquetry; perhaps she wanted to
test the real strength of this sudden thrall in which
she perceived, with her first truly tingling sense of
conquest, that she had secured a man whose atten-
tions were ranked as high favor by the most fastid-
ious of her sisters. . . .

"I think you were almost cold to him, mamma,"
she said, when Tremaine had left them, and while
her eyes followed the latter's figure, with its easy,
lounging walk.

"Cold, Leah?" murmured her mother. There
was a touch of perplexity, of worriment, in the
brief utterance.

"Yes," Leah continued, a trifle sharply. "It
was very polite of him to offer to send us invitations for the Casino ball on Monday night. Yet
you hardly thanked him; you left all the gratitude
to me."

"You seemed rather grateful," here broke in Lawrence Rainsford. They had begun to move; Leah was between himself and her mother as they prepared to leave the grounds. They were going toward the place of exit, away from the pavilion, beneath whose cool shade the band still briskly wrought its inspiriting melodies.

"I *was* grateful," Leah answered him, with increased sharpness. She turned her look full upon Rainsford's composed countenance, which he had somewhat drooped, as was often his wont. "Why should I not be, if you please?"

His response was very quiet. "I don't know why you should be," he said, evasively. "The Casino balls are quite dull, I have found."

Leah gave a high, clear laugh. "Good gracious!" she exclaimed. "Have *you* been to any of them? . . . Oh, well, I think there's a slight chance of their affecting us differently." She turned to her mother. "We are going, of course."

"Going, Leah?" said Mrs. Romilly, incredulously. "You can't mean it, child! You know how entirely out of society I have been for years."

"Oh, if you won't take me, Mr. Tremaine shall!" returned Leah, with petulant decisiveness. "I don't care whether it shocks people or not, mamma.

I did n't come to Newport to be mewed up with
invalid spinsters and lugubrious divines from
Brooklyn." She lifted one hand and swept it before her. "I like all this; I think it perfectly
charming. It makes me feel as if I were being put
back into my proper element." The next instant
her face was quite close to her mother's; a smile
had broken over it, and her brown eyes, that could
be so haughty, were sparkling merrily. "Dear
mamma," she said, "don't take me so seriously.
Don't try to drive me with a curb always. Throw
the reins on my neck for once, and let me have a
little gallop all to myself. Depend upon it, I
shan't run away!"

Leah's voice was music itself now, and her posture, while she leaned toward her mother and they
still walked onward, exquisite in its lithe, girlish
abandonment. Perhaps the rarity of these tender,
intimate changes made them irresistible; perhaps
they were stamped with an original and native
allurement, like that which so often gave an unex-
plained sweetness to her most wilful and imperious aspects.

Rainsford had scarcely heard these latter words.
But their caressing tones left him in no doubt of
their true import; he knew Leah in all her phases;
he had good reason for such exhaustive knowledge.

"I don't believe anything would induce you to go alone to the ball with Tremaine," he said, a little louder and quicker than he usually spoke. "But even if you went there with your mother on his invitation I should much regret it."

Leah at once showed him a frowning face and a curling lip.

"I can't help what you would regret or sanction," she retorted, with curt speed.

Rainsford looked very grave. He made the only reply that occurred to him, in his earnest singleness of motive:

"Tracy Tremaine is not a man from whom you should accept favors."

"What do you know against him?" she asked, with a ring of eager defence in her fleet tones. .

"I know of nothing *for* him."

"That is no answer," she said, an angry throb stirring her voice. "He pleases me exceedingly. I don't recollect ever having met any one whom I liked so well on a short acquaintance. He is the handsomest man I ever saw. And his manners are perfect. He may not paint pictures, or aim at being a great celebrity, but then everybody can't dedicate himself to immortality. There must always remain a few humble creatures who are content with respectable obscurity."

"Leah!" murmured her mother.

But Rainsford bore this volley of unsolicited impudence in perfect silence. It roused no resentment; it seemed only to augment a certain foreboding dread.

IV.

SO you think I was rude, mamma?" said Leah. This was a good quarter of an hour later. She stood before the mirror in her own room, with both arms lifted behind her head, as she gave some stroke of mysterious repairing handicraft to the back knots of her golden tresses.

Mrs. Romilly was in the next chamber, and answered through its open doorway.

"You were perfectly pitiless, as usual," she said. "But I do not believe Rainsford thought much about your treatment. He was too filled with concern at another matter."

Leah laughed scornfully. "I shan't pretend not to understand you." Her fingers were still engaged with her satin strands of hair; the loose sleeves, fallen from each arm, brought into solid relief both their slope and swell; the palms of her busy hands, turned toward the mirror, looked like the pinkish concaves of two small but deep shells, just above the faint blue lines that crossed either rounded wrist.

"No, I shan't pretend not to understand you,"
she repeated, with eyes fixed on her own comely
reflection, as though she were directly addressing
it. "You mean that I have presumed to actually
enjoy the society of some other than one particular
man."

"No, no, Leah," firmly contradicted Mrs. Romilly. As she spoke the last word her stately figure
had reached the threshold of the intermediate
doorway. Here she remained while continuing to
speak.

"No, Leah, it is not that. You cannot so mis-
interpret Rainsford; you have known him too
long. He professes no rights of supervision or
admonition except those of a friend."

"Why should he do so?"

"Why, indeed!" A faint sigh went with the
response.

Leah turned suddenly and met her mother's
gaze.

"Oh, I am so tired," she said, in repressed tones,
that betrayed dread of being overheard, while at
the same time filled with strong protestation—
"I am so tired of having you and Rainsford take
it superbly for granted that my matrimonial future
is in both your hands! Pray, how much longer
am I to be laid siege to, like a beleaguered town?

As if I did n't know that you and he were in perpetual stealthy collusion together ! As if I did n't
know that you, mamma, have a ready little rem-
edy for all my discouragements ! Why on earth
don't you marry him yourself if you think him so
perfect ? "

A moment afterward Leah had slipped to her
mother's side, and while putting both arms about
Mrs. Romilly's neck, had kissed her on the cheek.
It was an embrace that had nothing impulsively
affectionate ; there was even a matter-of-fact de-
liberateness about it ; you might have likened it
to the performance of some little half-heeded cer-
emonial.

" There, I did n't mean *that*, of course," she said,
while going quietly back to the mirror again and
resuming her former posture. " That was only a
bit of my impertinence, you know."

Several minutes elapsed before Mrs. Romilly
said : " Leah, it is an old story to you that I want
you to be Rainsford's wife. If you cared more for
any other man than you care for him, I should be
quick to dissuade you from such a marriage.
But I believe Rainsford could make you very
happy. As for there being any plot between
us, that is mere nonsense, child. Rainsford does
not like this Mr. Tremaine, and has given me

his reasons.   I think they are very fair and sensible ones."

"What are they?" asked Leah.   She had arranged her hair to her own evident satisfaction. She again faced her mother, with a demeanor that now had in it strong apparent intention to listen, tolerantly and peacefully.

"They are these," said Mrs. Romilly, with a brightening visage, as if glad of the new receptive conditions under which she could make herself heard.   "He is a man whose whole life is one of idleness and frivolity.   He is popular, in a certain sense, yet in no sense is he respected.   He has mental ability, yet he has let it all go to waste. His world is a narrow, almost a contemptible one. But he is wholly content with it; he sees nothing beyond, or rather he has long ago shut his eyes to any larger view.   But, worst of all, Leah, he is the slave of a shallow, flippant and worthless woman."

"Do you mean Mrs. Abbott Fortescue?" asked Leah, tranquilly.

Her mother started.   "Yes, that is the name," she said.   "Can he already have told you of this intimacy?"

"Never mind, please.   What does Lawrence Rainsford say of their relations?"

" Only what everybody says — that they are on terms which society should condemn and denounce."

" Is this Mrs. Fortescue a widow ? "

" No ; she has a husband living."

Leah shook her head slowly and sceptically. She was asking herself what Rainsford could really know of these easeful and resplendent circles, in which his sober figure was so seldom to be met. She felt herself assume toward Tracy Tremaine an indignantly defensive attitude. She grew sure that reckless-tongued scandal was doing him a signal injustice. Besides, the girl might have been dowered with a much slighter fund of self-esteem, and yet have laid at the door of jealousy Rainsford's dispatch in making her parent learn these invidious reports concerning Tremaine. Indeed, there was very little tinge of egotism in Leah's reflections on the subject of Rainsford's desire to marry her. She had got to think herself deferentially persecuted, and to wonder if some downright revolt on her own side might not, sooner or later, become necessary. As it was, she liked the young artist quite well enough to let him go on loving her. This is a species of allegiance which few women have ever been known to resent; indulgence is their usual order of treat-

ment, even when no trace of reciprocal passion
exists. What gives to Doris the sudden frown
and the unpitying sneer, is a tendency on the
part of her devoted swain to meddle with some
other little idyllic flirtation. Then Strephon abruptly becomes a nuisance; his hopeless pleadings
lose both their poetry and their pathos, and she is
angry enough at him for his determined wooing
to smite him roundly with her crook.

Matters, however, had reached no such lurid
climax with Leah, though she was not by any
means in the best of humors when her mother and
herself presently descended into the dining-room.
The meal was luncheon, not dinner, for Mrs.
Preen, the proprietress, had yielded, two or three
seasons ago, to that luxurious influence which has
been slowly taking possession of Newport like one
of its own ubiquitous fogs, and had surrendered,
through the introduction of late dinners, her last
stronghold of domestic provincialism.

The boarders were all assembled when Leah
and Mrs. Romilly took their seats. They had
been assigned places on the immediate right of
Mrs. Preen, who was a lady well past middle age,
with considerable flesh and a chronic smile. Mrs.
Preen's smile was her chief personal point. It
had a glowing amplitude; it seemed to overflow

her somewhat puffed and sallow face. It was seldom absent; the least temptation called it forth; it expressed an actual exorbitance of amiability. But it was accompanied, at the same time, by an enormous eleemosynary impulse. The word "poor" was pathetically frequent in her conversation. She was incessantly pitying everybody and everything, in her corpulent, beaming, oleaginous way. You felt that she was sincere, or at least sincere for the moment. Without that vague yet secure guarantee of amiability, you would have been assailed by a sense of repulsion. But the enormous kindliness of Mrs. Preen was an indisputable fact; to receive her facile sunshine was not to doubt the genuine source whence it had emanated.

"You've been seeing something of Newport, I s'pose," she soon said to Mrs. Romilly.

She had what is called the New England accent, and in spite of a short clip given to certain syllables, she readily conveyed the impression of a person who has been educated, and somewhat thoroughly.

"Yes," Mrs. Romilly at once answered. She had made up her mind to like Mrs. Preen, as she usually made up her mind to like all people; it was part of her philosophy to brighten with one of her own smiles the threshold of every new acquaintance. "We went to the Casino. We found it very gay and pleasant."

"Madam," suddenly said the Rev. Mr. Pragley, looking with an expansive stare straight at Mrs. Romilly, "did you not also find it *very* worldly?"

Leah at once broke into a full, careless laugh. This was the first time that Mr. Pragley had addressed either herself or her mother, although both had been formally presented to him on a first meeting.

"Worldly!" exclaimed Leah, before her mother could answer. "Of course it was! That was why we went."

An ominous silence followed. Mrs. Dickerson's dog gave a furtive bark. Mrs. Dickerson herself looked as if her spare body had been galvanized into a condition of statuesque decorum, while the sly, pert little head of the dog peered up from her lap as if it sympathized with the shocked feelings of its mistress. Both the Misses Semmes fixed their small, calm eyes upon Leah. The Mr. Yarde who dreaded malaria also gazed at her. But she was the recipient of one more bit of scrutiny, and this was, in its way, keenly significant.

The Reverend Mr. Pragley's wife had arrived an hour ago, rather unexpectedly. She was a lady of perhaps five-and-forty; she had a long, square-jawed face, eyes of a peculiarly lustreless leaden blue, and hair of that dull, drab shade which resists all the frosty attacks of time. She was a person noted for the extreme severity of her religious opinions, and it was currently stated among her friends that she had exerted marked influence upon her lord, in the way of urging him to the expression of his most violent and denunciatory views. She now regarded Leah with a look of mournful and shocked disapproval.

"I hope you don't mean what you say, miss," she declared, with a manner of excessive austerity. "I *hope* you are only joking. The love of worldliness is so great a human evil, that when I see my fellow-creatures openly professing it, I feel as if I were called upon by Providence itself to show them the true light — to — yes, to lead them forth from spiritual darkness."

"Indeed!" said Leah. "Did it ever occur to you, however, that your illuminative efforts might not be considered in just the best taste?"

Mrs. Pragley was a sort of idol among her constituents, and she was now in the company of at least five of them, her husband included. Leah's tone of serene sarcasm struck them as unpardonably audacious. They exchanged gloomy glances; Cigarettte gave a second little fragment-

ary bark, and then Mrs. Pragley tartly broke the
ensuing silence.

"I think, miss, it is always good taste to try
and save mortals from sin."

"Do you?" said Leah, tranquil and impervious.
"But have you ever reflected that all human nature is fallible, and that when we parade our own
virtue, we lay ourselves under suspicion as to its
real soundness?"

"I *never* parade my own virtue!" exclaimed
Mrs. Pragley.

"No, never!" echoed Mrs. Dickerson, so emphatically that her sharp chin struck against one
of Cigarette's perked ears, and caused the dog to
utter a little squeal of pain.

Mr. Pragley gave one of his coughs. "My
dear Amelia," he said, addressing his wife, "your
zeal carries you too far."

"Yes," shot Leah's quiet speech. "Beyond the
bounds of good breeding."

Mrs. Romilly laid her hand on Leah's arm.
"My daughter," she said, "I beg that you will be
silent."

"Come, come," now struck in Mrs. Preen, in
her customary cooing voice, "we had better not
talk of each other's faults and virtues. I'm sure,
Mrs. Pragley, that poor Miss Romilly didn't

mean to offend your Christian feelings. Young
people will be young, you know, and worldly
things are pleasant to them. Newport *is* worldly,
of course, in the summer — it is so filled with
fashionable people." After which limpid little
flow of commonplaces, Mrs. Preen gave her dulcet
laugh, which had rich notes in it, not unlike the
motherly cluck made by an especially contented
hen. She lifted one plump finger and shook it
playfully at Mr. Yarde; she was bent, it would
seem, on the restoration of peace among her
patrons. " Why, you poor Mr. Yarde," she went
rippling on, "if you don't look real alarmed, I
d'clare! It's just a shame to shake those poor
weak nerves of yours — now, is n't it, sir ? "

This rather sickly flash of humor was received
somewhat ungraciously by the cadaverous Mr.
Yarde. " I am much more shocked than alarmed,
madam," he returned, with acid brevity, and afterward fixed both eyes upon his plate.

" Dear me ! " piped the Miss Semmes with the
neuralgia; " I hope there is no occasion for *fear.*"

She stole a look at Leah, which the latter returned with a faint smile of satirical amusement.

" Oh, of course, I was only joking," burst forth
Mrs. Preen. "Still you can all scold poor *me* as
much as you want," she proceeded, with jocund

martyrdom. "I'm sure I shan't care a bit, as long as you won't disagree among each *other*."

Mr. Pragley slightly started, at this point, and gave a roll of his black eyes that seemed to the revering gaze of the Misses Semmes and Mrs. Dickerson positively apostolic in its grandeur. They supposed it to be the precursor of some such memorable rebuke as only their sainted paragon could administer; but Jove concluded not to hurl his thunderbolt this time, and the rest of the meal passed in low-voiced murmurs on the part of nearly every one present, to his or her immediate neighbor.

Only Leah and Mrs. Romilly kept completely silent, the first from apparent careless disgust, the last from an unwillingness to reprovoke in any possible way that unconquerable spirit of mischief which had already spoken so assertively.

"You need n't be distressed about me in the future," said Leah, when she and her mother had again retired to their own apartments. "I shan't notice any of these dreadful people after to-day. They are pitiable travesties on humanity. They have no right to exist in this progressive century. They belong to a hundred years ago, at least, with their nonsensical puritanic bigotries."

She kept her word. But the manner which she now chose to assume was one of supreme, uncompromising haughtiness. At dinner that same evening, she sat beside her mother with a posture and a look of repressed yet palpable contempt. There was no open hostility in her deportment; she contrived that no one should catch her eye, and yet she made it sweep the whole table, now and then, with a peculiar flutter of the lid, a peculiar accompaniment in the turn of her neck, that was far from pacifying her vigilant observers.

" Leah," said her mother, as they stood on the piazza afterward, in the twilight, "you are only adding fuel to the flame."

" For heaven's sake, mamma, what do you mean? " she asked, with unruffled hypocrisy.

" Oh, you understand. You looked everything that you wanted to say."

" I can't help that. I can't control my countenance as I can my speech. That has its separate indignation and resentment, I suppose. I confess that I realized for the first time what satisfaction Medusa must have had in turning some people to stone."

" Your simile is an unlucky one. Medusa was the type of a relentless cruelty."

Leah looked at her mother with a lofty im-

patience. "Upon my word, I believe you excuse
these persons!" she said.

"I think they are to be excused — yes. They
represent a particular force in society; they are
religious fanatics. But, after all, they have a
distinct sincerity of their own."

"The sincerity of extreme impudence," said
Leah. "I wonder whether Mrs. Dickerson considers it 'worldly' or no to decorate herself in
flounces and ribbons as she does. As if the attack
which this Dr. Pragley made upon you was not
clear enough in its motive! He remembers who
you are. He is one of your old enemies. He has
told them to treat you rudely, or try to reform
you, which is about the same thing."

"I am very willing that they should try to reform me," said Mrs. Romilly.

Leah almost stamped one of her pretty feet.
"Oh, certainly!" she exclaimed. "You would
actually stoop to pit your wisdom against their
cheap sentimentalisms. You would let them turn
your splendid philosophy into mockery with their
pietistic ignorance! You, who are more soundly
moral in your finger-nails than they, souls and
bodies all taken together, would let them tell you
that you are going to be roasted in eternal torments. I know just what you would do if you

were not afraid of my explosions. You would stand up before them as calm as marble, and answer their trivial assaults with arguments that they have neither the education nor the brains to understand. And the sole reward you would get would be to have them scream some such stock-in-trade word as 'infidel' at you because you had the presumption not to accept their sulphureous dogmas."

"I should not think that my life of study and thought was of any profit to me," came the slow answer, "if it disabled me from frankly expressing my beliefs to them in simple and direct terms. We should not garner seed except to sow it. I sometimes think that in these latter years of inactivity I have culpably hoarded truth whose dissemination I owed to my fellow-creatures as a precious trust."

Leah gave an aggravated moan. She did not speak for a moment; she was plucking from the dense greenery of the thick-twined vine just in front of her a little pearly spray of honeysuckle. She performed this act with swift movements of her agile white fingers, as though wreaking upon the helpless bloom the force of a strong irritation.

"I'm glad that I'm not great, like you, mamma," she presently said, while fixing the spray in the bosom of her muslin dress. "You make me feel immensely contented with my own little-ness, and as if cloudland, after all, could n't compare with my terrestrial comforts."

Mrs. Romilly caught her hand and pressed it. While she still held it, too, she spoke.

"Leah! Leah! you often say things at your very lightest, child, that seem to cast doubt on your own levity. There is often something in your words and deeds that frightens me."

"Why?" asked Leah suddenly, and with al-tered intonation.

"Because I feel that you will some day bend on life such different eyes! — eyes, I mean, that have shed tears, my daughter. Yours have shed none, as yet. Sorrow has not taught you one of her dreary tasks. She can tame us so terribly with her ferule of iron, while we spell out with sobs the hard texts in her stern little primer!"

When Lawrence Rainsford presently appeared, joining them on their special corner of the piazza, Leah chose to treat him with a delicious forgetful-ness of her own past incivility. He bore this valuable piece of indulgence with a stoic disre-gard of its condescension. He listened with great attention while she related all that had passed at luncheon. She gave him a very faithful

account, though one, at the same time, in which
her severities of epithet ran riot, bathing every
sentence, as it left her lips, in a lambent play of
ruthless ridicule.

"Now, you must not even hint that you think
me the least bit in the wrong," she finished.
"Mamma has greatly distressed me by inferring
it. I have engaged, however, to behave with
meekness in the future, provided the enemy fires
no more guns at either of us."

"You left out that proviso before, Leah," said
her mother.

"I am afraid, if she retains it," said Rainsford
to Mrs. Romilly, "that the war is by no means
ended."

"You mean that they will make another attack?"
questioned Leah. "Oh, well, let them. In that
case I shall certainly give them a few silencing
broadsides. In the name of all decency," she
went on, "are we to be persecuted like this for
the whole of the next month? I wonder what
they will say or do when they see mamma and
myself depart *en grande tenue* for the Casino
ball."

A silence followed. The piazza was now quite
dim with the increased nightfall. But Leah, after
her abrupt little allusion, managed to watch with

covert intentness the vague faces of Rainsford
and her mother. She saw these faces momentarily
turned toward each other, as though for the exchange of that same meaning look with which
past experience had so well familiarized her. But
Rainsford, when he now spoke, chose to say, in
quite his ordinary voice:

"It might be well to change your boarding-
place for more congenial quarters. I could easily
extricate you, I think, from present surroundings; and, indeed, I suppose it is my duty to make
the attempt, since I am innocently blamable for
having lodged you at Mrs. Preen's."

Before either Leah or Mrs. Romilly could
answer, a large figure was seen approaching this
end of the piazza in the uncertain light. It
proved to be Mrs. Preen, who held a letter in
her hand, which she at once gave Leah.

"This is for you, my dear Miss Romilly," said
the bland lady. As Leah took it, peered at it,
failed to decipher its superscription, and then
darted toward the lighted hall not far away, Mrs.
Preen went on addressing Mrs. Romilly and
Rainsford.

She appeared for some time to be commiserating
everything and everybody. She expressed herself
confident that the whole sad affair at luncheon

need not have happened if only her poor wits had
played the peacemaker sooner and more effectually. She was convinced that poor Dr. Pragley
had really meant nothing. As for poor, dear Miss
Romilly, her remarks had been impulsive, perhaps, but not really ill-meaning. And then poor
Mrs. Pragley was a lady of very high principle,
devoted to her husband's opinions and sometimes
defending them too sharply when supposing them
attacked, but at heart a most lovable creature;
she had just been assured of this by poor, sweet
little Mrs. Dickerson, who had been a friend of the
Pragley family for many years. And then poor,
mild Mr. Yarde, who had such a horror of the
chills, had expressed his sincere regret at the occurrence, as also those two poor, inoffensive Misses
Semmes had done. . . .

Rainsford found his heed growing less and less,
long before this compassionate monologue had
shown any sign of cessation. He was relieved
when Mrs. Preen ended, and withdrew her massive person, leaving behind it a kind of lackadaisi-
cally humane aroma.

He did not wish to discuss with Mrs. Romilly
this ponderous apologetic discourse.

"The poor woman is in a most bewildered state
of mind," he said. "You see, I instinctively bor-

row her own pathetic adjective when speaking of
her. But do not let us speak of her, — or of
this clique that has got into her house, and
wants so autocratically to regulate its moral atmosphere."

Mrs. Romilly looked at him with such gentle
fixity in the deep dusk that he saw the smile, joyless yet sweet, which edged her lips.

"You wish to speak of Leah," she said, "do you
not?"

"Yes; I always wish to speak of her."

There was a little silence.

"You are afraid?"

"I am afraid."

"You believe that we have committed an error
in bringing her, with her love for brilliant superficialities, to this place, whose superficialities are
so filled with color and glitter?"

"Yes. I think Newport has been a mistake."

"Ah, my dear Lawrence!" (She always called
him by his first name when they were alone together). "My doctor did not think that when he
sent *me* here."

"True," he answered, with an intonation of
apology, "but there are so many other seaside
places."

"Where Leah might have been kept comparatively hidden?"

"Yes. We are very candid with each other. We always are. It is best."

A breeze floated through the vines, moving them tenderly. The pulse that it made in their leafage was just audible and no more. But the moon had begun to mount, though still invisible, and her rich yet slow splendor was blackening the contours of trees and houses in the quiet streets outside, while turning the sky above into a golden haze.

Mrs. Romilly laid her hand on Rainsford's arm. "Why do you love her so?" she murmured.

"Good God!" he said, his quiet tones lending the words a fivefold intensity. "How can I help it?"

She kept her hand on his arm, but she did not answer him. He understood why she did not. He understood that it was because she had no comfort to give him.

"Did you tell her what I said of that man, Tremaine?" he asked.

"Yes. But she will not credit it. She says"—

And here Mrs. Romilly paused. Some one was rapidly approaching them. The next instant they both recognized the light, brisk step.

"I've been answering such a kind, charming note!" exclaimed Leah, as she joined them. Her voice had a defiantly merry ring; but while its merriment seemed genuine enough, its defiance had the effect, to these trained and loving ears which heard it, of being resolutely forced.

Neither Mrs. Romilly nor Rainsford spoke, and Leah went on:

"It was a note from Mr. Tracy Tremaine. It enclosed two cards for the Casino ball, and it asked me to drive with him on Monday afternoon. I have sent away my answer. Mrs. Preen is so obliging; she made one of her servants take it. I thanked Mr. Tremaine most heartily for the invitations, and I accepted with thanks his request to take me driving."

She seated herself as she finished. The moonlight had greatened so that she could see either face quite clearly. A silence followed, which Rainsford broke.

"Tremaine has excellent horses," he said. He brought the words straight from the inner pang of a heartache. The unexpectedness of their commonplace almost disarmed Leah. But an instant later she was her wilful and cruel self again.

"I am so glad to hear you say so!" she answered. "I shall enjoy my drive all the more on that account!"

V.

THE next day was Sunday. Leah and her mother intentionally breakfasted a little later than the rest of the household, thus avoiding Dr. Pragley and his adorers. But while they were busied with their coffee and rolls they heard the singing of a hymn in the adjacent parlor, and soon afterward Dr. Pragley's stentorian voice reached them in tones that made it plain he was fervently sermonizing.

Leah listened. She could catch nearly every word quite distinctly. But she presently left off listening and resumed her breakfast.

"Do you hear?" she said. "'Eternal punishment' — 'the vengeance of Heaven' — 'the wrath of the Deity' — 'the anger of the Most High' — oh, how horrible to love a God whom they believe so unmerciful! and how insolent to treat him as if they could really explain his works and ways! Do they ever reflect upon the irreverence of their own worship?"

"Volumes might be written on the impiety of

the pious," said Mrs. Romilly, almost as if she were speaking to herself.

Leah started. "Is that your own, mamma?"

"No, Leah. A greater mind than mine put it into language."

Leah looked at her with a composed fondness. "Remember," she said, "that I admit few minds to be greater than yours. Whose is the telling little axiom.?"

"It belongs to Herbert Spencer, my dear."

"How true it is!" Leah commented, sipping her coffee, while the resonant voice of Dr. Pragley still sounded. "Yes, I think I recollect meeting it. It is in the 'Lay Sermons and Reviews,' is n't it?"

"Huxley wrote those, Leah."

"Oh, yes, so he did. I remember now. But, good gracious! why are not all these great modern thinkers dead? They ought to be."

"Why do you say that, my child?"

"Oh, because they are so majestic, most of them, that they deserve the final majesty of death itself. Even some of my nonsense would be less stupid if I should die. Death would give it a kind of classic touch. A few people would get to think there had really been something in it, because they could never hear any more of it. . . . Yes," she went on, as if entertained by the quaintness of her own reflections, "I suppose that if Mrs. Dickerson's repulsive little dog should suddenly expire in a fit we might find ourselves deciding that it had once or twice barked melodiously. . . . Oh, dear, I wish that he would n't do it quite so loud!"

This last bit of irreverent vernacular referred to the continued rolling periods of Dr. Pragley. Leah and her mother soon afterward finished their breakfast and went out on the piazza. Each took from a table in the hall a book which she had left there since the preceding afternoon. That corner of the piazza which they had already fallen into the habit of occupying was very near a large window, whose green blinds, at present shut, could be opened directly upon the parlor in which Dr. Pragley was still making himself rhythmically audible. Leah fixed her eyes upon the pages of her book, remaining silent for some little time. Mrs. Romilly began likewise to read. But presently, as she turned a leaf of her own volume, something slipped fluttering to her feet.

Half instinctively, at first, Leah stooped, reaching forth her hand. Securing what appeared to be several small sheets of printed matter stitched together, she cast her look upon the print itself. Then she uttered a faint, abrupt cry. The next

instant she had almost snatched away Mrs. Romilly's book, and had glanced at its title.

" Oh, mamma ! this is outrageous ! "

" What, Leah ? "

" Do you see ?　They have dared to put a tract
in your book !　It is called ' A Staff for the Lame
and Sight for the Blind.'　Is not this *too* much ?
Are you going to endure it ?　If you are, *I* am
not ! "

Leah had risen, by this time.　Her eyes were
flashing ; she had thrown back her head, while
turning her face with a look of accusative anger
straight toward the near apartment.

Mrs. Romilly remained seated.　" Leah," she
said, in earnest undertone, " I can endure it very
well.　Pray, do not excite yourself for such a
trifle."

" Trifle ! " repeated Leah, ominously, below her
breath.　But a moment later she had raised one
finger, with her gaze again fixed upon the neighboring window.　" Listen ! " she went on, with
her lips pressing together and her face turning
pale.

It was easy to listen.　The voice of Dr. Pragley
had seldom been more vigorous and oratoric than
now, outside the spacious walls of his own famed
tabernacle.

" Yes, my friends," he appealed, " let us pray for the perverted soul of that once notorious and still unrepentant woman ! Let us not *judge* Elizabeth Cleeve Romilly — that is not our province, not our prerogative. But let us implore the Holiness which she has offended to confer upon her the mercy of a blessed remorse, even though it may be a tardy one ! Let us implore " ——

It is possible that Dr. Pragley just had time to finish his next adjuring sentence before Leah, fired with an irresistible purpose, had succeeded in opening the broad blinds of the adjacent window. She burst into the room after that with quite enough force to make her entrance a prophecy of storm and outcry among the persons gathered in mute and rapt absorption about their fluent pastor. But if they all expected that the scene of yesterday was to be tenfold intensified by this fearless young antagonist, Leah now disappointed them with the extraordinary equipoise and calm of her demeanor.

She stood quite still, at a distance of scarcely two yards from the window by which she had so impetuously entered. Through this a wide shaft of the outer daylight had shot itself across the floor of the big, gloomed chamber; she stood centrally within the scope of its brightness, which gave to her dilated figure, her incensed eyes, and

the pale refinement of her visage, a prominence
otherwise lost. She looked at Dr. Pragley, and,
with very slight hesitation, spoke. Her voice was
rather unwontedly vibrant than loud. Her agitation and ire were plain, but it was also plain that
she had good mastery over both.

"I had made up my mind," she commenced, "to
give you, your wife, and your friends, sir, no
cause for any further personal rudeness while
we remained within this house. I did this at
my mother's anxious request, and not because
I am not quite able at all times to hold my
own with those who annoy me by verbal sharp-
shooting, of whatever sort. But you have
shown me this morning that such a course
is quite beyond my powers. In the first place,
you, or some of your clique, impertinently placed
a tract in mamma's Herbert Spencer. That was a
very officious and objectionable thing to do; but
it does not compare, in point of pure insult, with
the fact of your daring to call mamma names, under the disguise of praying for her, and in a voice
of such volume that you are certain it must
reach her ears and my own. I do not doubt, sir,
that I am giving you a very needless piece of information when I tell you that you ought to be
ashamed of yourself; for, though you could prob-

ably preach for hours about modesty or gentlemanly courtesy, I believe that both are as foreign
to your nature as the demands of your profession
make them really requisite ! "

Leah half turned toward the window, with one
of her most queenly gestures, and would at once
have quitted the room had not Dr. Pragley's tones,
full of sonorous lamentation, sounded a prompt
response.

He had thrust his right hand into the breast of
his close-buttoned coat; he had drooped his head,
and was shaking it from side to side with immeas-
urable regret in the oscillation.

" Oh, most unfortunate young scoffer ! " he
mourned. " And it is with such wanton abuse as
this that you return our patient, Heaven-inspired
efforts ! "

Just then Leah saw the light of the window
darkened, and looking round, she perceived the
forms of her mother and Lawrence Rainsford
crossing the threshold.

Rainsford's appearance gave her a sense of rein-
forcement, so to speak, but it played havoc with
her self-repression as well. Here was somebody
who would doubtless offer her the sympathy that
her distress merited, — who would aid her in the
defensive stand that she had taken. As a conse-

quence she did what no amount of dire conten-
tion on the part of the Pragley faction could have
forced her to do. She immediately burst into
tears, — they were the hot tears of hysterical
wrath — and addressed him in wailing tones, that
had lost every trace of their former continence.

"Did mamma tell you what these dreadful
people have been doing? As if that old shout-
ing sensationalist had any right to call my dear,
good, noble mother what he did! I shouldn't
have minded half so much if he had had the impudence to pray for *me*. But *mamma!* who is so
much above him, in mind, in soul, in goodness,
in charity, in *everything*, that it would take him
his whole noisy, wrangling lifetime even to — to
understand her!"

The final sentence, gathering toward its passionate rhetorical climax, was flung in a sidelong manner at Dr. Pragley. And then Leah,
like all with whom to weep is rare, saw the ludicrous side of her perturbation, and hurried
toward her mother, hiding her face on the latter's
shoulder, while her tears changed themselves into
almost convulsive sobs.

"Leah," she heard her mother's voice say, low
and sweet in its firmness, "come with me, child;
come away with me." . . .

Nothing was quite clear to Leah after that, until she and Mrs. Romilly were seated, side by side, on a corner of the piazza opposite to the one which they had formerly occupied. Then she again became aware of her mother's fervent, persuasive voice.

" Leah, do not take it so much to heart. Rainsford is speaking to those people now. He has already told me that he will arrange for us to leave this afternoon. There will be no further annoyance. We can go to the Aquidneck House in a few hours."

They did go. What Rainsford said to Dr. Pragley and his côterie he never communicated afterward. The disappearance was managed very quietly. Mrs. Preen came to her two departing boarders with a lachrymose visage and a mien of genteel matronly despair. Mrs. Romilly held converse with this bereaved lady, and made the inevitable leave-taking as brief as possible. Leah, with her eyes dried and glittering rather hard, maintained a sturdy silence. Rainsford supervised all the petty details of their withdrawal. By about four o'clock that same day, they were installed within two very comfortable rooms at the Aquidneck.

" This is delightful " said Leah, who was now

thoroughly herself again. "Why should we not remain here until we leave for good?"

"I fear it is too expensive," said her mother. And then Mrs. Romilly named the price which Rainsford had told her that they would be charged.

"Nonsense, mamma!" exclaimed Leah. "Why talk as if we were paupers? When have we spent our full income?" She named the amount of money which they had decided to be their limit of expenditure while in Newport. "Besides," she went on, "there are those few extra bonds which you wished to sell just before we came here. I fancy that we shall like the Aquidneck. It has a sort of homelike look." Here she gave a decided memorial shudder. "*Anything*," she went on, "would be better than that wretched place of Mrs. Preen's."

A little later she said, as if suddenly recollecting: "Oh, by the way, now that I am here I must write to Mr. Tremaine. I mean about tomorrow's drive, you know,—that my address is changed."

Mrs. Romilly made no answer, but Leah wrote a brief note, and when she went downstairs with her mother she paused at the desk and gave her directed envelope to the clerk, saying that she wanted it sent immediately. The clerk, who chanced to be a functionary of effusive politeness, assured her that the missive should be dispatched at once, and added that Mr. Tremaine lived only a short distance away, in the same street. "It's the old Tremaine house, miss," he continued, answering affably Leah's surprised look. "Nearly everybody in Newport knows it."

Leah afterward told her mother of their nearness to her proposed escort of the morrow. Mrs. Romilly scarcely responded at all; but when, that same evening, Rainsford appeared, meeting her in the lower hall of the hotel, some temporary absence of Leah gave her the opportunity to tell him both of the note sent and of the neighboring residence.

"I forgot he was so near," murmured Rainsford, as if to himself. "She is contented here?" he went on, in much less preoccupied tones. "She likes it?"

"She wants to stop here permanently. The hotel pleases her."

"It is much less public and populous than the Ocean House," said Rainsford.

Leah presently made her appearance. For a reason that both she and Rainsford understood, though it was concealed with not a little tact,

Mrs. Romilly soon left them. They walked out together on the piazza, so much broader and ampler than Mrs. Preen's.

"Your mother says you like it here," ventured Rainsford.

"Oh, yes," said Leah, positively. "Very much. We shall remain. It is decided."

"Will you sit down, or shall we walk?" Rainsford had paused beside two chairs while he thus spoke.

Leah gave a little laugh. "I shall stand," she replied. "But only for a short time. I am tired. I want to go upstairs. You know what has tired me." She turned her head away from his watchful face while she spoke, and looked in at the wide illumined hall.

A few people were scattered about in seated groups, here and there. But he and she were comparatively isolated where they now stood.

A hundred things that he might say swept through Rainsford's mind. But he hit only upon one.

"Leah," he began, looking at her intently in the dusk, "is there not something that you are willing to tell me?"

Her eyes seemed to gaze across his shoulder out into the dark street beyond. "I want to thank you so very much," she said, with an evasive frankness, "for having got us away from that shocking place."

" I do not mean that," he faltered helplessly.

" Well," she returned, with a ring of resignation in her voice that would have been comic at another time, " what *do* you mean, please ? "

"Have you not guessed, Leah? " His tones deepened, and seemed to throb a little. "I mean that I want you to tell me you will be my wife."

There was a silence, during which they both heard the sighing of the gloomy trees on the near lawn.

"For the last time, I hope," Leah said, measuredly, but by no means coldly, " I must answer you that this is not possible."

"Not possible," he said, repeating the words, yet scarcely knowing that he did so. It was almost as if a condemned prisoner had automatically murmured over an adverse sentence just pronounced.

" It is final — quite final," Leah went on. "But we must always be good friends. In time you will not care ; at least, I sincerely hope not. You will marry some charming girl, — and you will love her very much. You will tell me all about her, and we will laugh together over the past."

She laid her hand, very lightly, on his arm. All her former hard brilliancy had vanished; she had grown very womanly and winning; you would not have believed her guilty of the least rigor, the least cruelty. Her eyes, as they dwelt on Rainsford's face, were full of a rich, humid light.

"I think it better," he said, with the effect of forcing speech between shut teeth, "that we should never see each other again after to-night."

"No, no," she objected. She still touched his arm. There was a flash of the old imperiousness in her veto, softly as it was given; and yet this was mixed with a strange, uncharacteristic candor. "I like you to like me. I don't want you to desert me because I care for you less than you care for me. I promise always to be your friend. Friendship has its demands, its conditions, its obligations. You and I are to be friends — no, I mean you, myself, and mamma. There; it is settled. You are not to go away permanently. I cannot spare you. As I said, it will all end in time, — you know to what I refer. I hope she will be charming and high-bred. If so, I shall be very fond of her. Look, there is mamma coming. Act nicely." She withdrew her hand from his arm at this point. "Act as if everything had *not* been arranged, once and for all." Just at

this point her voice, before ending, hardened a
little. . . .

The weather was full of moderate breezes and
the best sunshine on the following day. Leah
took a short walk with her mother in the morning,
and passed a certain spacious, attractive dwelling,
which she informed her companion was the Tremaine homestead. Mrs. Romilly did not ask her
how she had obtained this knowledge. But the
fact that Leah had secured the exact information
was not without its saddening result.

The Aquidneck House charmed Leah. Before
mid-day she had drifted into conversation with a
certain lady whose appearance pleased her. The
name of this lady was Mrs. Forbes, and her remarkable information on the subject of Newport
and Newport doings afforded Leah the most potent
entertainment. She insisted that her mother
should share her new acquaintance, though Mrs.
Romilly, who found the lady in question somewhat vapid and unsatisfactory, did not long remain
in Mrs. Forbes's company.

" I think mamma is not very well to-day," said
Leah, when her mother had made an excuse to
withdraw from the large, shady, pleasant sitting-
room in which the introduction had occurred.
"She came here for her health, you know. You

must find it a decided change from Peoria, don't
you? That is so far away—I mean it looks so on
the map. Isn't it in the Rocky Mountains, or
very near them?"

"Oh dear, no!" said Mrs. Forbes. She gave a
blithe laugh. "You Eastern people are always
supposing that we Western ones come from the
most unearthly places. But don't let us talk of
Peoria. You can put it as far west on the map as
you please. I'm almost sorry that I told you I
was born and raised there. I've been abroad ever
so long since I saw it. I was married abroad. I
married an Englishman."

"Yes?" said Leah, with interrogative suavity.

She liked everything about Mrs. Forbes except
her voice. The lady was plump, pretty, and of
excellent style in the way of attire. She had a
tender pink-and-white complexion, a little, reced-
ing, piquant nose, and a mouth as small and sweet
as a crumpled red flower. But her voice, her pro-
nunciation, struck Leah as shockingly nasal. It
was so unmelodious, so coarse, in fact, that it con-
trasted most dissonantly with the agreeable *per-*
sonnel to which it belonged.

"Yes, my husband is an Englishman," Mrs.
Forbes continued. "We lived in England and
France for nearly seven years after we were mar-

ried. Then something happened with regard to
my property; I have a great deal of property in
the West. It was this trouble that brought us on
here, but we find that there has been a sort of
false alarm, and we shall probably stop in Newport
until the end of the season. Poor pa died in Peoria three years ago; he had been with me in Europe
when I was married, but afterward he had gone
back. He died quite suddenly; it was a dreadful
blow. Bertie thought it best that I should n't go
back right away. He said it would be different if
mother was living. And I am the only child.
By 'Bertie' I mean my husband, of course. His
full name is Bertram Chetwynde Forbes. He is
the first cousin of the Marquis of Chetwynde, you
know."

This latter statement was made with a slight
straightening of the jaunty little body, as though
it concerned a question of the most notable import.

" Oh," said Leah, "then you are one of the
Americans who have married among the English
aristocracy? I have often heard about those kinds
of marriages."

Mrs. Forbes nodded her head with more sociabil-
ity than seemed quite the proper accompaniment
of a lady in such close matrimonial nearness to a
marquisate.

" Yes," she said. And then, like a little oft-repeated formula, she murmured: "Bertie is first cousin to the Marquis of Chetwynde."

Leah did not wish to be too interrogative on so short an acquaintance. She felt very curious, however, regarding Mrs. Forbes, but contented herself, for the ·present, with saying:

" You go out a great deal into society here, don't you ? "

" No," said Mrs. Forbes, " I don't. Bertie does, though." And here she noticeably brightened.

" Your husband goes without *you ?* " murmured Leah. . . . " You have told me so much about the manners and customs of Newport that I supposed you had been a good deal among the great people."

Mrs. Forbes laughed. Her laugh, like her voice, was extremely harsh. She was so modishly and brightly robed that she reminded Leah, while listening, of those splendid-plumed tropical parrots which satirize their feathery loveliness by the utterance of hoarse screams.

" Oh, Bertie describes it all," Mrs. Forbes now said. " *He* goes everywhere. He thinks it best that I should n't be gay. There are the two children, you know, Enid and Gwendolen. Don't you think that those are pretty names? *We* think so. Enid is named after Bertie's sister, the Countess of Breadalbane, and Gwendolen is named after his mother, who was the third daughter of Lord George Maskelyne."

Leah recalled two pale, sickly children, who bore not the slightest resemblance to her new rotund, healthful-looking friend, and who had clamored peevishly round Mrs. Forbes on the piazza about an hour ago, until drawn away by a gaunt French *bonne.*

" They are both quite delicate," continued the mother of Enid and Gwendolen. "They are not at all like Bertie and me. Bertie says that they require all my care. I suppose he is right, of course. But then there are the two French nurses, you know, Aline and Françoise. Still, I dare say a mother should be motherly and domestic."

Leah had by this time acquired a pronounced dislike of "Bertie." Her drive with Tracy Tremaine was to take place at four o'clock, and very punctually at that hour a dog-cart, drawn by two heavy, stylish bays, drove up to the door of the Aquidneck. Leah, attired simply, but with a taste that well became her slender figure and lovely face, was soon ensconced at Tremaine's side. Mrs. Romilly saw the departure from an upper window; she somehow chose not to descend and greet Leah's new escort.

"It was so good of you to come with me," Tremaine said, while the bays were starting and the footman was leaping into his seat behind. "I was so afraid that you might refuse. Your little mention of a row at your other place has made me immensely curious. Do pray tell me all about it."

Leah began her narration. She gave it with certain touches of her old sarcastic humor that caused Tremaine more than one burst of hearty merriment. And, meanwhile, she noticed the faultless nicety of his toilette, in which, from the shining boot to the high drab hat, there was care without finicality, and elegance without foppery. He seemed to Leah a very finished human expression; he satisfied her in every way where Rainsford had fallen short of satisfying her. Nor was she at all sure that this pleasure was not one of mental as well as physical approval. He was not very often in earnest, but then Rainsford was always too much in earnest. He had no superior views of life, but then Rainsford's views were in a manner superior to the maintenance of agreeable permanent intercourse. There lay Rainsford's trouble in the eyes of Leah — he was too extraor-

dinary, too exceptional, without in the least pre-
tending to be so. But Tremaine, on the other
hand, though quite as exempt from pretensions,
had an art of putting things, a manner of living,
a grace and taste of deportment, that were all
delightfully on a level with the everyday usages,
pastimes, or occupations. Leah felt an exhilarated
relief in his society. She could not help compar-
ing the two men; they were the only two men
who had ever wakened in her the slightest definite
regard. The one whom she knew best was forever
commanding her respect; the other represented a
cheerful relaxation from this silent but continuous
levy. Not that she failed in respect for the latter,
but in him the moral tribute did not incessantly
thrust itself forward with wearying prominence.
Tremaine was an unpedestaled figure, so to speak;
there was nothing august about him; one's sight
need not be lifted too high to span his dimensions.
But, on the other hand, neither had it to be in the
least lowered. Leah felt contentedly certain on
this last-named point, notwithstanding what she
had recently heard with regard to Mrs. Abbott
Fortescue.

"That Pragley fellow must be the most shocking old duffer," said Tremaine, when she had finished her piquant recital. "It's not necessary, I

suppose, for me to tell you that I think your conduct was entirely proper."

But Leah soon forgot her grievance. They had reached Bellevue Avenue, and had begun to feel the fresh breath of the near sea.

"It is enchanting," she said, looking almost gleefully to left and right. "This, then, is the real Newport. I see it at last! I have so wanted to see it!"

VI.

THE abodes had lost that close-neighboring aspect which marked them in the older part of the town just left. They rose on either hand, in countless varying structural designs. A few — and these were quite occasional — had the smartly-assertive air of the American villa; but by far the majority of them were either noble and stately, or rustically simple in a way that left it plain as to the generous means of their owners and lessees. The popular name of "cottages" was rarely applicable. They were mostly mansions of grand and massive proportions. Their lawns lacked the amplitude usually found engirding similar English homes, but many of them, in spite of such disadvantage, satisfied the gaze with a beautiful manorial majesty.

"I suppose the great people live here," said Leah, giving full play to a childish admiration.

Tremaine laughed.

"Oh, yes," he replied. "Here are to be found our American dukes and duchesses."

"And are these people, so constantly driving past us, to so many of whom you bow," she questioned, "all what is called the cream of Newport society?"

Tremaine gave a much louder laugh.

"Oh, what a delicious phrase for this awful rabble!" he exclaimed. "Come, now, Miss Romilly, I am sure you got that straight from the newspapers."

Leah was too preoccupied to dream of being offended.

"Why do you call it a rabble?" she said, as carriage after carriage, in every conceivable shape, from the monumental four-horse drag to the small two-wheeled tilted cart, swept multitudinously past them. "I think everything is so prosperous, so glittering, so undemocratic! It all seems to me like a region in which poverty is quite unknown. As we drive along now we seem to be in a kind of gentlemanly and ladylike paradise."

"Oh, there is money enough, if you mean that," Tremaine answered, in his loitering, half-indifferent way. "But you must n't judge of this Bellevue Avenue parade by outside appearances. A few years ago it was quite another matter. Then Newport was really a special and peculiar place. Now it is overrun by people from heaven knows where. We used to have from thirty to forty families here, who all knew each other and entertained each other. It was a blessed refuge, then, from such rowdy spots as Saratoga and Narragansett. But something has changed all that of late. There are various explanations given; for my part, I am convinced that only one is to be credited. I mean that wretched Casino."

"Oh, don't call it wretched!" dissented Leah. "It is so lovely!"

"Yes, that is what everyone said when it was first built. But *I* consider that it has ruined Newport. It has done away with all the old quiet, conservative charm of the place. It has made Tom, Dick, and Harry flock here with their wives, daughters, and sons. It has destroyed all our atmosphere. The old residents can't be rude to people who *will* get introduced to them at the Casino, and *will* bombard them with hospitalities afterward. They are forced to make some return. As a consequence, it has become customary to give great dinners at the Casino restaurant — could anything be better evidence than that of the lowered tone of the place? All the fine, select atmosphere of Newport has gone. The really swell women don't drop- in upon each other of a morning as they used to do; that charming mix-

ture of home life and fashionable life, — the lady's
morning visit, once so distinctive a feature here, —
has almost completely vanished; everybody sees
everybody else, nowadays, at the Casino. Then,
again, if somebody like Mrs. Chichester, of New
York, or Mrs. Parkinson, of Boston, wants to
throw open her palace of a house and give a ball
to guests whom she knows and has known for
years and whom she desires to compliment by a
superb piece of real civility, she straightway
trembles in her boots, poor woman, at the prospect of having about two hundred extra invitations asked for the moment her regular cards have
been issued. Now, I maintain that the Casino is
responsible for this new abomination. It has
turned Newport into a watering-place. It never
was one before; they used to call it so, but it
never was. People would go to the Ocean House,
and stay there a week, and go away bored, who
now remain to struggle and push and elbow
themselves right into cottage society. For that
matter, there is no cottage society any longer;
it has become a mere memory."

Leah was so interested by this glimpse into an
unknown world, that she never gave the least
egotistic thought to her own isolation and aloof-
ness from it. She showed, on the contrary, her

relish of Tremaine's *dilettante* complaints by a laugh that pealed out sweet and silvery in the crisp marine air.

"Truly," she said, "it's like the wail over Babylon, or some great ruined city of the past. If there were only more willow-trees in Newport, how pretty it would be for all you old cottage-people, as you call yourselves, to decorate them with croquet-mallets and lawn-tennis bats, just as the poor Israelites hung up their harps, you know!"

"An excellent idea," he said, echoing her laugh. "I should like to commemorate our downfall in precisely some such picturesque way."

But now Leah spoke in decidedly altered tones. She had remembered at last what it was so like her to remember, sooner or later.

"By-the-bye," she said, very seriously, and with a little heightening of her delicate head, "I suppose it has not struck you that *I* might be ranked among your condemned pushers and strugglers, has it?"

He replied instantly, and with apparent shocked astonishment. If counterfeited, nothing could be more deft.

"Miss Romilly, is it possible that you are not joking?"

Leah felt the balm at once touch her hurt, which, after all, was a mere scratch.

"Well," she admitted, with her grand, cool air, "it is true that you sought an introduction to me."

"I was compelled to seek one."

"Compelled?"

"Assuredly. You understand, of course."

"But these very exclusive personages," she went on, "whom I don't know, and whom you know that I don't know — what will they say when they see us together?"

He leaned his face for a few brief seconds near to her own. The bays were so well broken as not to require great vigilance.

"Ah, what *would* they say," he murmured, "if you should choose to meet and mingle with them?"

"I am sure I can't tell. Can you?"

"Quite accurately, I think. They would say that, with all their exclusive tendencies, they had never denied their courtesy to beauty, wit, and refinement, when those three gifts met notably in the person of one woman."

Leah thought this, as it was spoken, — we might also add, as it was looked, — thoroughly delightful. It so entirely banished her resentment that when, a little later, Tremaine asked her whether she

would prefer to visit the polo-grounds or to quit
the wagon and walk a little way along the Cliffs,
she readily answered:

" I will leave the preference to you. Whichever
you choose I will choose."

Her mien of condescension, blended with her
unaffected ease and her brilliant beauty, affected
him very pleasurably.

" Let us go to the Cliffs," he said, thinking how
he should like to walk at her side for a little
while.

When they reached the end of Bellevue Avenue,
he signed to the groom behind him, after stopping
his horses. The groom sprang out and held their
heads, while he assisted Leah to alight.

They were presently strolling close to the edge
of the sea, along a hard, smooth path, beneath
which sloped in rugged, rocky acclivity the extreme ocean-limit. On their left was a seemingly
interminable line of palatial edifices ; on their
right the sea broke, with its immemorial music
and its vast, pure distances of lustrous color.
But sheer down from the porticoes and verandas
of the adjacent dwellings, directly to the verge of
old Atlantic itself, ran a carpeting of green lawn,
as sleek and even as a leopard's fur. It met the
grim top of the precipitous headland and there

ended with an abruptness that was like a happy
truce between nature and art. The ocean seemed
to have grumblingly granted this peaceful com-
promise; it washed the granite bases, many feet
below, with a sort of leonine submission. Perfect
culture never before blent so harmoniously with untamed wildness. The residences themselves were
those past which Tremaine and Leah had already
driven; but seen on this, their shoreward side,
they acquired a new meaning, a new vantage.
Their encompassing lawns not only flowed toward
the coast, but flowed into each other with an
untrammeled pastoral freedom. You felt, as you
looked into their vague doorways, their curtained
casements, that the salt, invigorating breeze
wandered at will through each luxurious interior.

"It is something that I have never seen before,"
said Leah, with a peculiar thoughtful enthusiasm,
as they moved onward for hundreds of yards and
found always the same sweep of emerald grass
touch the austere gray rock on one hand, and the
same line of imposing abodes gleam to them on
the other. "It charms me, delights me, and yet
it has a certain cruelty."

"Cruelty?" repeated her companion.

"Yes. Do you know, it makes me think of the

miserable people who are starving in crowded cities not far from here. I don't know what puts such a thought into my head at such a time; but it has come; I can't help having it."

No one would have called Leah cold or haughty while she thus spoke. Tremaine looked at her in surprise.

" Are you so humanitarian, so philosophic ? " he asked.

She suddenly frowned.

" Yes; if I choose to be," she said, annoyedly. " There is a cruelty of luxury about these cliffs, as you call them. They are *too* lovely. I mean that while so many people are shut in hot garrets, not knowing where they shall get their next crust, all this pomp and comfort seems like an injustice,— an outrage ! "

She was instinctively thinking the thoughts that she knew her mother would have had if they had come here together. But, more than this, she was thinking the same thoughts because of hidden depth in her strange, capricious nature that even her mother had not possessed the skill or acumen to fathom.

Tremaine disliked her unforeseen mood, but in most moods she had begun so potently to please him that he chose, with a sure tact, to thwart and alter this one.

"You say truly that you have never seen anything like it before," he softly ventured. "Neither
has anybody, I think. Not long ago I walked
this same path with — well, I can't dream of pronouncing his name; he is the Russian Minister,
and a very good fellow. He has seen three-
quarters, at least, of the inhabited sphere. I
asked *him* if he had ever seen anything like our
Newport cliffs before, and it was very amusing to
watch him, with his encumbering foreign prejudices, muse and meditate until he had answered
me, in his halting, precarious English, that there
was a summer resort on the borders of the Crimea
which reminded him of our present ramble, and
yet was actually far less fine. I suspect, myself,
that it can't hold a candle to this, wherever and
whatever it is. I've knocked round a great lot,
myself, but I have met only one Newport — that
is, from this one *point de vue* of external superiority."

After a little more strolling they retraced their
steps toward the attendant vehicle. The sun had
now dropped to its partial extinction, and the sea,
under its level rays, had begun to take darker
wrinkles upon a surface of deepened blue. Along
its horizon the sky showed a ring of that faint
rosy haze which betokens the ripeness of summer,

and tells that the sharp autumn evening is not
far away. As they drove back through the
delicious early dusk, Leah said, "Are there many
English people here at present?"

"Yes, a few."

"Great swells?" she questioned; and then
laughingly added, "As *you* would say."

"Not many great swells; no." He mentioned
the name of one British nobleman, and then
paused, as if he could think of no one relatively
distinguished.

"Do you know a Mr. Forbes?" asked Leah.

He turned quickly, with a smile: "Bertie
Forbes? Of course I do. Oh, yes; I recollect.
He is at the Aquidneck. Have you met him al-
ready?"

"No," said Leah, gravely; "but I have met his
wife."

"Ah," said her companion, with an odd
accent upon the monosyllable. "I know Mrs.
Forbes slightly."

"Tell me about them," demanded Leah.

"About them?" he repeated, with a quizzical
mystification. "Do you mean who and what they
are?"

"Oh, no. I have learned all that from the poor
little lady herself."

"Why do you call her a poor little lady?"

Leah was transiently silent. "Because," she soon said, with emphasis, "I have an idea that she is shamefully neglected."

"Well, I must allow that you're right," returned Tremaine, with a swift sidelong look into her face. "But *she* has n't complained, has she?"

"Oh, no. On the contrary, she seems to think that she is enormously honored by being married to a man of close connection with the English peerage, and who never takes her anywhere. A man who is ashamed of her, in fact."

"Well, you are about right. She was a great heiress. Bertie married her in England. He had n't a penny. I never knew such a case of unmurmuring conjugal devotion. She might be made presentable enough, if he would only introduce her. But he does n't. He spends her money instead — sometimes even gambles it away at cards, I'm afraid — and keeps her always persistently in the background. It's shocking of him, of course."

"I should say so," answered Leah. . . .

A little later, after Tremaine had assisted her to alight at the hotel door, and had said a few low words concerning the Casino ball, at which they were soon to meet, Leah passed into the hotel on the way to her mother's room. But before reaching the staircase she came face to face with Mrs. Forbes.

"I saw you come back from your drive," said this lady, in her brisk, nasal way. She looked extremely pretty; she was dressed quite showily, yet tastefully, for dinner. "Did you enjoy it?" she went on.

"Oh, very much," replied Leah. "Did *you* not drive this afternoon?"

"No. Bertie took some gentlemen out. But I usually drive — that is, when he does n't want my particular horses. We have only four with us, this year; we were not sure how long we should stay, you know; and one of Bertie's has gone lame several times since our arrival."

"So you let him keep you at home?" said Leah, with a dubious levity, while her brown eyes dwelt very firmly on the little woman's gay, kindly face. She lifted one finger and shook it with smiling admonition. "Ah, Mrs. Forbes, if I were you I would manage things very differently!"

Mrs. Forbes could not feel offended. Her intimacy with Leah had been rapid and almost wholly of her own making. Besides, Leah greatly attracted her; she thought her one of the most beautiful young creatures she had ever seen; and

she had a pronounced liking for beauty in her
own sex. Apart from all these considerations,
too, the girl had given her little burst of famil-
iarity with enough jocose carelessness to render it
safely non-committal.

"How would you manage things?" asked Mrs.
Forbes, with a sudden earnestness that struck her
hearer as a little short of wistful. "I'd like to
know. I've been *wanting* to know."

Leah promptly became serious. She slipped
one hand into one of Mrs. Forbes's plump hands
as she spoke, while still maintaining her fixed
regard.

"You ask me that question," she said. "I don't
know what precise answer you wish, but I will
give you a frank and sincere answer. It is this: I
would go to the Casino ball to-night. It means
more than it says, that slight answer of mine.
There's a good deal behind it."

Mrs. Forbes's color grew slowly from its usual
pink into a much richer shade. But she did not
withdraw her hand from Leah's.

"You — you mean against *his* will?" she said,
hesitatingly.

Leah pressed the hand that she held. The rec-
ollection of Tremaine's words now keenly recurred
to her.

"Oh, Mrs. Forbes," she answered, every trace of her customary secure reserve having fled, and a fervent, sincere cordiality replacing it, "I don't know if I am not unwarrantably officious! I expected that you were going to snub me, and I should n't have minded it if you had! . But, yes, really, I *do* mean against his will, since you *ask* my meaning. I would not stand being made — oh, well," she suddenly broke off, "I can't say it! We have got to be very good friends, of course, in this little bit of a time — but still I can't say it! You can understand if you choose." Here the speaker looked as grim as her fine-cut and clear-lined face would permit. "And upon my word," she pronounced, with her voice as gutturally bass as she could make its naturally soft tones, "I do hope that you *will* understand!"

"I think that I do understand," said Mrs. Forbes.

Leah had not heard her speak with anything like this decisiveness before. The new tone startled her.

When, after dining, Leah went to her room, she found a large knot of fresh pink roses waiting on her dressing-table. The bouquet was shaped with perfect skill for a corsage. She fixed it in the bosom of her white dress, knowing well who had sent it. Mrs. Romilly also knew. Mother and daughter dressed together, almost in silence.

"By the way," said Leah, when they were both about to go downstairs, "did Rainsford speak of accompanying us?"

Mrs. Romilly's face flushed a little. She was clad in a robe of filmy black, whose sombreness Leah had insisted on relieving with a few of her large pink, gauzy-petaled roses.

"Leah," she murmured, "how can you expect *that?*"

Leah tossed her head.

"I don't expect it," she answered. An instant later her eyes, which had got an excited spark in their velvety brown, wandered toward her mother. And then she went straight up to Mrs. Romilly and put both arms round the lady's neck.

"You're a perfect picture!" she exclaimed. "I never saw you look so bewilderingly handsome. Kiss me!"

Her fresh red lips were within an inch of her mother's, but she held her lightsome, flower-like head obstinately backward, waiting for the kiss to be given. Mrs. Romilly gave it, with a faint sigh that Leah's quick, gay laugh might have drowned to the girl's own ears.

"You'll have a splendid time," she exclaimed. "I know you'll be admired. *I* expect to be. And I made you come with me, poor, dear mamma, did n't I? I got the best of you. That is the way of the world; the little people always get the best of the great ones, I begin to think. . . . But you'll have a splendid time, as I said. . . . I *intend* to have one myself."

Leah did. The ball of this evening was especially brilliant in the way of patrician attendance. Mrs. Abbott Fortescue was there, loudly but becomingly dressed in a gown of some yellow-and-black tissue that suited her tawny complexion beyond cavil. But Tremaine was not at Mrs. Fortescue's side. He adhered devotedly to Leah, who refused to dance with him.

"I don't dance at all," she told him with positiveness. "I never could learn, and I shall never try to learn any more."

"Dancing is a frightful bore," he said. "I am so glad you hate it. I do."

"I don't hate it," said Leah, looking at the forms, masculine and feminine, which were moving across the waxed floor. "I think it is charming to be able to dance. I envy those who can."

"A swan walks ungracefully," said Tremaine, having a smile in his dark-blue eyes which his

mouth, shaded with its long, blond moustache,
gave no sign of. " She can only swim."

" Please don't call me ·a swan," said Leah, with
arch impatience. " I don't like it. It is so near
being called a goose."

" Oh, *I* did n't call you so," returned Tremaine.
"Somebody whispered it just now. Shall I tell
you who? It was the great Mrs. Chichester —
the reigning power, one might say, of both Newport and New York. And I don't know how many
men," he went on, "have asked to be presented.
I 've promised them all that I would get your per-
mission. Do you grant it? I wish you would
say 'no,' but I am very much afraid you will say
' yes.' "

Leah creased her straight white brows reflect-
ively. " I want to see how mamma is getting
on," she said, turning her head swiftly away from
her companion, "before I either consent or refuse."

She saw her mother, seated in a portion of the
large ball-room that was reserved for dowagers and
non-dancers generally, in converse with a white-
haired, sweet-faced lady, who seemed glad of her
society.

" With whom is mamma talking ? " she asked of
Tremaine.

"With Mrs. Lydia Holt Morrison," he at once answered.

Leah recognized the name. "Oh, yes," she said. "Mamma knew that she lived in Newport — or somewhere near. They met years ago. She always wanted to meet her again. I know all about her; mamma has told me. I am so glad that they have got together. I assured her that she was to have a splendid time. . . . Well, on the whole, I conclude that I will let you introduce those gentlemen." She said it with a laugh of almost insolent condescension. He thought how exquisite she looked, too, as she said it, with her half-curled lip and her softly flashing eyes under the dense, back-drawn gold of her hair. . . .

A little later she was the centre of quite a throng of gentlemen. She found some of them tiresomely stupid, and almost told them so, with her ready speech, full of apt utterance and easy repartee. But others she found attractive, and bent on these her most indulgent smiles.

Tremaine presently dropped away from her. He was irritated at her wish to know other men. "She is already a great belle," he thought. "It was certain to happen. The men are flocking about her like sheep. One presents another." He repressed an inward oath of discontent. He was ready at oaths when annoyed and sure that no woman overheard him.

He went out on the big porch, where a breeze was blowing, and where people were moving about.

Suddenly, a very familiar voice met his ear. He started, and saw Mrs. Abbott Fortescue standing quite near him, in the dusk. Her olive skin and her black-and-yellow braveries harmonized well; but even in the dusk Tremaine's eye could see that she was both pale and angry.

" You 're alone?" he said, still more annoyed, not knowing what to say.

" Yes; I saw you leave the ball-room," Mrs. Fortescue answered. Her black eyes were riveted on his face. " I slipped away to meet you. It was my only chance. You have not spoken to me this evening. You drove this afternoon with that girl. What does it mean ? " ·

They were standing together now in a very obscure portion of the spacious and shadowy place.

Tremaine looked sullenly, even defiantly, at the woman who thus addressed him.

" It means anything you choose," he said. " It means that I am tired."

" Tired ! " she repeated, drawing back from him a little.

"No," he answered, with a sudden, sinister gay-ety, "not a bit of it! I'm refreshed! I shall ask Leah Romilly to be my wife before an hour has passed. She will refuse, of course. But that will not matter. It will prepare the way for my acceptance hereafter. It's time I married. And I mean to marry *her*."

"You mean to marry *her?*" said Mrs. Fortescue, very softly, looking at him intently in the dimness with her black eyes, that now seemed to burn his own gaze as they met it.

"Yes."

As Tremaine uttered the word, he turned on his heel and passed once more into the bright-lit ball-room.

He so rarely committed the least discourtesy toward a woman that this act was, in its way, fatefully momentous.

VII

$M^{RS.}$ ABBOTT FORTESCUE went back into the ball-room with a beating heart and an angry soul; but she was very far from believing that Tracy Tremaine had actually meant his recent words. Men may love at first sight, but the intention of matrimony is a more deliberate affair, even with the most amorous of suitors.

Tracy Tremaine had, indeed, spoken at random. And yet he felt certain regarding one point — that he was exceedingly, however suddenly, in love with Leah Romilly. Her new belleship told him this in forcible terms. He watched other men watch her, smile upon her, be smiled upon in return, and his quickened pulses told him the truth. No such sensation had ever entered his being before. He measured it by his past caprices, and felt the folly of resisting its intense headway.

Mrs. Abbott Fortescue was in many respects a clever woman. She had thus far succeeded in doing a very difficult thing with success; she had braved scandal, and yet held her own as a leader

in the fashionable world. Her dinners were not
only models of culinary skill; the people whom
she allowed to eat them were such as did not sow
their courtesies broadcast. She had made one
arch-enemy by her daring indiscretions. She
knew this, and in thinking of the great power
which that enemy held she sometimes trembled
for her future position. She was a woman who
had always skated on thin ice, and enjoyed the
excitement of the peril. Her good name was very
dear to her for the prestige that it brought, and she
liked to remember, now and then, that she had been
a poor country clergyman's daughter when she
married Abbott Fortescue, and that he had been
an obscure young stock-broker. It pleased her to
think that her wit and energy had pushed him
into his present high place as one of the Wall
Street millionaires, while it had lifted herself
among the social celebrities of New York. She
knew perfectly well that her "tone" was thought
to be vicious, and yet that in every practical sense
this evil repute harmed neither her prominence
nor her power. She understood that her one
great safeguard was her husband; as long as she
kept him loyal in his adherence and belief, she
could easily breast the tides of assailant gossip.
Thus far she had so kept him with an unwavering

security. He was a man of considerable brains, and yet he never suspected in her the least approach to absolute infidelity. He used to say offhandedly that Serena liked her fun, and it was all nonsense for a woman to cage herself merely because she was married. But it never occurred to him that he was even reposing confidence in her. He was no longer very fond of her; they had no children; he liked her way of presiding at the head of his household, and he was proud of the individual distinction that she had won. He knew of her enemy, and regretted the quarrel, as he chose to term it, though there had really never been any quarrel at the root of this noted antagonism.

The name of the enemy was Mrs. Chichester, of New York. Hers was a very different gentility from that of Mrs. Fortescue. That of the latter might perish in a day; a sudden *esclandre publique* would sweep it away, as a tornado sweeps a rosegarden. But the standing of the former was indestructible in its august stability. The Chichesters owned blocks of houses in New York. The aggregate income of the family was enormous. Their name had for several years past been one of the shibboleths of our groaning socialists. Mrs. Stephen A. Chichester, as it was customary

for the society-columns of the newspapers to
entitle her, was the acknowledged head of her
very wealthful house. There were other Mrs.
Chichesters, all of whom shared the magic that
engirt this race of mighty capitalists; but she, for
reasons which concerned her lord's vast posses-
sions, yet not for these reasons entirely, reigned
lofty and alone. Those who declared the Chichesters to be monopolist upstarts, even while
glad and proud to know them, could fling no similar slur upon this particular lady. She had been
a Miss Vanderveer, and an heiress of large fortune, before her marriage. Everybody knew the
Knickerbocker soundness of the Vanderveers;
that implied a solidity like the foundations of
Old Trinity itself, near which many of this note-
worthy race lay buried. Thus Mrs. Chichester
held all the advantages of colossal opulence, blent
with the talismanic charms of a brilliant pedigree.
She bore these double honors with great modesty
and sense. She was now nearly fifty years of
age, but the necessity of bringing three daughters
out into society had caused her to remain an active participant in its pomps. The daughters were
now all married, but Mrs. Chichester continued to
"entertain." It must be conceded that she entertained with a lavish splendor, tempered by the

most faultless good taste. Her house at Newport
was a roomy mass of gray stone, towering above
the sea, and appointed with incomparable beauty.
Her new mansion, near Central Park, was one of
our metropolitan marvels, both without and within.
It has been stated that her age verged upon
fifty; but she failed physically to show, by at least
ten years, this material advancement. She had
been a very lovely maiden in her youth, and she
was now a somewhat stout matron, with masses of
curly chestnut hair, into which time had slipped
only the most lenient silver, and a complexion
whose natural creamy freshness yet withstood the
aggression of all serious wrinkles. Her neck and
arms were phenomenal in their chaste and just
moulding, and though report spoke with bated
breath of the precious jewels in her possession,
she rarely wore as much as even a thread or band
of gold about throat or wrist. She had the repute
of being a martinet as regarded decorum, and had
been known more than once to strike from her
visiting-book the names of certain young men who
had offended her by their indifference, their laziness, or their self-esteem.

She had struck Mrs. Abbott Fortescue's name
from her visiting-book, and had indeed once cut
this lady on meeting her face to face, with that

freezing avoidance which looks past, above, below you, but never straightly encounters your waiting gaze.

Mrs. Fortescue at length understood. She had been dropped by the great regnant dignitary. She invented a falsehood as the reason of the terminated acquaintance, and endeavored to make its cessation appear the result of a mutual rupture. No one believed the falsehood except her husband, whom no one attempted to disabuse of his deception. It reached the ears of Mrs. Chichester, and hardened her more than ever against its author. She had cut Mrs. Fortescue on strictly moral grounds, and for no other cause. She had the charity, however, not publicly to proclaim this; she made, with unpharisaical wisdom, the whole affair one between herself and her own conscience. Of course Mrs. Fortescue profited by her reticence. If the great lady had chosen to head any hot faction against her she could ill have held her own with so formidable a foe.

Mrs. Chichester liked Tracy Tremaine, though she disapproved of him. There was at one time a rumor that he had become engaged to a daughter of hers, but events soon disproved this fallacy; she would never have permitted such a union. Still, as recorded, she felt the spell of Tremaine's *bel air* and indolent attractiveness. His dead father had been a beau of her own in past ante-matrimonial years. Tracy reminded her of those years; he won her reluctant indulgence; she deplored his intimacy with Mrs. Fortescue, and would have given much to break it.

Once or twice Tremaine had shown signs, during a few recent seasons, of snapping the bondage in which his charmer held him. But Mrs. Fortescue had brought him swiftly back to her side. She stood, presently, fanning herself with a big gorgeous fan, attended by one or two of her inalienable male devotees, and wondered whether she could now resume her sway as easily as on former occasions.

She had an ominous dread, however, lest she might fail. Half the assemblage was talking about Leah; scores of eyes were riveted upon the girl; she had made what is called a sensation. Mrs. Fortescue, clearly perceiving this, spoke of her with a gentle admiration in which there was no ring of the irritated foreboding from which she suffered. While she stood thus, unable to keep her glance from straying toward the new belle, Mr. Bertie Forbes sauntered up to her side.

They were very good friends. They had met abroad not many months ago, when Mr. Forbes

had secured her the *entrée* to several rather difficult foreign houses.

"She's not bad," he drawled, after the talk had
inevitably drifted upon Leah. "I exchanged a
few words with her. She's at the Aquidneck, you
know, so I thought it would only be civil to let
Tremaine present me. Besides, she's got in with
my wife."

"I saw your wife here," said Mrs. Fortescue,
surprisedly. "Is n't that something very unusual ?"

"Bertie," who had a mindless, inanimate face,
over which his hair was so glued to his narrow
head on either side of a white, accurately central
parting, that it made him look as if he wore some
kind of glossy black satin cap which clung with a
wonderful skin-fit, now shifted his lank, loose-
jointed body a good deal sideways, and gave vent
to a discontented groan.

"Good gracious," he said, grumbling the words
to Mrs. Fortescue alone, in surly confidence, "it's
all this girl's doin's, don't you know? She's put
a lot of stuff into Lucy's head about my neglectin'
her. Only farncy! Arfter a few hours of acquaintance ! . . . I went to the 'otel to dress mee-
self to-night, and there. was Lucy in teahs. She
was ready to have a dreadful raow with me unless

I brought her heah. She said there were two
nerses to mind the babies, and that I never treated
her as a husband should, and oh, a lot of rot like
that, and then ended by sayin' she'd met a real
woman, of real spirit, who'd opened her eyes to
the propah respect thet was dew a wife, ye know.
Now, let me arsk you, could anything be maw of
a baw?"

"Do you mean that there has been a domestic
insurrection," asked Mrs. Fortescue, "and that
this young lady has brought it about?"

Mr. Forbes struck the black broadcloth of his
thin thigh with a pair of kid gloves that he carried, clutched together in lavender limpness.

"Yes; that is precisely what I do mean. Did
you ever heah of such beastly officiousness?"

At any other time Mrs. Fortescue would have
secretly exulted over her friend's discomfiture,
and regarded it as a surpassingly good joke. But
now it dealt her a new wound; if Leah were clever
enough to turn the tables upon this abominably
selfish young English snob (for it was thus that
Mrs. Fortescue had always considered him), what
subverting changes might she not already have
wrought in Tremaine?

"I should think it a very imprudent way of beginning her Newport career," said the dusky little

lady, "by mixing herself up in matters which do not concern her. That is, if she is going to *have* a career. What do you think?"

"A careeah?" repeated Bertie. He glanced toward the dark-coated throng which almost concealed Leah's fair young figure. "It looks awfully like it. I carn't see what they see in her, for my part."

He could, perfectly. The wife whom he had made support him for several years in moneyed sloth, and whom he had shown the manly gratitude of treating a little worse than though she were the nursery-governess of his children and her own, had needed but a straw to test the capacity of her patience. Leah had supplied this straw, and the petty spirit of Mr. Bertie Forbes hated her accordingly. "Her mothah, you know," he went on, "is really a very objectionable, public sort of person. I don't think any of the women will take her up on this account."

But before the evening was over, both foes had the somewhat questionable satisfaction of seeing Leah in close converse with Mrs. Stephen A. Chichester.

The truth flashed, then, through Mrs. Fortescue's ired mind. Her old enemy had gone silently but effectively to work. She was setting upon this new preference of Tracy Tremaine's a *cachet* which her own acquaintance could almost singly bestow.

Mrs. Chichester had proceeded with perfect tact. She had admired Leah in the hearing of Tremaine, but she had by no means allowed the latter to make the desired presentation. In speaking to her of Leah, Tremaine had recently said: "She comes from New York. Her mother is with her here at the Aquidneck."

"They have not cared to go about much, I suppose?" said Mrs. Chichester, who always spoke very guardedly on all matters of social degree.

"No," returned Tremaine, who understood the words in their precise import. This import was just as plain to him as if Mrs. Chichester had said outright, "They have no position in society, since I have never heard of them, and since they yet live in New York."

"The mother is a sort of literary woman, I believe," he continued. "Her name is Elizabeth Cleeve Romilly. You have probably heard it."

"It has a vaguely familiar sound," said Mrs. Chichester; "and yet" . . . Here she shook her handsome head. "No; I can't place her."

This was surely a most credible circumstance. The speaker had dwelt, through all her fifty years

of life, hedged in by every stout encompassment
of orthodoxy that the most conservative principles could possibly rear between herself and that
loud, radical world in which Leah's mother had
once shone with such meteoric radiance. But
when Tremaine said, " Mrs. Romilly is talking now
with Mrs. Lydia Holt Morrison, and I believe they
are old friends," his companion gave an approving
nod. She liked the white-haired, sweet-faced Boston woman, who had transgressed the usage of
upper circles, it was true, and yet who had been
one of the Holts, and whom she considered charming and high-bred, notwithstanding her " advanced
views."

But it was not through Mrs. Morrison that she
secured the flattering introduction to Leah. The
Misses Marksley chanced to be hovering in her
near neighborhood, attended by one or two of those
unpopular male revellers to whom the pleasure of
reflecting that they have enjoyed fashionable life
is compensation for nights and days of tedious dis-
countenance. Mrs. Chichester knew the Misses
Marksley, or rather remembered that for a slight
while past she had had the option of recognizing
them or not, at her royal inclination. It had fallen
from Tremaine, in some chance way, that Leah
knew these young ladies. Mrs. Chichester, who

was never without at least two or three waiting
escorts, contrived to have herself placed not far
from the sisters. A little later she amazed them
both by addressing one of them. The honor made
both tingle. Two excitedly civil faces were lifted
to her own. It became rapidly evident to Mrs.
Chichester that she would have no difficulty whatever in being accompanied by gentle sidelong approaches toward the neighborhood of Leah.

And then the introduction followed. Each of
the Misses Marksley gave it, in a sort of fluttered,
demoralized duo. They were so impressed by the
idea that Mrs. Chichester had condescended to
address them at all, after a fortuitous and unex-
pected meeting during the previous week, that
Leah scarcely understood their real intention from
their eager and half-coherent words, until, as it
might be said, she found herself face to face with
majesty.

She conducted herself in a thoroughly unawed
way. She was agreeable, and this, at all times
with Leah, meant to be fascinating. Mrs. Chichester's trained perception read her keenly. She
saw the girlish egotism, the uncalculating pride,
the haughty self-confidence. But she liked Leah,
nevertheless, and was so allured and enticed by
something in her smile, her contour, her voice, her

attitude, that when she had pressed the slight hand
in her own full-palmed one, and asked her to drop
in at Steep Rock any morning, this sovereign lady
felt that, after all, she had conferred no unde-
served compliment.

Nor would Leah have thought so if the Misses
Marksley, still sensibly tingling, had not assured
her with loquacious vehemence that she had made
a most signal conquest. Leah listened amusedly
to the voluble congratulations of the sisters. She
had no thought of taking offence. There was
something ludicrous and yet pitiable in the amiable envy with which they regarded the great
lady's recent action.

"She can make it so monstrously pleasant for
you, my dear," declared Louisa. . . . "Oh, yes,
Leah," continued Caroline; "she is perfectly
adored and worshipped in Newport, you know,
and anything that she says is just *law*." . . . "If
she chose to take up a red-handed assassin she
could make him a swell," struck in Louisa. . . .
"Oh, she has shown that you have set her mad
with admiration," resumed Caroline; "and, upon
my word, we're not surprised at it, for you do
look simply ravishing to-night, my dear, and it's
no wonder a bit that the men are all insane to be
presented." . . .

This species of convulsive exaggeration was continued in spasmodic asides, until Leah began to weary of it. She felt relieved when the Misses Marksley withdrew themselves and their cordial hyperboles.

"I think I can see why they are not a success," she said soon afterward to Tremaine, in her placid, even voice. "They are too anxious to please. And then the way in which they hurl their superlatives at you! It's funny, but rather tiresome. Are many of the Newport maidens like that?"

"Oh, no," he returned. "The volcanic style is n't much in vogue. But the Marksleys are very typical, — very representative. They belong to a class. They are essentially American, somehow. No other country on the globe could ever produce them. Everything that they do, they overdo. . . . But I'm not going to abuse them," he continued, appreciably softening his tones; "I can't afford to. They were the means of our getting acquainted. . . . Here come at least four men whom they frightened away from you. Don't you think it was extremely nice and heroic of me to stick beside you in the very teeth of your persecution?"

"Oh, I was not persecuted," said Leah. "I should never have stood it so long if I had been. Patience is by no means one of my few virtues." . . .

That evening was a memorable one with Leah. She told her mother so frankly, and with an unaccustomed fervor, after they had regained the hotel.

"I feel that I was made for this life, too," she proceeded.

"No one was ever made for such a life," said Mrs. Romilly.

"Oh, nonsense, now, mamma! *You* enjoyed it! I saw you having a delicious time with Mrs. Morrison."

"Ah, my dear, *she* is a woman quite out of place in all that empty whirl. I don't think that she endorses its futility; she merely accepts it. I told her so to-night."

"I hope you did n't lecture her," reproved Leah. "She is a power in her way. She is somebody whom I wish to have on my side. You see, I know all about her. I have inquired. She was once something like your dear self. I mean she had opinions, and publicly aired them."

"She was born in a different sphere from mine."

"I know — of an old, influential Massachusetts family. She married a man of wealth and position."

"Position in the fashionable world, my dear."
Leah gave a positive little gesture.

"That is the only sort of position one should
prize, I begin to think," she affirmed. And then
she burst into a laugh of merry fulness. "Don't
look at me, please, as if I were a hardened sin-
ner! . . . I 'll take it all back, mamma. Believe,
if you choose, that I did n't mean a word of it!"

"She means too much of it," thought Mrs.
Romilly, before answering these words of random self-exculpation. . . .

It was not long afterward that Mrs. Romilly and
Mrs. Morrison sat together, in a chamber of the
latter lady's residence, which overlooked a breezy,
ocean-skirted lawn. Books, in plenteous array,
lined the walls; every appointment was quiet and
yet of distinctive charm; it was evidently the
favorite haunt of one whose pursuits and habits
were scholarly.

"Yes," Mrs. Morrison said, continuing a conversation which had interested both, "I do manage to
reconcile my studies and my contemplations with
the other life that you have called so flippant and
weightless. I do come to Newport, as you see. I
do meet these aimless and unthinking people. If
you ask my excuse, I can only tell you that I find
in their outward felicities a something that satisfies

artistic feeling. And I have never outgrown that. All my ethics have never killed it in me. I like to think of Plato's Academe as a place where the walks were kept well-tended, and where the disciples wore togas that drooped gracefully."

She spoke this last sentence with a low, musical laugh. She was a woman who had attempted great things, in her day, when the white locks that now shone above her aged but fresh-tinted face were full of dark gloss. In the popular phrase she had been as much a failure as Mrs. Romilly herself. But in another sense she had succeeded. Born within circles where fashion reigned predominant and where the key-note was one of frivolity, she had asserted an influence that told and obtained. Long ago she had contented herself with being a force gently to improve, not a force dominantly to destroy. After all, she had plucked better fruit from life than the deeper-minded sister with whom she now sat in reflective colloquy. She had found for herself a certain *métier;* she had not sunk into entire obscurity with her theories and impressions. If her metaphysical poems did not sell, if her profound essays remained unread, she had still secured an intellectual vantage-ground, though it might have been termed only that of a lovable old lady with whom light and elegant people often liked to talk, as a safeguard against the vague remorse resultant from their own protracted indolence.

" We shall never agree with regard to there being the least use and worth in that idle throng," firmly but softly answered Mrs. Romilly. " Let us speak of more concrete things. You know to what I allude."

Mrs. Morrison laughed her melodious laugh. " Yes, . . . to Mr. Tracy Tremaine. Surely, he is very concrete; there is nothing at all abstract about him." She remained silent for a little while. Then she looked earnestly with her dim, kindly eyes at her companion, and added: "My dear friend, I would take my daughter away from Newport at once ! There is my advice, plain and candid."

· But Leah had no intention of leaving Newport. She was now in the full zenith of her triumphs. Mrs. Chichester had nodded, and if society did not tremble it certainly obeyed. Leah might have striven through three seasons, and then without avail, for admission to houses that now opened prompt and willing portals. Under the shadow of her new protectress's broad and strong wing, Leah was shielded from every blast of adverse treatment. Society looked at her astonishedly

through its eye-glasses, so to speak, and murmured, " Who is she ? " a good many times. But
that did not prevent its smile from being of the
blandest, or its welcome from being of the most
effusive. She has entered, with an abrupt yet
tranquil advent, straight into the midst of a community as distinct in its conservatisms and traditions as anything of the sort which has ever
existed. True, it is constantly supplied with re-
cruits, but these must bring with them the cre-
dentials of great wealth. Only to the possessor of
millions will our Newport aristocracy proffer any
rapid cordialities. As a rule, for those who would
gain its complete endorsement, it presents a hundred different and devious paths toward victory,
not seldom so baffling to the most resigned patience that a final cessation of effort despairingly
ensues.

A great deal of genuine homage fell to the
share of Leah, which she accepted without abat-
ing by a jot her former reposeful *aplomb*. She
received it all as though it were quite her due.
She looked very much the same when throned on
the box-seat of some drag driven by an owner of
high degree as she had looked when seated beside
her mother on the piazza of Mrs. Preen's boarding-house. She would not even permit Mrs. Chi-

chester to patronize her. Perhaps, if she had
done so, the latter, who had got to like her very
much, would have liked her very much less. As
it was, she retained the lady's full adherence.
This was clearly seen, and it surely, if gradually,
transformed her, in the eyes of many watchers,
from a mere ephemeral favorite into one estab-
lished and permanent.

The days glided along. They were days of
infinite enjoyment to Leah. She drove in stately
equipages to watch the madly topsy-turvy game
called Polo, undertaken by rash boys on marvel-
lously well-broken ponies; she attended dinners of
great state; she moved through ball-rooms of
bright-lit magnificence; she played lawn-tennis on
spacious and shaded lawns; she sat near cool windows, at afternoon receptions, with always a bevy
of male courtiers ready to applaud her newest
clever epigram — and some of her epigrams were
undeniably clever; she did, in short, all that the
mirthful throng of Newport pleasure-seekers do,
and yet retained among them a saliency, a dis-
tinctness, a maiden-like leadership, which caused
her name to be printed in a hundred newspapers,
and even made her the subject of more than one
sententious "watering-place letter."

Meanwhile, mother and daughter remained at

the Aquidneck. For hours at a time Mrs. Romilly would not see Leah. There was nearly always some other voluntary chaperone. "Mamma,
you need not go," had become an oft-used sentence on Leah's lips. Mrs. Romilly remained at
home with relief, and yet with anxiety. She saw
Lawrence Rainsford frequently — much more so
than Leah did. He told her the general drift of
comments regarding her child. The bitterer ones
he spared, or sought to spare; sometimes Mrs.
Romilly would detect their unspoken presence in
his mind, and plead for their utterance. They
usually reflected upon herself, and either Mr.
Bertie Forbes or Mrs. Abbott Fortescue was sup-
posably at the bottom of their propagation. "Let
them sneer at *my* past life as they will," she more
than once said. "I do not care for that, as long
as they spare her the least slander."

But Leah evoked no slander. She quickly won
the reputation of being extraordinarily cold.
The hate of Mrs. Fortescue was always waiting
its chance, but none came. Bertie Forbes, whose
wife had now asserted a very bold independence,
would have abetted Leah's couchant detractor at
the slightest opportunity. He was brimming
over with spleen; he felt an accumulating debt of
vengeance toward Leah with each new entertain-

ment at which his wife aired what he considered
her abominably second-rate American manners.
But Leah blunted his wrath as ice blunts wind.
She took Mrs. Forbes under her especial care, and
saw that the pretty little person, with her nasal
voice, received exceedingly respectful treatment.
She even went so far as to induce Mrs. Chichester
to smile upon her friend. This last exquisite
piece of mischief—if it deserves no more generous explanation — caused Bertie to gracefully
succumb. He was so arrant a snob that he could
no longer disdain a wife whom the potentate of
Newport had condescended to favor. Leah also
set herself another task — though her sovereignty
made it too easy for that term. She conceived
the idea of popularizing the Misses Marksley.

"They're a black draught," said Tremaine to
her one day. "You're a great belle, as everyone knows, but you can't make people swallow
the Marksleys."

But Leah differed with him. "I shall try," she
said. She did try, and succeeded. The Marksleys issued invitations for an "evening." It crept
about that everybody would refuse. Leah made
a point of quietly publishing the certainty that
Mrs. Chichester and herself would be present.

"And oh," she once or twice said, in loitering

afterthought, "I know of several others who will surely go. . . . Let me think. There is Mrs. Schuyler Sheldon, Mrs. Livingston Maitland, and Mrs. Courtlandt Sinclair." All these ladies were near kinswomen of Mrs. Chichester, and obeyed the mandate of their chieftain. . . . Leah knew that she dealt with actualities. The Misses Marksleys' "evening" was a brilliant success. The sisters were *lancées* from that occasion thenceforward. Their amusing struggles had ceased for evermore.

"You did it," acknowledged Tremaine, afterward. "But *why* did you do it? From charity or mere caprice? I confess that I suspect the latter."

Leah did not tell him what she actually more than fancied — that it was because the Marksley sisters were inseparably concerned, in her own thoughts, with the first meeting between himself and her.

Toward the close of August her engagement to Tremaine was widely discussed as a settled fact. It had not been corroborated by a ceremonious announcement, and yet it was firmly believed. Other men devoted themselves to Leah, but none with the changeless assiduity of Tremaine. Others, too, began to give way before him. Perhaps Leah, with all her equanimity of demeanor, could not hide the passion he had inspired.

She had met Mrs. Fortescue. Their meeting had been a fatality, since both now revolved, as it were, in the same orbit. But Leah had been decently polite, and no more; she had defined her civility by a very keen limit. Mrs. Fortescue felt the chill under the thin surface of conventional decorum. It stung her, as cold will often sting.

" That Chichester woman has done it," she reflected. " It is she who has set her up to it. *He* would not. His *rôle* would naturally be one of silence."

On a certain evening, toward the close of the season, she appeared at a ball given with much splendor at a private dwelling of special expanse and adornment. It was an important ball, and she chose to robe herself importantly. Her dress was of crimson silk, with various ornaments of silver, one a broad, polished zone about her waist, and two more being broader bands on either arm. In her dead-black hair she wore some tiny butterflies, shaped of the same metal. A number of ladies pronounced the costume hideous, but every one noticed it, and had an opinion concerning it. There was no doubt that she looked extremely well. The voluminous crimson enshrouding her

figure suited her tawny coloring to perfection.
For some eyes the silver struck a note no less
discordant than novel, but in a general sense the
apparel was considered a striking success.

Leah, dressed in simple white, with a big knot
of roses in her bosom, sent by Tremaine a few
hours before, was also a guest at the ball.

Tremaine had not spoken to Mrs. Fortescue for
three weeks. But he spoke to her that night.
Leah saw them leave the ball-room arm-in-arm.
She saw them a little later, seated together on
a broad veranda that gave upon the sea. For
the first time in her life she knew the sickening
bitterness of jealousy. When Tremaine, toward
the end of the evening, at length rejoined her,
she turned upon him a look of freezing unconcern.

He perceived the truth. It chanced that they
were presently standing alone together. Strains
of rich music sounded near them; dancers were
gliding across the waxed floor not far off.

"It is warm here," he said; "won't you come
out and get a breath of fresh air?" She took his
offered arm.

They were presently walking in the darkness.
They could not see the ocean, but its salty waft-
ures came to them, and they saw the stars shining
white and still over its concealed immensity. She

had not, thus far, spoken to him. He knew that her having taken his arm meant a surrender which her pride, if once hurt, would have given to no man but himself.

"You are angry at me," he broke silence; "you are angry at me for talking with that woman. People have told you stupid things. But it's all nonsense. I'm awfully sorry you don't like my chatting with her even once in a great while."

Leah withdrew her arm. He could just see her face, and no more.

Her voice broke palpably as she answered him. Perhaps she was too agitated to know of this. "I am not angry," she said. "Why should I care if you speak with some one whom you like?" Then she suddenly added these words:

"What right have I even to think of your affairs? I know of no right. You have given me none."

"I give you every right," he swiftly said to her. "I give it you, Leah, because I love you!"

She realized then what she had uttered. She paused, and he saw her eyes flash in the dimness. "I — I drew that forth from you!" she stammered. "I — I made you say it!"

He put both his hands about both her own. "If you did — and I don't grant that you did," he murmured, "thank God, all the same, that it is true!" . . .

A day or two later all Newport rang with the formal and positive engagement of Leah Romilly to Tracy Tremaine. Leah had made peace with her mother. Mrs. Romilly knew of her daughter's love for the man with whom she had plighted troth. That fact helped her to be tolerant and acquiescent. She even said to Rainsford, during one of their morning talks, when Leah was absent:

"She loves him. I am certain of that, Lawrence. For her future, it may mean so much!"

"Or so little!" said Rainsford.

She looked into his grave face, which, as she truly felt, hid an actual agony, and replied, "Let us hope for the best. You know what I wanted, Lawrence. But it cannot be. Still, let us hope, now, all the same. I know your heart is big and warm enough to do that. I know that because the love she gives him isn't the love she might have given you, a generous regard for her happiness in the years to come still sways you!"

"Yes," he answered, after a pause. His face was lowered as he spoke the one little word. But Elizabeth Romilly knew the sound of it to be good and stanch, like its speaker.

"Oh, Lawrence," she broke forth, softly, "who

but you would have pronounced that small but pregnant answer at such a moment!" . . .

It was on this same morning, and but a short time later, that a card was handed to Mrs. Romilly. The card bore the name of Mrs. Ogden Tremaine. The lady who desired to see Mrs. Romilly, said the servant who had brought the card, was waiting downstairs.

"It is his mother," said Mrs. Romilly, after giving the card to Rainsford. "I might ask to have her shown up here. This little sitting-room will not shock her, I suppose? It is better, for such an interview as that which she intends, than the public parlor below."

"Much better," replied Rainsford, "for such an interview as that which she intends."

Mrs. Romilly raised her brows. The second portion of this sentence seemed to startle her. "What do you mean?" she questioned.

Rainsford had meanwhile slowly risen.

"You shall see," he said. His face never looked more serious than now.

"I shall see?" repeated Mrs. Romilly, with soft amazement.

"Yes."

"What do you mean?"

"Request Mrs. Ogden Tremaine to be shown

here. I am going. I shall not disturb your coming talk."

Mrs. Romilly spoke a few words to the servant, who at once departed after hearing them. Rainsford then took her hand. " Be strong and brave during this interview," he said. " But I need not tell you to be either — you are always both." After he had gone, and while she waited the coming of her guest, Mrs. Romilly wondered what he had really meant. She soon had ample reason for knowing.

VIII.

IN a very few moments after the departure of Rainsford, Mrs. Romilly found herself face to face with a spare, faded woman of about sixty, dressed in mourning. She had a narrow, colorless visage, over which the scant white tresses were worn rolled backward, thus increasing, if possible, a natural expression of superciliousness which dwelt you could scarcely tell where; if it had not its home in the small, light-tinted eye, it lay either in the high, curving nose or the shrivelled mouth, whose lips were almost as thin as paper, and loved to close themselves in pursed tightness after the delivery of each new sentence.

"I am very glad to meet you, Mrs. Tremaine," said Leah's mother. She was about to extend a welcoming hand, when something in the lady's attitude prevented this gesture — perhaps a little heightening of the contracted shoulders, or an elevation of the slight head on its slim support of wrinkled throat. Instead of offering her hand, Mrs. Romilly made a bow, quiet and stately, while pointing to a chair.

An extremely awkward pause followed. Awkward, at least, for Mrs. Tremaine's hostess, who felt herself quietly devoured from head to foot by a stare which had in it what she began to consider an element of hard belligerence. Both ladies were now seated.

"We are somewhat near neighbors, I believe," again said Mrs. Romilly, breaking the silence in gentle desperation.

"Yes," came the reply, accompanied by a faint yet shrill cough. "I rarely leave my house except in a carriage. I live very quietly here. I am compelled to do so. My health makes it absolutely necessary."

Mrs. Romilly perceived that she was being held at arm's-length. The tones of her guest were as inflexible as if all her words were strung upon a rod of steel.

"I am very sorry to hear that you are so unwell," she said; and then, with the motive of shattering what might be, after all, but the half-timorous reserve of an invalid, she added: "I think that your son, Tracy, has more than once mentioned your being in ill-health — I mean before he became engaged to my daughter. I regret, by the way, that she is not in the hotel at present."

Mrs. Tremaine looked down at the slender hands

crossed in her lap and clad with long gloves of black kid. Then she raised her chilly little eyes and said, resuming her stare :

"1 know that your daughter is not here. I am aware that she is driving with my son. I am obliged to tell you that this is my reason for calling upon you now. Your daughter's absence — I feel forced to say it — gives me my desired opportunity."

Mrs. Romilly's doubts had vanished. Here was surely no timidity, no reserve. It looked more like the blunt prelude of open warfare.

"Opportunity?" she repeated, and then sat with her calm brows raised and a spark of inquiry, but not resentment, in her clear hazel eyes.

"Yes. That is just the word. I wished to speak of this engagement. I wished to tell you that I, and that all my connections — unusually large, as you perhaps know, madam — must refuse to sanction it."

Mrs. Romilly turned pale. But it was not with anger. Her thoughts had flown to Leah. "And why?" she asked, with no displeased ring in her voice.

Mrs. Tremaine started in the aggrieved way of a person with abnormally sensitive nerves. "Why?" she iterated, almost in a plaintive treble. Then she raised one dark-sheathed hand, and waved it once or twice before her narrow face. " Oh, pray do not ask why. I want this interview to be peaceful, quite peaceful, if you please. I think that you must certainly understand my reasons."

" Indeed, I do not understand them. I sincerely hope, however, that you have sought me with no intention of insult."

"Insult!" repeated Mrs. Tremaine. Her tones were a peevish whine. " That is the way with you people! One cannot even refer, before you, to one's superior position, without being accused of insult!"

Mrs. Romilly rose. There was a very sweet and womanly dignity in her bearing now, but it was quite lost upon the callous individuality she addressed.

" I shall not inquire of you by what right you presume to think your position in any way superior to mine or that of my daughter," she said, with even firmness. " Such a question would be as trivial as your own recent words are vulgar. But I must request you either to make full explanation and apology for what you have just said, or at once to leave my apartment."

Mrs. Tremaine rose flutteredly from her chair. She was in a visible tremor. She looked pitiably small and mean beside the handsome, tranquil woman whom she now faced.

"Oh, I was prepared to find you very clever. I had heard of that.. It is your profession to be clever. I won't attempt to cross wits with you. Tracy has been fascinated by your daughter. Very well--let him marry out of his set if he pleases. But you will gain nothing, madam, by such a union. I think we will *none* of us acknowledge it. I wished to talk peacefully with you, but you make that impossible. When I say 'we' I mean our whole large family. The Tremaines and Tracys have been noted for their sensible marriages. We have scarcely had a single *mésalliance* for four or five generations. I shan't appeal to your sense of justice; I don't suppose you have any. You want to be received by us, and that is all. Such a union is to me horrible — horrible! I can't tell you just how horrible I think it. Ours is the first family in America. I was a Tremaine myself; I married my second-cousin. The Tracys, the Ten Eycks, the Hackensacks, the Spuytenduyvils, the Van Corlears, the Van Horns, the Amsterdams, the Manhattans — they are all more or less cousins of mine, but there is not one of them who will not yield precedence to the Tremaine blood. Our record stands alone, and speaks for itself. We were an illustrious race in England five hundred years ago, and since we landed in this country we have produced statesmen, generals, clergymen, diplomats — all of the very greatest distinction. And now to think that my son, Tracy — the only child I have left — should marry the daughter of a person who used to give public lectures about all sorts of shocking subjects! You see, madam, I remember you. I did not at first, but when I thought about your full name, and how familiar it sounded, I recollected how my poor dead papa once whipped my poor dead brother, Ten Eyck, for going when a boy to hear you say your horrid things against religion and matrimony, and all that decent people hold most sacred! And now I must endure seeing Tracy link his name with yours! Oh, if you have the least shame left, you ought to help me save him!"

Mrs. Romilly was still paler than before, but a smile touched her lips as this unforeseen outburst ended. And her voice never faltered from its admirable composure as she said:

"It is very sad for me to witness how the ancestors of whom you boast have produced a descendant so unworthy of their distinction — a person, in fact, without the common rudiments of good breeding." Here her wide, fair brow grew cloudy and her voice took a stern note. "I have no more to say, and shall permit you to say no more in my hearing. If you do not instantly leave this room, Mrs. Tremaine, I shall myself retire from it."

She passed toward a door that communicated with her bedchamber, and placed her hand upon its knob. If she had heard a sound from the wan, quivering lips of the woman whose insolence had just met her rebuke, she would have disappeared at once. As it was she had not long to await Mrs. Tremaine's departure. . . .

Leah returned from her drive about an hour later. She had taken off her hat and was swinging it carelessly by the strings, as she entered the presence of her mother. The air had given her cheeks a pink flush, and disordered her gold hair about forehead and temples; but it was something else that had put so rich a sparkle into her brown eyes and softened the outline of her lips as though a coming smile had cast its shadow before. Only a brief while ago the change in her had appealed piercingly to Mrs. Romilly. It was like that time in the life of a rosebud when the coil of its balmy leaves will so loosen and relax that if you watch closely you can see new interspaces for the breeze to search or the dew to brim, while the heart of the flower itself still remains jealously screened.

It seemed to her mother as if Leah would never
be proud again. All her spiritual lines appeared
to have lost their rigidity and to have become
curves. Her wit would flash as of old, but it
rarely stung. Humanity held a new meaning for
her; she felt kinned to its large throbs of love
and hope, and more indulgent of its faults, without pausing to consider why. There are two great
gateways through which our chief woes enter the
world; they are love and death; yet the foot-
prints of each are sympathy, and were these
blotted from off the earth it is hard to tell what
giant evils would spring up in their place.

Leah had laid one hand on her mother's wrist
before she detected that anything was wrong; and
even then her misgiving was not defined.

"We had such a lovely drive," she said. "Not
by the sea, this morning, but along country roads,
you know. I shall be so sorry to leave here.
But our time is nearly up. Tracy says that they
all rush back home by the first of September."

"I think we had better go before then, Leah.
I should like to go to-morrow."

"Something has happened, mamma!" exclaimed
Leah, peering into her mother's face with startled
gaze.

"Yes, something *has* happened. Don't be

alarmed, child. Sit down here at my side, and I will tell you everything. I believe I can repeat it word for word."

She did, almost. Leah shivered once or twice during the recital. She held her mother's hand, pressing it tensely all the time. Then, at the end, she rose and walked to a window, staring straight out upon the shaded street below. Her face, just glimpsed by Mrs. Romilly before she averted it, was fixed and hueless.

Suddenly she spoke, turning toward her mother.

" You don't advise me to break the engagement, do you?" she asked. There was a wistful wildness in her look. " You can't advise *that!* He loves me. I know it! I know it so well! He has told me about *her*. Is she to ruin our happiness? Answer me, mamma! I am confused — I don't know what ought to be done! I have been very wilful with you, often and often. But now I have no wish to do otherwise than you say. You are so strong — you remember how strong and splendid I always thought you! Oh, mamma, I leave everything to *you!* "

Leah put both arms forward as the last sentence left her lips. Her mother had risen, and was approaching her. During those few short moments memory was busy in this mother's mind. She saw

Leah as a little child, clinging to her because of some fancied grief or terror. Her great heart quivered under the stress of motherhood — that lovely force which transcends all other human emotions.

When she reached Leah she took the girl in her arms, and put her head upon one shoulder, smoothing its tossed hair, before Leah herself could lay it there. And then she felt the form that she was clasping sway and pulsate. Very soon afterward there came a storm of sobs.

" Oh, mamma, my own, dear, strong, fine mamma, tell me — tell me what it is right that I should do ! "

" This is right, Leah," came the answer, which cost the speaker no slight effort to give: " We will go back to New York soon — to-morrow, or perhaps next day. You will see Mr. Tremaine to-night. The wedding must take place at once. I think it had best take place at once — or not at all. . . . There, my love, don't be so distressed. It *shall* take place. We owe it to ourselves to despise this coarse treatment. *He* will be ashamed — yes, I am certain that he will. Why should you really care? You love him, and you tell me that he loves you. That will be enough. I will stand by you, darling. Oh, I am sure that

you feel and realize that! . . . Stop sobbing so,
Leah. . . . Why should you care what a childish
old woman has said? I felt it my duty to tell
you all. I could not keep anything back. But
you know that nothing can ever part you and me.
If he really loves you, and will be a man, a gentleman — as you say he is — then this little bitter experience will prove only the beginning of a happiness
which I, too, shall feel nearly as much as yourself,
watching it, rejoicing in it, believing in it, dearest,
because it is yours!" . . .

. That same evening Tremaine made his appearance. Mrs. Romilly was not present when they
met. Leah could scarcely keep back her tears, at
first. They strolled together along the vague
outer street, where the dusky tree-boughs waved
and rustled below the shining stars. Leah told
him everything. He listened without a word till
he had heard all. Then he said, very tenderly:

"Leah, I am so sorry! What *can* I do? This
thing is mother's mania, and I regret to add that
nearly all the Tremaines are possessed with the
same madness. What she said to your mother
was frightful — infamous! I won't deny to you
that it has serious significance. I don't think that
this country contains a more shocking set of snobs
than my own family. They are all banded to-

gether by the one ruling idea — their own birth. There's no doubt that we have it. If we didn't their nonsense would be more excusable; there would be a certain pitiable braggadocio about it. . . . Regarding those remarks made to your mother, I have no way of expressing my disgust for them. But surely, Leah, you can't dream that it will ever make any real difference between you and me! Let the whole clan rise up against us. Why should we care? We will not care. Leah, nothing on earth shall part us! I am ashamed of my race. I beg you to despise this abominable treatment. Good God! *I* am not to blame for it. Don't hold me blamable! If you want, I will never speak to any member of my family who does not recognize and receive your mother and yourself!"...

Two days later Mrs. Romilly and Leah left Newport. Meanwhile Rainsford had heard from the former just what had passed.

"He has made every possible concession, Lawrence," she had said. "He hates the indignity offered me. He has behaved very well. His mother's line of action pains him beyond measure. They both wish the wedding to be soon. I, too, think it best. We shall have a very quiet wedding. Every member of Tracy Tremaine's family

shall receive cards; he will give me the list of all
his kindred, and I shall omit none. Afterward it
can be seen just what course they all intend to
take."

" They will all take one course," said Rainsford,
in his slow, thoughtful way. " At least, I imagine
so. They usually stand by each other. Their
pride of name is something preposterous. Yes, I
think it quite probable that they will all, in a
disdainful body, refuse to be present."

But Rainsford was in error here. Three weeks
later the wedding occurred at Mrs. Romilly's small
and pretty residence in Thirty-Fourth Street.
Tracy Tremaine had power enough with not a
few of his relations to induce their attendance.
Without exception they all disliked the marriage.
But in the sense of practically recognizing or
ignoring it, the house of Tremaine was for once
divided against itself. Four or five of his aunts,
as many more uncles, and not a few cousins, condescended to witness the ceremony. It was all a
most bitter ordeal for Mrs. Romilly. Not even
the look of supreme happiness on Leah's face
could dispel the regretful ache that lurked dull
and unaltering in her heart. She felt that her
daughter was passing forth into paths of hazard
and venture. The more that she saw of Tracy

Tremaine the less she believed in him. That he passionately loved Leah she could not doubt. But she distrusted his matrimonial future with Leah for a wife. The girl was blinded by her love to all Tremaine's faults. She insisted on thinking him an almost perfect man. The awakening must ultimately come. She must one day realize that his whole nature was set in a key of meretricious vanity. Leah would soon demand and not receive. She would reap a deadly harvest of disappointments. The glitter of fashionable life would soon lose its charm for her. She would see dross and tinsel where she now saw gold and gems.

"With Rainsford," she thought, "all would have been so different! Every new year would have brought its precious income of increased contentment. His love would have been to her like an arm on which we lean at first lightly, then a little harder, and at last grow to treasure as an inestimable supporting strength!"

Rainsford was absent from the wedding. To have appeared would have cost him agony, and at the suggestion of Mrs. Romilly herself he made the excuse of being called to Boston, where he remained for several subsequent weeks. He sent Leah a gift of value, accompanied merely by the conventional card.

It had been arranged that mother and daughter should now live apart. The separation gave Mrs. Romilly many pangs, acute though secret. And yet she told herself that this plan was by far the best. Tremaine did not like her; he had more than once shown her so by his elaborate attempts to conceal the aversion. Why had it arisen? With silent misery she again and again asked herself that question. For Leah's sake this admirable woman would have made almost any conciliatory overtures. But Tremaine prevented such a step. He was constantly making overtures himself; and these were so severe in their studied civility as to lift a perpetual barrier against less formal terms.

If Leah guessed the truth, she strove to give no signs of having done so.

"I have yielded to Tracy's desire about our renting a separate house," she said, a little before the wedding, "because it most probably springs from his intense fondness. He wants to see me the mistress of my own establishment. Well, for my part, you must know, mamma, dear, that I should like always to have you with me. But we shall see each other every day; of course I shall be very particular on that point. Tracy will prefer it, too. I am sure that he likes you very much. You have not any *doubts* of *that*, mamma, have you?"

"Oh, of course not, my dear."

On another occasion (still previous to her marriage) Leah said : "Mamma, you never speak of my leaving you *alone*. Now, tell me — tell me candidly : are you not sorry?"

"I do not wish to be sorry if you are not, my daughter."

"What an answer!" cried Leah. Her eyes flashed, as if in anger, but the next moment they were filled with tears. She put her arms about Mrs. Romilly's neck; she was getting to make these tender revelations far oftener than ever before.

"I've been deceiving you!" she said, while her voice broke. "I've made you think that it will give me no pain. This is not true. But Tracy wishes it; I must yield to him, you know. It would be such a bad beginning if I did not. Besides, isn't it only just and fair that he should like to rule in his own house? Of course you would rule here; this house is yours. I'm afraid *I've* done a great deal of the ruling heretofore ; and you've let me, without a murmur. Oh, mamma, I fear I have been dreadfully wayward and headstrong! I feel it so keenly now, when our dear old life together is going to end! This thought sometimes makes me very miserable in spite of all my happiness. And I *am* happy — that is, most of the time. I read you so clearly; you don't suspect that I do, but I do. You blame me in your own heart for putting such faith in Tracy. You can't bring yourself to trust him as I trust him. Oh, but you are quite wrong! He will prove that you are. He worships me. We are going to be a model husband and wife. We are not going to live for fashion at all; we shall have a few nice social friends, and dine with them now and then, or get them to dine with us. But we are not going to any of the big affairs. We are both a little tired of the whirl. Of course he has seen years more of it than I have seen. But I told him only last night that I had begun to be a good deal disillusioned. I spoke as boldly as you please — yes, truly I did! I told Tracy that these fine people were not a bit what I had first supposed them. I said that many of them struck me as merely conducting themselves with an air — that it was all in their air — that behind the air there was nothing a particle different from the principles and habits of persons whom they would sneer at as vulgar, and not fit to walk the same floors with them!"

"So soon!" thought Mrs. Romilly. "It was
sure to come, and now it is here! This pure
young spirit is finding out its mistake more
quickly than I expected, with all my ominous
forebodings."

But aloud she said nothing, and Leah hurried
on, as though she were making a swift confession
that some new mood of reticence lay in wait to
interrupt.

"I fancied Tracy would be annoyed, mamma —
he has lived so long in this atmosphere, you know.
It was rude and reckless of me — at least, I feared
he would think so. But he surprised me by
agreeing with me. I was so glad that he did.
And then he spoke so charmingly. He said that
it was all sounding brass and tinkling cymbals.
We laughed together over that phrase. It hits
off so many people whom we have both met in
Newport. I couldn't help but reflect that perhaps the worst tinkling cymbal of them all was
his own mother. But, of course, I didn't say so.
I felt how her outrageous actions have made him
suffer . . . and I never mean to notice her unless
Tracy should specially ask it, and she herself
should specially ask as well."

Leah need not have made this latter proviso.
Mrs. Tremaine failed to solicit the acquaintance

of her daughter-in-law. If a monomaniac, she at
least remained a consistent one. But monomania
would doubtless too charitably have defined her
conduct. This had rather emanated from another
quite explainable source — a meagre intellect,
acted upon by massive inherited prejudice. She
stood in her day and her country as a dreary
anomaly, a pitiful, discouraging contradiction.
That she could exist at all in a land bought from
monarchism with blood, and consecrated by great
dead patriots to a very beautiful future, meant, if
it had any meaning, some fatal national weakness.
Such Americans as Mrs. Tremaine are either a
disease or a development. If the first, they challenge cure; if the second, they prophesy disaster.

L EAH'S wedding-tour lasted nearly a month. She wrote to her mother very regularly during this interval of separation, and every letter breathed of perfect happiness. When husband and wife returned, they went at once to their new residence. It was small, but charmingly appointed. They had made certain economical calculations, and had decided that their present income would permit of only judicious expenditures. Both were amazed, a little later, to find that Mrs. Romilly had taken a most decisive step.

She had ceased to rent the house in which she and Leah had dwelt for a number of past years. She had engaged apartments in a boarding-house adjacent to Fifth Avenue, and near her daughter's new home. And she had done this for a reason which Leah too well understood when a cheque of no mean amount was put into her unwilling hand.

"Yes, Leah," came the soft yet insistent words. "I had no use for the house all to myself. I shall be thoroughly comfortable in those other quarters.

Every year you shall receive just the same amount
that I have now given you. Remember, it was
your father's money. Some day all must be yours.
I shall have my books; I shall live in complete
comfort. But you, presiding over a larger household, will, of course, need larger resources. . . ."

That same evening the first shadow crept over
Leah's devout love for her husband. They had
dined together, and laughingly discussed the
somewhat lame way in which their new *ménage*,
with its new servants and its general tentative
atmosphere, had thus far thriven. But presently
Leah had referred to her mother's generosity.

"It will make matters so much easier for us,
Tracy," she said. And then she looked with sudden fixity into his face, while he sat close at her
side, smoking the cigarette that she liked to have
him smoke almost any time in her presence, because he was fond of it.

"Oh, Tracy," she broke forth, "I am so sure
that mamma would love one thing to happen,
above all others!"

"What?" he asked, with a slight start.

"She would love to have you ask her to come
and live with us. I mean, if she thought you
really meant it, — if she thought I had n't induced
you to make the request."

He was silent for some time, while her eyes dwelt on his profile. Then he said, with crisp brevity:

" I don't mean to ask her."

Leah bit her lip. " Tracy ! " she exclaimed, in reproach, "you speak as if you disliked mamma! *Do* you?"

"I dislike the idea of having her live with us. That is all." Leah fancied that she saw coldness in the look which he now turned full upon her saddened countenance; and she had never even remotely had this fancy before. He was smiling, however, as he proceeded:

"I supposed the matter quite settled. If you persist in reviving it, I must assume that you place too slight an estimate on my opinion of what is most advisable."

" No, Tracy — not that ! " began Leah ; "I " —

But he at once rose, the smile leaving his handsome face.

" I shall not be able to argue the question with you," he said.

And then she knew that she had offended him, and was miserable while he stood examining some new books, which lay disordered on a near table, not yet having been shelved in proper fashion. But soon afterward he broke silence in ordinary

tones on some ordinary topic. Mrs. Chichester, a
few days later, sent them an invitation to one of
her ceremonious dinners. The invitation (all
except their own name and the date) was en-
graved on heavy white paper that bore arms and
crest.

" I will write our refusal to-morrow," said Leah,
in a matter-of-course way.

" Our refusal ! " echoed Tremaine. " What can
you possibly mean ? "

" Why," returned Leah surprisedly, " did we
not both agree that we were to go very little into
society ? "

He laughed.

" What a memory you have ! " he said.

" Do you mean that you want to go ? " she
asked, prepared at once to give her own acquiescence.

" Enormously," he replied. " It is best to break
that resolve in a gradual way, and not wait for the
sudden rupture of it that is certain to come. No
human honeymoon ever yet lasted forever, and I
don't imagine that ours will prove an exception."

His words were softly jocular, but she felt a stab
of fright pierce her as she heard them, and knew
that she was growing pale. A moment later she
told herself that such serious interpretation was

folly; but while the beats of her own heart sounded in her ears, the quiet voice of Tremaine sounded above them.

"Besides, you know, Mrs. Chichester's dinner-invitations do not usually go begging. It is not customary to refuse them except for a very good reason; and I don't think that we have even a bad one."

"We have one that I thought would seem excellent," answered Leah, steadying her voice. "We had both decided that a life of fashion after marriage would suit neither. *I* had seen enough of it, even during my brief experience, — and what *you* said made me confident that you were sincerely fatigued."

"Oh, I have been taking a rest," he answered, with another laugh. That laugh, amiable though it was, had an edge with a cruel cut in it.

They went to Mrs. Chichester's dinner, and to many more of equal or lesser splendor through succeeding weeks. Leah constantly saw her mother, but often their meetings were snatched from the claims engendered by frequent festivities. She had her visiting-book, her "day," her calls of courtesy. Meanwhile she was popular as ever, and firmly placed by her marriage on a level with the most "careful" sets. But Mrs.

Romilly had divined, some time ago, a weariness in Leah no less manifest than were her efforts to conceal it. This weariness did not mar her beauty, still fresh and captivating; it was mental, not physical, and therefore the mother's almost clairvoyant eye detected it while wholly elusive for others. Leah's step was elastic as of old; her neat-clinging, quick-rustling robes ensheathed or draped her flexible figure in faultless unison with its lines and movements; she had lost that assertion which once marked the pose of her small head on its slender yet queenly shoulders; she had the tamed look of a bird that has been taught repose though not inured to durance; she was no longer maidenly in mien or gesture; and yet no actual touch of matronhood had rounded or relaxed her still girlish delicacy.

Mrs. Romilly waited for some avowal, but she waited a long time before any came. At length she one day tempted it by saying:

"Do you enjoy all this excess of gayety, Leah?"

"No, mamma," was the slow reply; and as Leah spoke she drooped her eyes.

"Then why do you let it hurry you along?"

"I do so on Tracy's account. He wants it. He thinks it best. He thinks it right."

Mrs. Romilly repeated this answer to Rainsford,

with whom she still had her long talks, and whom
Leah rarely saw. He had won added distinction
in his art. Money, for which he had not real
need, had flowed in to him, and with it a fair
share of no despicable fame.

"He has shown her his shallow soul," said
Rainsford. "She understands that what she
thought so durable, so individual about him was
the merest veneer. And she has made this discovery regarding him as a kind of sarcastic ter-
minus to the other discoveries made regarding
those vainglorious worldlings among whom she
first met him."

"But she is still fond of him, Lawrence. I am
sure of that."

"You would not know it if she had ceased to
be — at least, not for a long time," he added.
"But you may be right. I am ready to grant that
her love, when once given, is of the inalienable
sort — or *should* be!"

After more than a year of marriage, Leah began
to assume a course of strange reticence toward her
mother respecting Tremaine. Mrs. Romilly had
occasionally dined with them at first, but of late
she had received no invitation to do so. She felt
that her son-in-law was alone concerned in the cessation of these requests. But she made no in-

quiry of Leah. Perhaps it was solely because she
dreaded to receive the wounding truth. She seldom met Tremaine. When they did encounter
each other, she had no fault, and yet every fault,
to find with the clean exactitude of his urbanity.

But Leah had been reticent in other ways. The
absolute selfishness of her husband had now become as well-known to her as the wretchedness
which this final realization caused. He had not a
personal whim, howsoever slight, to which he did
not, as time wore on, demand unqualified allegiance. She nearly always gave it; she even tried
at first to justify it; she hated to face the bare
ruin of her own charming ideal. For a long time
her very pride made her uniformly compliant; it
was so hard to admit that she had been entirely
deceived in him! But at length a most brutal
shock came to her. Rudely enough her eyes were
opened to what she deemed a horrifying fact. . . .
"I will not tell mamma," she reflected, after the
first misery of her new knowledge had passed.
" And perhaps it will never happen again. He
says it has very seldom happened in his life. . . .
Very seldom," she repeated aloud, quoting his own
words with a shudder, and feeling the stinging
sense of *what it was* that had happened.

His mornings were usually spent at one of the

two or three clubs to which he belonged, and often his afternoons as well. When they dined alone together, and there was no engagement which called them both from home afterward, he would now nearly always leave the house, often not returning until the small hours. At such times she was given to understand that he was "at the club;" but she did not know which club, and more than once, on inquiry, had received answers of such laconic rebuff that there seemed almost a slight and a slur in them.

The plain truth is that Tremaine now frequently drank to excess. Leah had only seen him on a single occasion when wine held him well in its degrading grip, and perhaps the affright and tears which she had then shown had repeatedly, since being forced to confront and console both, made him wary about the hour of certain home-comings.

His vice was of the sort which sometimes overtakes, abruptly and almost unawares, men of precisely his character and temperament. They appear the last men of whom one would prophesy any such downfall. They have drifted into the habit of taking stimulants freely — indeed, too freely — at certain convivial times. They are seen intoxicated after a "stag" dinner; they are

known to have sat late over jovial beakers; they
have been observed unsteadily to hail cabs near
dawn at the doors of their select clubs. But no
one accuses them of any overt inebriety. It is an
intemperance very temperately condoned. "Every
man does it now and then," runs the facile comment, and that they are constantly met, morning
and afternoon, in spotless broadcloth and with no
thirst more compromising than one which a moderate potion can satisfy, is a fact fit to blunt suspicion and put friendly warning in the light of an
impertinence. Besides, they are such cold-blooded
sorts of fellows. A hundred tongues, even among
those associates whom their frigid conventionalism
has most suited, and their patrician nonchalance
most pleased, are always prompt to quote these
traits of imperturbation as special safeguards against
real danger. But for just such men — decorous,
aristocratic, indolent, and beset with a worship of
form and caste, — will now and then lurk a vigilant
fury who has fashioned her scourge out of their
own egotism. They have for years kindled a flame
before the god of Self, and one day the flame leaps
devouringly into their own faces. They have for
years yielded to every appetite, and one day it
is an appetite which rises to master, perhaps to
slay them.

It was thus with Tremaine. His passion for
Leah had passed, as such a passion nearly always
passes with such a nature. He regretted his marriage, and would have given worlds to undo it.
He meant to be a good husband. He thought it
unpardonably vulgar to be a bad one — to have
brawls at home — to let people see that you were
not happily married. But he was discontented by
a bondage which had till recently been a thrilling
happiness. Perhaps this same discontent served
to accelerate the baleful growth of a desire already
carelessly indulged. Twenty times a day he would
tell himself that he was never the man to have married. He still thought Leah a very beautiful creature; his pride in her had somehow strengthened
as his love decreased, and a good share of a certain kind of pride had fallen to him by maternal
inheritance. He became possessed with the idea
that his household was not being made difficult
enough of ingress; Leah had too few dislikes; her
list was too expanded; she was showing a tendency
toward democratic liberalisms. . . . Well, this was
in her blood, Tremaine argued; it must be exter-
minated in time. ·

"I notice that you see a good deal of that little
Mrs. Forbes," he said.

"She is my *protégée*," laughed Leah. "Besides,
she amuses me considerably."

"I think her abominably vulgar. She talks through her nose, and is a bouncer besides. Then one meets the greatest riff-raff at her house. You did an unfortunate thing for poor Bertie Forbes when you gave her that longing to know people. After all, he was right. He has forgiven you, but I don't doubt that he feels the injury still."

"I have not forgiven *him*," said Leah, with a touch of her old haughtiness. "I never shall forgive him for being contemptible."

A hard spark came into Tremaine's eyes. "Extend your pardon or not, as you please. But I wish you to drop his wife."

"No," she answered, "I shall not do so."

He frowned now, and his voice was sharp. "I insist," he said.

Leah looked at him, and slowly shook her head.

Her silent resistant firmness roused a wrath in him which she had never before seen. But she was somehow prepared to see it. Her idol had tumbled earthward. Her idolatry, too, was now daily jeering her with the emptiness of its own perished fervor.

"There are those Marksley girls also," he proceeded, with dry, low voice. "You chose to popularize them, and in a manner you attained your object. But they are still merely endured, and

everybody laughs at their grotesqueness. I will
not have them lunching here, or happening in so
intimately every two or three days. You are los-
ing tone by letting such people know you on such
close terms."

"Then I shall continue to lose it," replied Leah,
with a laugh so icy and defiant that he started as
he heard. "Yes, I shall continue to lose it until
it is all gone. I like Lucy Forbes, and I like the
Marksley girls. I don't exalt them above the rest
of humanity, but I place them, both in morals and
intellect, well above a good many persons whom
you think it proper for me to know. And I *will*
know them — I *will* be intimate with them. I
have chosen to make them all three my friends;
they are all three honestly fond of me, and I would
not abate my friendship or my civility one jot for
any inducement that could possibly be offered."

Through that emphatic yet composed little
speech she was like and yet unlike the Leah of old
— the Leah who had bearded Dr. Pragley and his
côterie at Newport with flashing eyes. But her
eyes did not flash now; they were full, instead, of
a sad courage. She was the woman who withstood an attempted wrong — not the girl who
resented an irritant impertinence.

This interview had taken place at dessert one

evening, while they sat over their fruits and coffee, after the retirement of the servants. This was the second winter of their marriage.

Tremaine rose as her answer ended. He had grown white, but a smile broke from his lips. "How you remind me of your mother at times," he said, measuring each word. " You have the true spirit of the female lecturer. What a pity that fate should have drifted you away from a platform ! "

He was preparing to pass out of the room as he finished, but he could not reach the door until her fleet retort had been uttered. And yet, although fleet, it was filled with a secure self-control.

" You can pay me no such compliment," she said, "as to compare me with my mother, just as you can scarcely ever lower yourself so much in my esteem as when you fling any paltry slur at her beautiful life."

Leah shed hot tears, a little later, after he had left the house and she was alone. But soon her natural force asserted itself. This new rift must not widen. It would be horrible. She and he had years yet, perhaps, to live out together. No doubt other women had made just such mistakes as hers, and been forced to face just such consequences. He was slowly proving to be everything that she had felt convinced he was not. She thought of him as he had looked to her when they were married, and his merely physical stature rose retrospectively like that of another man. Even his love had vanished; she had seen that weeks ago. And her own love? She shivered as she tried to assure herself that this had not vanished as well — that it had not been swept away in the general ravage of hope, trust, respect. For how could their future be made tolerable to either if *both* must plod along lovelessly through uncalculated years?

Leah resolved to do her best, and did it. In the previous summer they had not gone to Newport, but in the following one they again went. They rented a cottage there, and lived the life which she had now almost grown to hate. Still, its excitement deadened her reflections. The youth in her veins made her enjoy almost against her will. She often wondered why people liked her as they did; but this very self-questioning showed that she was unconscious of her own graces and charms; and such unconsciousness increased both, winning her admirers and devotees of either sex whom she had not put forth a finger to attract.

Meanwhile Tremaine gradually slipped deeper and deeper into intemperance. But his indulgent

periods were brief though frequent, and in almost
every case they occurred while Leah slept. He
and she now occupied separate apartments; the
cottage was commodious enough easily to allow
this plan; Leah seldom knew at what hour he returned, after late stays with cards or billiards in
the upper club-regions of the Casino.

She noticed that he wore an unhealthy look, that
he had grown thin, and that his eyes were sometimes darkly ringed. She was not quite sure of
the cause, yet her suspicions verged upon certain-
ties. She constantly blamed herself for not sim-
ulating enough warmth during their hours of
meeting, and yet it is doubtful if she was often
truly culpable. They had their frequent quarrels
now, yet these were incessantly of his making.
Leah would not let him crush her in trivial argument; she would use one sarcasm of her own to
at least ten of his, but hers, though it nearly always
told with silencing power, was reluctantly given.
There was no longer a shadow of affection on either
side. But Leah had the voice of duty to chide her,
and used her stoutest efforts to obey it.

Mrs. Romilly had remained in New York that
summer. The separation was an added trouble to
Leah; but she wrote her mother nearly every day,
if it was only a line. And in those notes and let-

ters she would sometimes lay the whole bitter truth bare, while adding some such merciful after-comment as this :

"We can have no·actual rupture, however, because I shall always struggle to prevent it, unless he should make some important demand that quite transcended all possibility of concession. . . . And as for the life he is leading, I must grant that he never shocks me with any of its immediate results. I have never seen him really in wine except once, though much oftener than once I have felt sure that he was the worse for it. . . . I think I can go on like this for a very long time. Other women are doing so every day — why not I? And do not even fancy that I am any great martyr. My only trouble is that I can't do what other women are continually doing under the same circumstances. . . . You understand what I mean? It shames me even to think of writing it."

Rainsford, who was living his usual quiet life at Newport, would repeatedly see Leah and bow to her. But they were never brought together that summer in any conversational way. Where she went he never went. Indeed, he went nowhere, as the phrase goes. He painted his pictures and strove to get from them the high peace which art will so often give a hurt soul when it serves her truly.

But he would sometimes make a flying trip to
New York, and then he always saw his dear friend,
Mrs. Romilly. During a visit which he paid to
her late in August, Leah's mother showed him the
lines just recorded, which had been received three
days ago.

"Oh, Lawrence," she murmured, "what is the
real meaning of those words?"

"Despair," he answered.

"Can she go on living with him in this joyless,
mocking way?"

"She will, and very bravely. It is like her to
be brave. Life is trying her now, and she stands
the test. Her former pride and arrogance were
merely the surface-flash of her innate womanly
sincerity. Below all that harmless discord she
rang true. She is ringing true now. She sees
herself bound for life to a vicious fop. She will
accept her destiny with stoic fortitude." Then,
after a moment he added: "She will accept it
without the least weak complaint, unless"——
And there he paused.

"Unless?" questioned Mrs. Romilly, intently
watching his strong, meditative face.

"I refer you to her own words," said Rainsford.
And then he quoted, with grave slowness, a portion of what Mrs. Romilly had just read him, show-

ing how it had all bitten into his memory. " 'Unless he should make some important demand that quite transcended all possibility of concession.' Let us both trust that he will not — for her sake."

"You believe that he will, Lawrence ? "

"I have not said so."

Mrs. Romilly gave a long, heavy sigh, as her hazel eyes, still so youthful, searched his own. " But you mean so," she persisted. " You mean that Leah has herself foreshadowed the results of her own pathetic misjudgment."

There is often a dramatic neatness in the occurrence of everyday events which almost puts to shame the deft manipulation of the nicest playwright. Just as Mrs. Romilly finished speaking those words, a knock sounded at the door of the room in which she and Rainsford sat. The knock came from a servant, and the servant brought a telegram.

"It is from Leah ! " exclaimed Mrs. Romilly, after she had torn open the envelope and swept her glance across the message.

"Well ? " queried Rainsford.

" '*Something has happened*,' " read Mrs. Romilly, striving to repress her agitation. " '*I will be with you to-morrow evening. I leave to-morrow for New York, alone !* ' "

"Alone!" echoed Leah's mother, as the paper dropped in her lap.

Her eyes met Rainsford's. "It has come," he said.

"'It has come'? What has come?"

"That of which we have just been speaking."

"Do you mean that he has insulted her?"

"No. She would bear insult. She would resent it, but she would bear it. He has made that demand. He has required, and she will not concede."

Mrs. Romilly stared at him mutely. Her face was full of misery. Both knew the futility of further words. Both knew that they must wait.

X.

THE great Mrs. Chichester drove with her own
hands, that summer at Newport, a pair of
thorough-bred bays, and drove them very well.
She was passionately fond of horses, and it was
stated that the new fashion of ladies driving
themselves had received its chief support from
her zealous concurrence. Plainly and trimly
dressed, with her curly chestnut hair gathered
well beneath a dark riding-hat, with a fragmentary
gossamer veil drawn across her remarkably fresh
face, with her gloves of just the proper fit and
texture to handle the reins easily, and with her
whip held at just the approved angle, this lady
presented an appearance in which ostentation had
no part whatever, and in which even those critics
who morosely condemned her pet pastime as un-
feminine could not but admit that she had a very
simple and dignified way of indulging it. She
usually preferred to drive in the morning, and
would sometimes call at the Tremaines' cottage
for Leah to accompany her. Leah liked well

enough to go. She stood in no awe of her friend's social grandeur, and would talk as familiarly to Mrs. Chichester as though she were one of the Marksley girls. Indeed, Miss Caroline and Miss Louisa had once, in that exaggeration of speech which so rarely forsook them, professed their joint wonder at this undaunted self-complacency.

"I believe that is why Mrs. Stephen A. dotes on you so," said Caroline. "Nearly everybody else grovels to her, you know. She is tired of being grovelled to."

"I should think it would be a very tiresome experience," laughed Leah.

"But we don't see how you hold your own with her in that superb style — do we?" proceeded Louisa, nodding toward her sister. "Why, Carrie and I have a feeling as if electric currents were darting up and down our spines whenever she speaks to us!"

"You know she is such a perfectly terrific swell," resumed Caroline. "She *awes* us — does n't she, Lou? We don't see how you can look her so straight in the eyes."

"Do you think I ought to watch her through a piece of smoked glass?" said Leah, "as we watch the sun?"

She was so firmly assured of the honest natures underlying the eccentricities of these girls, that she had grown to regard their present foible in the light of a diversion; and not seldom she found it a very effective one.

In the morning of the day before that on which her mother received Leah's alarming telegram, Mrs. Chichester gave her young friend a delightful drive behind the neat-stepping and well-broken steeds. The day was almost perfect; they went by the Ocean Avenue way, where huge rocks lifted their black bulks against the dazzling noon-tide sea. None of the great houses are here, and, indeed, scarcely a dwelling of any sort meets your sight as you glide over a road whose hard, finely-tended level makes the horse-hoofs ring almost as if they struck against metal. This road is the sole sign of art which marks the lovely, desolate region. The sea-grasses thrive here, in rugged coves and by ponderous ledges, as they may have thriven a thousand years ago. The strong waves have no ministry to perform on this unpeopled stretch of coast; they do not bear gifts of color and light to the doorways of fair abodes, or wash headlands green with smooth lapses of watered sod; the shore on which they break is untamed as themselves; this so-called avenue, one of the

glories of Newport, strikes a rich, clear note amid
the scale of her delicious variability.

The two ladies went back to Steep Rock after
their drive, and lunched together in a sea-fronting
room of that fine mansion. Leah, while she
watched the strangely youthful face of her hostess, felt a furtive thrill of envy. "Here," she
thought, "is a life in which plenty and peace have
ever gone together. What earthly trouble has
this woman ever known? And does she realize
her complete happiness? Ah! do we. ever do
that until it is past?"

Then Leah thought of her mother, and the
envy, becoming more generous, deepened. Between Marion Chichester and Elizabeth Romilly
what intellectual distance lay! Both were good
women, yet the virtue of one had been a mere
dormant receptivity; she had accepted dogma
and homily, questioning neither; she had bowed
all her life at the shrine of propriety; she had
tacitly held that regarding the most vital human
questions thought was sin. And yet how great
was the place that she possessed in this American
society where she reigned, and where the lines of
provincialism were being yearly more and more
obliterated. Why had not Elizabeth Romilly a
place like hers? Why did she, born a queen by

right of genius, dwell without a crown, without a
courtier? What supreme benefit might *she* not
have accomplished for her race with these millions that had gone to rear only the airy and un-
durable scaffolding of a ballroom sovereignty!
How might she have proved to the world that
certain dreams of her youth, chimerical as these
had seemed, could be substantiated in golden
realities!

While Leah's involuntary reflections took more
or less the meaning just given, words shaped
themselves on her lips of whose delivery she was
almost unconscious until she heard Mrs. Chichester's full, rhythmical voice answering what
she had uttered.

"You ask me if I have not always been happy,
Leah? Well, I feel as if it were a crime to say
'no,' and yet I am tempted to say it." She
smiled, stirred a cup of frothy chocolate with her
little spiral-handled spoon, for an instant, looked
thoughtful (she who so seldom looked thoughtful), and then added: "Do you know, my dear,
that great prosperity has its own peculiar discom-
forts?" Leah was actually startled by this simple
sentence. A funny fancy crossed her mind; she
wondered whether the Marksleys would have
remained free from hysteria if subjected to such

an imposing bit of royal confidence, since Mrs.
Chichester had never been known, in the experience of her most intimate devotees, to mention,
however indirectly, the mighty fact of her own
wealth and state.

"For example, my dear Leah," she now continued, lowering her voice as though some possible ambuscaded servant might overhear so
weighty a confession, "I never know what it
is to want anything. Ah! my child" (and she
sighed here with a distinct pathos), "there is so
much in that — *to want a thing!* When I put on
a new gown I occasionally have a most desolate
sensation. I am on a kind of dead level of luxury. It is all as commonplace as *la pluie et le
beau temps.* No, I mean it is all *beau temps;*
there is no *pluie* whatever. I wish that there
only were, but there is not. I need not ask the
price of my new gown; I need not even concern
myself with how many of them I have. You
don't know what a bore it becomes to have no
personal desires ungratified."

The lady said this with a truly immense earnestness; Leah had never seen her so earnest
before. Her tone and expression were precisely
those which might have been the fitting accompa-
niments of extreme indigence unbosoming its

woes. She tried to look sympathetically interested; she tried not to let the hint of a smile mar
her attentive seriousness; she wanted to get the
whole rare satire of this new species of distress.
For the time she forgot even to be shocked. The
exquisite absurdity of extreme opulence deploring
its overplus in the same strain as that of some
meagre-pursed starveling who craves charity,
touched only her sense of humor, and very
keenly.

"But it is the same with dress as with everything else," proceeded Mrs. Chichester. She had
now left off stirring her chocolate; its ropy,
bronze-brown liquid appeared to have palled upon
her taste; she moved her head sorrowfully from
side to side, and stared straight past Leah at a
breadth of tapestry which hung by gilt rings on
a gilt rod.

"Dress is not my only trouble," murmured this
afflicted millionaire. "Oh, no, indeed! There is
the wretched bore of having a *chef* and two or
three assistants who require no orders in the matter of dinners. It would be so perfectly charming
to make out one's own *menu* when one asked
people to dine. But our man, Claireau, whom my
husband specially imported, and whom he pays
several thousand a year, would regard me in polite

amazement if I presumed to *order* anything. The 'ideas,' as he has the impudence to call them, are submitted to me, and I am expected unqualifiedly to approve them. I always do; Claireau is so monotonously capable. Of course he combines with his skill a great deal of handsome humbug. He talks of his dishes as if they were poems, and of his courses as if they were stanzas or cantos. He assured me, the other day, that one kind of soup had much more sentiment than another, and that a certain *entrée* was full of lyrical tenderness — '*pleine d'une tendresse lyrique, Madame.*' . . . Think of that! . . . And thus it goes on, my dear. I have no real comfort in living, because I live too comfortably. I could recount a hundred other little miseries to you, all springing from the same cause. But I will not. Let us talk of something else, my dear." Here Mrs. Chichester became herself again, and began to stir and sip the beverage before her with a kind of repentant briskness. " Let me ask you with whom you shall dance the german at my ball, next Thursday? It is such a pleasure to speak with a friend who has not written me asking invitations for two or three other friends. *There* is a new little misery — and not so little a one, after all — which I forgot to record! My ball will probably be as

mixed as one of the poor late President Lincoln's.
I am prepared to have it criticised as the most
broadly democratic entertainment ever given in
Newport. But what can I do? My own friends
betray me. I can't say 'no' to them. . . . Ah,
they don't reflect what hard things I say when I
write 'yes!'" . . .

Leah afterward had her ruminations as she was
driven homeward in a spacious open equipage of
Mrs. Chichester's. She had ceased to feel amused,
she was silently ired.

"How preposterous seem these dainty griefs,"
she thought, "when one reflects upon them!
Where are that woman's almsgivings? You read
of them in the newspapers — a conspicuous cheque
is donated to this or that asylum or institution.
But what more? . . . She broods over the tyranny
of her cook because he feeds her faultlessly — of
her tailor, because he clothes her beyond reproach!
And yet this woman is a Christian, and goes to
churches where, if you plied the question close to
them, they would say, with Dr. Pragley, that my
great-hearted mother is an atheist!"

Leah reached home to-day in no pleasant mood.
It was about four o'clock. The domain of Bellevue Avenue had begun to fill with its usual throng
of carriages. Polo was played this afternoon, and

many of the vehicles were hurrying toward the
grounds where that madcap game had its especial
theatre of revel. Leah's dwelling was in Kay
Street — that realm of close-crowded cottages,
nearly all unobtrusive, and yet all informed with
a special home-like fascination. There, on the
roadside, just opposite her gate (for the nearness of all these houses to the public turnpike
admits of no entrance within their lawns), she
found Mrs. Forbes, seated in a barouche, quite as
grand as that of Mrs. Chichester, which had just
brought the guest of the great lady back to her
cottage.

"Oh, I am so glad, Leah!" exclaimed Mrs.
Forbes, leaning vivaciously forward. "I wanted
to see you. Come — let's go to the Polo grounds
— or anywhere you please — I don't care. But
you must come with me. They said here that you
were off somewhere with Mrs. Chichester, and I
was just on the point of driving to Steep Rock
to try and get you. I must have you. Now, don't
refuse!"

Leah demurred not a little after alighting, but
presently permitted herself to be persuaded. She
had had quite enough of driving for that day, but
there was a nervous eagerness in Mrs. Forbes's
manner which made her suspect that it had origin

in some mental trouble. For this reason she consented.

At first her suspicion seemed very far from confirmation. The elegant equipage in which she was now seated soon passed from Kay Street into Bellevue Avenue. But, although Mrs. Forbes had a great deal to say on the various topics which concerned the present rush and swirl of things, she made no allusion to that particular matter which had appeared on the verge of disclosure.

"Lucy," at length said Leah, quietly, "you're talking in quite a random way, and I know there is something you really want to tell me. Pray, what is it?"

Mrs. Forbes laid one hand on Leah's, pressing sensibly with her gloved fingers.

"Oh, Leah," she said, "don't ask me quite yet!" Her unalterably nasal tones somehow made this appeal more plaintive than it might otherwise have been. "We'll get to the Polo grounds in a minute. Don't ask me till we're driving back. . . . Or, if you say so, we won't go in. I'll tell James to turn round. What do *you* say?"

"Oh, well," answered Leah, "we are so near, now, that we might as well enter."

Polo was an oft-told tale to her, and she thought

it an extremely stupid amusement for the crowds
that flocked to see its petty battles lost or won.
Still, she owned there was attraction in noting the
various faces and costumes, if nothing more ; her
eye was quite as quick as formerly to seize on all
comic points in either, though her tongue was
much less ready to record the effects of such ob-
servation.   Their carriage now entered an immense space of deep-green, elastic turf, inclosed
by a wooden fence of thrice the ordinary height.
A very wide margin on every side of this fine
amphitheatre was given up to visitors in equipages
of countless sorts, while here and there moved
equestrians of both sexes.   Many of the carriages
had stopped, and words were being interchanged
by their occupants.   Others were in motion,
making two continual streams that flowed past
one another.   To-day had brought what was
esteemed a very full attendance ; it was a specimen day, so to speak, and as usual in any
large gathering at Newport the winsome faces
of beautiful young girls were a brilliant pre-
ponderating feature.   The bustle and animation
of nearly everybody, their smiles, their brisk nods
or more stately bows, their peals of laughter,
their bursts of careless or mirthful speech, con-
trasted happily with the rich radiance of female

apparel, the neat smartness which marked the
gentlemen's attire, the style and airs of the cock-
aded, booted flunkeys, the flash of silver or gilded
harness, the fragrance and glow of roses knotted
at the bosoms of charming women, the keen blue
of the afternoon sky, the vigorous breeze that blew
straight from the sea across this splendid expanse
of turf, and lastly the blithe music of a band
stationed as centrally as possible, and doing its
rapid, vociferous best when each game was started,
as though to stimulate the players in their feats of
supple horsemanship.

Remarkable indeed were these feats. The clipped
little ponies that their riders bestrode with such
tough adhesiveness, would now press four or
five of their volatile bodies together in a wriggling
mêlée, now swerve mutually from collision when
on the apparent verge of it, now describe the most
breakneck zigzags or wheel in the most giddy revolutions; and all the while one tiny ball, struck
at with plunges of the mallets, dashed for with
headlong swoops of the ponies, continued the
cause of these onslaughts, tilts, shocks, sorties, or
retreats. The great distance which separated
players from spectators made this ball often invisible amid the tumult, as it made the pigmy steeds
themselves assume proportions hardly larger than

those of some big-framed mastiff. Suddenly a lucky stroke would send the ball leaping far away from the massed contestants, and then, fleet as wind, a pony would dart to where it had fallen, his sitter eager to strike it out of bounds with the final victorious blow. But perhaps he would stoop, aim, essay the swinging hit, and yet miss at the decisive second. Then some adversary, hot in pursuit, would perhaps halt straight at the important spot just passed, with enough suddenness, you might think, to unseat a centaur. Like lightning the obedient pony would veer about; like lightning the new implement would meet the ball and send it flying back among those glad or chagrined at its return, and fired with zeal to fight for its possession. Perhaps it would soon be hurled toward the opposite bounds from those so nearly reached a brief while since; perhaps the same ill-fortune would here repeat itself with the other foe, or possibly a strenuous, rushing *coup* would abruptly end the struggle and decide the conquest.

"You need a telescope to provoke any lively interest in Polo," said Leah, as she and Mrs. Forbes were driven at a gentle pace along the usual turfy, circular route. "Don't you agree with me, Lucy?"

" Yes," said Mrs. Forbes, in rather absent tones. The game bored her, as it does most women ; besides, her thoughts had excuse for wandering just now. " I always did think that Polo was made for children," she continued. " How few men ever play it! They are nearly always boys of twenty or thereabouts. After that age they begin to respect their bones and joints; dyspepsia warns them that they're not immortal; they discover that while discretion is the better part of valor, so is prudence the sworn friend of longevity."

Leah laughed, as she often did, at the sparkles of pleasantry that came from her friend. Mrs. Forbes's speedy way of delivering her bright things, and the nasal voice which never failed to utter them, stamped them as individual and characteristic.

But Leah had already plainly seen that she was by no means her merry self to-day. Just as they were driving away from the Polo grounds, about a quarter of an hour later, Mrs. Forbes surprised her by a swift, sharp laugh, and a motion of the head toward a rocky elevation of land, whose highest portion commanded an evident view of the game and its assembled watchers. Here a few nurses with children were to be glimpsed, and many more persons of both sexes, shabby in guise and clearly members of the working-classes.

"That is Deadhead Hill, you know," said Mrs. Forbes, after her laugh. "Oh, dear, it reminds me of such a funny adventure of mine, summer before last! Bertie — as usual then — had gone off with some swell man or woman to see Polo. *I* wanted to see Polo, too. I had n't my horses yet; we had just got here, and did n't know how long we should stay, on account of that money fright in Peoria, of which I told you. So I concluded I would take a walk to the Polo grounds. They told me it was n't far from the Aquidneck — at least I think somebody said so. I found it pretty far though, and when I got here I saw people standing just as they 're standing now, and that broken fence where they get in, and I said to myself, 'This must be the way you go when you go on foot.' So I marched up, and clambered along till I had a good place for seeing, and then I saw. It did n't occur to me that I was n't particularly among people of my own kind. I had a rather good time; I did n't think much of Polo, any more than I 've ever thought of it since. But when I got home and told Bertie where I 'd been, you should have seen his horror." Here all Mrs. Forbes's humor vanished. She spoke with positive acerbity; Leah

had never before seen her exhibit so much bitterness. "'That was Deadhead Hill,' he informed
me, in the most shocked manner. He hoped no
one had seen me there. It was horrible to think
of his wife having gone where nobody except servants and common people ever dreamed of going."
At this point Mrs. Forbes gave another slight
laugh, harsher than before. "Oh, I know what I
might have said, Leah, and what perhaps I *ought*
to have said — I mean that Deadhead Hill was
much more suited to him than to me, since I was
n't living in conceited laziness on my husband's
money, as he was living on his wife's."

Leah saw the truth at last. She let a little
silence elapse, and then she stole her hand into her
companion's.

"Lucy," she said, "you 've had a serious quarrel with your husband. Come, acknowledge it.
That is what you wanted to tell me."

"Serious?" said Mrs. Forbes, turning her face
on Leah's, and lifting her pretty brows in mock
astonishment; "that is no word for it, my dear.
I intend arranging for a separation."

"Really," murmured Leah.

"Without the least doubt. I 've stood his ridiculous airs long enough. I 've had the British peerage substituted for the family Bible *quite* long

enough, too, not to mention its being occasionally
fired in my face when his majesty chanced to be out
of humor. But, more than this, Leah, I have become business-woman enough not to allow the fortune pa left me to be gambled away at the Metropolitan Club in New York and the Casino here.
I told him *that* very squarely last night. I said:
'Go your way, sir, and I 'll go mine.' I am to see
my lawyer in a few days, and I told him *that*, too.
I suppose there 'll be a scandal, but I don't care.
I have n't an atom of regard left for him — not an
atom ! He has treated me vilely ; he has used me
(the mother of his children, Leah !) as a mere con-
venience and cat's-paw. I 've borne it all, for
months past, only from a sense of decency. Now
he 's gone too far, and he shall feel it. After this
we live apart. I 'll put him on an allowance ; I 'll
give him three thousand a year ; not a penny more
— and that 's more than he deserves. . . . He insulted me grossly last night. The fine gentleman
vanished when he found I would n't pay his gam-
bling debts ! The rare old Chetwynde blood ac-
quitted itself most aristocratically ! He called me
a common little Yankee, Leah. He said that my
poor, dear, dead father had been a cad. . . . Oh,
then I gave him a few plain truths — be sure I did !
I have never been so furious before in all my life,

and I hope I shall never be so again. I let him understand that he had come to the end of his tether — and he *does* understand it. He 's frightened now. Let him stay so. I 'm firm as steel; I mean to show him good cause for fright. He 's great friends with your husband, by the way. I suppose he has told Mr. Tremaine everything. I 'm so fond of you, Leah, that I hate to think of anything unpleasant rising between us."

"You need have no fear of anything unpleasant rising between us," said Leah, quietly. "Whatever side my husband takes is of no import to me. . . . You are wretched, Lucy, and not yourself. You must dismiss the carriage when we get to Kay Street, and stop and dine with me."

Mrs. Forbes demurred, but Leah insisted, at length carrying her point. As the two ladies passed up the short lawn-path leading to the piazza, they saw Tremaine standing there.

It was nearly dinner-time. He wore full evening-dress, as he had done at this hour almost from boyhood. He bowed with perfect suavity to Mrs. Forbes, who at once passed indoors. Meanwhile Leah lingered for a moment.

"Lucy dines with us this evening," she said.

His face clouded. "Have you asked her for the purpose of annoying me?" he replied. "I don't see what other motive you can have. Bertie has told me of their quarrel. You know he and I are friends. I detest that woman, and you know that also. I will not have·her at my table."

"Shall I tell her so?" asked Leah, calmly.

"Yes," he answered, sullenly. below his breath. "You can, if you choose."

XI.

A SMILE of irony touched Leah's lips as she left her husband standing on the piazza and rejoined her friend. Not long afterward dinner was announced, and when Leah and Mrs. Forbes appeared in the dining-room they were met by Tremaine, who had chosen to assume a cool, careless manner, although indignation burned not far beneath its decorous outer crust.

The talk flowed rather freely, though aimlessly, until dessert was served and the attendants had retired. Leah had been speaking in a vein of light ridicule regarding the troubles which Mrs. Chichester had confided to her that day at luncheon.

"Some of the people who are crying the Chichesters down as shameless monopolists ought to hear of Mrs. Stephen A.'s distresses," said Mrs. Forbes. "It might comfort them a little. . . . I wonder if there are many married women in Newport this evening who have less actual grievances."

She gave a sidelong look toward Tremaine as she spoke the last sentence.

"Oh, most married women have very serious grievances," he said, with his eyes drooped upon his plate.

"Yes, and they are always foolish ones, of course," said Mrs. Forbes, with a kind of mournful satire.

"Not always," Leah broke in propitiatingly.

"Oh, yes, my dear Leah, *always!*" declared Mrs. Forbes, turning with great earnestness toward her friend. Her lip trembled a little as she spoke. A glance from Leah silenced further words.

"The longer that men live in the world," said Tremaine, with his drawl, beginning to peel a peach, "the more they are led to conclude that it wasn't entirely made for the other sex. They want a small corner of the big sphere — only a corner, you know. And they take the liberty of being annoyed when that moderate demand is interfered with."

"I don't know what you mean!" exclaimed Mrs. Forbes, who had no parry of words, no power of duelling with wit. "You *can't* allude to *me*, surely! I don't think there ever was a woman who endured quite as much downright imposition as I did from my husband. I suppose he has told you what has happened. You always sided with him, Mr. Tremaine, and no doubt you do so now."

᠆ "I heard there had been trouble," he said, a trifle bluntly, "and of course I have my opinions."

Mrs. Forbes gave a peevish, exasperated sigh.

"Well, keep them to yourself, I beg," she responded, rather tartly.

"I had no intention of airing them, really."

"If you have finished your coffee, Lucy," now said Leah, "we will go into the drawing-room."

"What! and leave me?" said Tremaine, softly, with a fleeting smile that had not a ray of humor.

"Yes — to your cigar," she answered.

"Ah," said Mrs. Forbes, in tones more sad than angry, though both, while she lifted one plump forefinger and shook it at Tremaine, "I'm afraid you're glad enough to have *me* go."

"I must be polite enough to disagree with you there," he promptly said, "no matter how great danger I may run in doing so."

It was somehow not a rude speech as he pronounced it, though on other lips the implication, at such a time, that to disagree with her was dangerous, must have seemed openly assailant and harsh.

Thus Mrs. Forbes chose to deem it, however, from the present speaker; her nerves were shaken by the recent domestic tornado; they were still vibrating under an acute sense of indignity. She had not merely the feeling that everybody who was not with her was against her, but that everybody who was against her must base such antagonism upon the most malicious injustice.

"No one runs any danger in disagreeing with me!" she exclaimed. Tears were in her voice, and a good deal of spleen besides. "But when I have been abused and insulted for years it is a different matter."

Tremaine looked at her with a cruel tranquillity. "Upon my word," he said, "I have made no inquiries into your family history. Why do you volunteer these interesting details?"

"Why?" echoed Mrs. Forbes, brokenly. "Because I am a very unhappy woman through no fault of my own, and because I see that you are bent upon taunting me."

Tremaine gave his head a slight toss. His voice was hard and arbitrary now, though not loud. "If you want to be canonized as a martyr," he replied, "I am not prepared to perform any such ceremony. I confess that I lack the requisite faith to do the anointing. You must seek somebody more blameless — more like yourself."

"Tracy," broke in Leah, firmly and decidedly,

at this point, "you will please say nothing more. Lucy is miserable, and you know it." . . . She rose and went toward her friend, whose tears had begun to flow, and whose form was trembling. She laid one hand upon Mrs. Forbes's arm. "Come, Lucy," she said, "come at once into the drawing-room." Mrs. Forbes quitted her chair. But her eyes, reproachful and shining with resentment through the moisture that had beset them, were fixed upon Tremaine. A sudden impulse assailed her; she yielded to it; she spoke with almost violent heat.

"*I* never pretended to be blameless, Mr. Tremaine, and *you* have good reason not to call yourself so!"

His brow darkened. He left his chair, and went several paces toward where she stood.

"What do you mean," he demanded, with challenging directness.

"I mean," answered Mrs. Forbes, with the look of one goaded into heedless rage, "that it would be well to reform your own conduct before you fling slurs at mine! All Newport knows that you spend hours at Mrs. Fortescue's house, and that you have revived an intimacy which is shameful to yourself as it is disrespectful and unmanly toward your wife!"

Tremaine turned very pale. His eyes swept
Leah's face; then he gave a scornful laugh, turned
on his heel, and passed from the room. . . .

About a half-hour later he and Leah met in the
lower hall. Lights had been lit; the dusk had become night. Leah was on the point of passing
into the rear drawing-room. But she paused as
she saw her husband descend the stairs.

He held a collapsed opera-hat in one hand.
Across one arm he had flung a light overcoat.
As his step left the staircase, Leah, still standing
exactly where she had first paused, said to him:

" Were you going out? "

" Yes. Has that woman gone? "

" Mrs. Forbes has gone. . . . I wish to speak a
few words with you."

They faced each other. Tremaine coolly took
out his watch and glanced at it. " I have an engagement," he said, with matter-of-fact brevity.

" What I wish to say will not detain you long,"
returned Leah.

He gave a faint shrug of the shoulders. " Oh,
very well. As you please."

She at once passed into the drawing-room. Two
lamps in shades of rose-colored silk starred its attractive, modish interior, where you noted the
warm gleam of a rug or two strewn on light-

tinted flooring, the luminous oval of a Venetian mirror, or the airy outline of a gilded bamboo screen.

Tremaine threw himself into a commodious chair and waited. Leah moved toward one of the small tables on which a lamp was burning. The pink tinge flung across her countenance decreased its pallor, but in her close-joined lips and unwavering gaze lay subdued yet distinct resolve.

"I said that I would not detain you long," she began. "Unpleasant things are best spoken quickly; they are also best referred to by suggestion rather than detailed statement. Mrs. Forbes's very plain accusation saves me from doing more than mention it, and enables me at once to ask you, Is her charge a true one?"

There was a dead silence of several seconds. Tremaine stared down at one of his glistening boots while it lasted. Then he raised his head and met Leah's answering eye.

"Do you want to make a scene?" he asked.

"It is what I wish to avoid. My question can be very well answered without one." Her tones were ice itself. Her flinchless look made him avert his own.

"You have made up your mind that I shall answer? Suppose, then, I refuse?"

She instantly said : " I shall, in that case, assume that you *have* answered by an affirmative."

She saw a sneer commence about his mouth, under its blond shadowing growth, which he was now stroking quickly with one hand. " And if I totally deny this charge ? "

" Then I shall be certain that you have uttered a falsehood."

He sprang to his feet with a suppressed oath. She had pierced the crust of the fine gentleman. " Do you suppose I will stand being made sport of in this ridiculous style ? " he said. " So you intended to set a trap for me, did you ? Well, believe that vulgar little Western minx, if you please. I 'm sick of her and you, both."

" I set no trap," said Leah, with her words as swift, now, as her tones were controlled. " I merely gave you the chance of admitting your guilt."

" Guilt ! " he exclaimed. " Bah ! " He raised the finger and thumb of one hand, and audibly snapped them.

" I gave you the chance of admitting it," she went steadily on, " so that the promise I shall now exact of you might naturally ensue from such admission. I have known this thing for months. Lucy Forbes's outburst pained me, but it did not bring me any new tidings. All in all, I am glad that she spoke as she did. She has marked for me the limit of my own patience. We can no longer live together on terms that will make such an affirmation possible from a third party. I exact a sacred promise of you. It is this: that from to-night henceforth you shall never enter the doors of a certain woman, and shall in every way avoid even the exchange of a word with her. Let me be still more explicit. Let there be no least risk of misunderstanding. The woman to whom I allude is Mrs. Abbott Fortescue."

He threw back his head with a laugh of irony. " It 's astonishing," he declared, " what precious fools we can sometimes make of ourselves without knowing it ! "

" To be uncivil is not to give me your reply."

He repressed another laugh, equally full of contempt. " Please allow me a few days to reflect," he said, in mockery, going to the chair which he had quitted, taking from its side his overcoat, re-flinging this lightly across one arm, and then moving toward the door.

She glided several paces after him. She had uplifted her right hand. " I want the promise or the refusal to promise, now — at once ! " she said. And there was so stirring a solemnity in her man-

ner and intonation that it put all his assumed
jauntiness of scorn into prompt disarray.

Half-turning, he frowned very darkly at her,
over one shoulder. "You'll wait for a long time
before you get either!" he retorted.

The key of Leah's voice heightened then; the
immobility of her manner changed. She made a
gesture of excited force — a sweep forward of both
hands, followed by their rapid withdrawal. "You
refuse, then! I have no more to say. To-morrow
I rejoin mamma in New York. Afterward I return to your house but on one condition — your
promise, as before described."

She wheeled away from him then. But he
followed her, angry almost to madness.

"You will dare to take this course — you!"
he said, below his breath, and with hoarseness.
"You'll forget what name I gave you when
I married you! —— what a place I raised you
to!"

His hands were clenched at his sides while he
spoke. But she did not see this; the light was
too irregularly disposed about the room, perhaps,
or it may have been because she was regarding
him across her shoulder, as he had done with her
but a few moments since.

"You raised me to no real place," she said, still

calmly, yet as if between shut teeth. "I care nothing for what you call position. I thought it something far finer and purer than what it has proved. I despise in it all that you respect. I see that what you think sound and high is flimsy and low. You must leave that woman once and forever, or I will not live with you. You know that I have *been* living with you for none of the old reasons. Those are gone. But there should have been a maintenance of respectability — de-cency, between us. You have failed to meet even these last requirements. I exact that promise in the hope of making its fulfilment a barrier against the separation which now seems certain."

By this time Tremaine's anger was cooled. He saw the reality of the indignation that thus ad-dressed him. At the same time he recalled the exacted promise.

"Do as you please," he said. He immediately passed from the room. . . .

There was a reception that night at one of the great Newport houses. Leah did not attend it. She retired to bed at a late hour, but lay sleepless until nearly dawn, thinking sad thoughts, telling herself that hers was a wasted and ruined life. Such a short time ago she had been so credulously and trustfully happy! And now her soul had a

black past to look back upon, and a blank future
to foresee. Her resolve remained unaltered. She
would leave for New York early on the following
day. Before seeking her bed she had dispatched
the telegram of which we know; she had also
packed certain portions of her wardrobe and all
her jewels. She did not believe that her husband
and herself would ever live together again. She
meant to return to him on a single condition; he
might perhaps make her return possible; she did
not much care whether he would or no; he had
become despicable in her sight. The man whom
she had loved was now a dim, memorial shadow;
the man whom she no longer loved rose before her
as an almost hateful actuality. She shed but a
few tears, and these were provoked only by reflections on her mother's coming pain, her mother's
rich, waiting sympathy. "Poor mamma!" her
lips whispered, again and again.

Strangely, and yet not strangely, the grave,
strong face of Lawrence Rainsford shaped itself
to-night before her mental vision. She did not
know whether his love for her yet lived or not.
But she remembered what that love had been.
And she thought of the stanch, manful nature
whose devotion she had held at so slight a worth.
Why could she not have loved Rainsford? Her

mother had been so right in wanting her to love him! If only she could live that vanished time over again, aided by her present dolorous experience! Might she not then see, understand, appreciate, and so love? Yes, beyond doubt! And how different it would all have been! No bleeding wound — no shattered ideal — no palsied hope!

It was almost dawn when she heard a carriage stop at the gate below. Then she heard voices of men, now loud and now faint. She rose and went to the window, peering forth. She saw three figures moving up along the garden path. The central figure walked insecurely and in a tottering way; it was supported, apparently, by those on either side of it. She guessed the truth, though she had not recognized her husband. She withdrew from the window, loath to see more. Then she waited. A step presently sounded upon the outer stairs. It was so unsteady that it suggested the most perilous insecurity; it was indeed a succession of irregular stamps. But the sounds gradually grew nearer. A little later she heard them in the hall. Tremaine's apartment was at the head of the stairs. He had but a short space to traverse before reaching it. To Leah, while she listened intently, it seemed as if the staggering gait must soon end in some sort of overthrow and collapse, so noisy a stumble had it now become. A moment later this fear was verified. A dull, heavy fall now followed. She stood irresolute for a little time; then she lighted a candle and put on a loose wrapper over her night-dress. Very quietly, though she was shivering as if a cold gust had assailed her, she went out into the hall. The light that she carried presently showed her an inert form, lying prone across the threshold of an open doorway. She regarded this form for a longer time than she knew, while holding the candle uplifted in one tremulous hand. The face, with its closed eyes and the stentorous breathing that issued from its half-shut lips, fascinated her by its familiar beauty, once so treasured as the symbol of an exceptional spirit!

It was a terrible moment with Leah. Memories swept through her, each piercing in its dread appeal. She recalled her past estimate of this man; she revived her old belief in him; she saw again those graces and charms which had won her to link her own life with his. And yet there he lay, prostrate, incapable, an incarnate denial of her faith, a dumb refutation of her respect. She gazed upon the merciless evidence of a misjudgment that must vibrate through all her future life. What savage irony it seemed that this grossness should lie before her as the palpable product of a romance, a sentiment, an enthusiasm!

There are brief intervals in many a human experence when the soul almost proves itself an incorporal force, unconditioned by flesh; it grows very wisely and drearily old while the body yet remains young. . . . Leah stooped and touched her husband's shoulder; but it would have taken a rougher grasp than any which she could employ to rouse him from that despised stupor. Still, she had a fair store of strength, and shame now gave a spur to its use. She set down her candle on the floor of the hall. Then, clinching her teeth as we do when a task that we abhor confronts us, she again bent down and clutched either shoulder, so seeking to drag the supine frame farther into the bedchamber. She might have succeeded better in her pathetic effort, had not a weakness — born perhaps of humiliation and disgust — suddenly overcome her. As it was, she moved the fallen shape only a few inches. That nerveless desperation which in some feminine temperaments is the prelude of hysteria, rushed over her as she desisted from the attempt. She felt like screaming aloud — like perversely bruiting her forlorn pain abroad amid the darkness and silence!

But immediately this wild impulse fled; it had transiently jarred her sanity, and nothing more. Fresh and cooler energy resulted from it. She saw that the disposition of the limbs now chiefly prevented the door from being closed and the whole body hidden within the room. Still, the body itself required further displacement. Not long afterward she had made her second trial with success. . . . The door just grazed Tremaine's dragged bulk as she closed it. Then she locked it on the inside, and at once passed, by other means of communication, back into her own chamber.

When she had reached it her emotion underwent a new and odd change. She burst into soft, uncontrollable laughter, while the tears stole down her white cheeks. Nor was even this manifestation one of hysteria. The sense of humor, always strong with her, had abruptly intruded itself, like a daring and unbidden guest, upon her dumb, desolate misery. The indulgence of this weird mirth, at so intensely unreasonable a time, went with full perception of its ghastly discordance. She made a most woful picture, seated with her lovely hair half loosened in the dim candle-light. That fearful, mute laughter was like the farewell of her own dying youth. It had a strange and darksome consistency, too; it was a mournful echo of the old girlish fault, so alert to see and ridicule any decisive failing in her fellows.

Her beauty was never the same after that night. Its freshness had vanished. It was tenderer, more appealing, more poetic — as though the erect delicacy of the alder had been gently given the downward curve of the real willow. People afterward said of Leah that she had faded. This was true, and yet the difference held a wistful interest. Her. face told you that she had lived; her brown eyes burned as if they had known tears; her fair, chaste brow looked as if sorrow had shadowed it; her smile, no longer brilliant, beamed with that autumnal sweetness which we all know in the quality of a sun-ray when its warmth has ebbed yet when its light has grown mellower.

Leah started for New York at an early hour on the following day. She did not see her husband before leaving the house; she was not even aware if his vinous torpor had ceased or no. She hated and yet loved the thought of meeting her mother.

When they did meet, which was happily in the presence of no observer, she clung to Mrs. Romilly's neck with a prolonged paroxysm of sobs. Then, after the calm had followed the storm, she narrated everything.

"Did I do right, mamma?" she questioned.
"Tell me! I have lost the old wilful way of
always judging for myself. I want you to judge
for me, with that wisdom of yours which I have
sometimes treated so irreverently. But I never
meant to treat it so — I never *did*, really — I
only pretended. Tell me, mamma! If you blame
me, I will believe you! If you approve me, I
will believe you! Which is it to be? How am
I to act? Shall I break my resolve? Shall I go
back to him before he makes the promise? If he
never makes the promise, shall I still go back to
him? Ah! that will be hard; and yet your answer, however given, shall be my law. You knew
so well at first! You advised, you remonstrated,
but I heard and yet would not hear! If only I
had heeded and obeyed! How few women have
ever lived who have had such a mother as I!
And how I have undervalued you! Now, when
it is too late, I see the headstrong folly of it all!
I don't ask you to forgive me. You are so large
in soul and heart that you always forgive easily.
I would have said 'too easily' in those other days.
But I don't say it now. I see you in your full
perfection. Tears clear the eyes so — you once
said something of that sort to me — it was not
very long ago . . . do you remember? I'll lean

on you like a staff, if you'll only let me. And I
know you will let me. Ah! talk of love! I
never loved any one but you, and never shall!
That may have been my real error, mamma, darling! I was in love with you — yes, only you —
and did not know it!"

"Leah," said Mrs. Romilly, after this soft tirade
had ended, "you must not go back to him until
he gives you the promise. You were right. I
shall tell him so when we meet — if we are destined soon to meet."

They were so destined. Two days later Tremaine presented himself at the house. He asked
for Leah, but Mrs. Romilly received him.

He was dressed with his former precision. He
looked extremely aristocratic. He spoke with all
his best nicety and composure. "I am forced to
tell you," he said, very early in the conversation,
"that I wish to see my wife, and no ambassadress
between herself and me."

"Your wife will not see you," replied Mrs.
Romilly, firm as stone.

He quietly nodded. "I see you have counselled her."

"I have. And yet my counsel was needless, I
think. Her leaving you was a proof of that.
She exacts a promise. You must give it, or she
will never notice you again."

He looked at the speaker with a polite scorn. "If I were not a gentleman," he said, "I should call you a very officious and disagreeable mother-in-law."

"You are not a gentleman," said Mrs. Romilly, softly. "You have shown it beyond mistake."

Tremaine pressed his lips together, and his eyelids lowered. Rage, though held within bounds, was never expressed more surely.

"You want a separation—perhaps a divorce," he said.

"I want a reformation," answered Mrs. Romilly.

He drew a long breath. "Ah!" he murmured, "you advocate morality now. You have deserted your former laxities of opinion."

At this insult Mrs. Romilly gave a faint, pitying smile. "If I had not already told you that you are not a gentleman," she said, with quiet dignity, "you might have cause to fancy that your insolence troubled me."

Tremaine looked at her with repressed disdain. "It seems to me," he answered, "that we address each other from wholly different standpoints. I don't think I should like your idea of a gentleman. Would he wear long hair and preach communism?"

Mrs. Romilly shook her head. "I don't know

how he would arrange his hair," she replied; "but
he would respect his marriage vows, and he would
abstain from drunkenness."

Tremaine bit his lip. His mild eyes flashed for
an instant. He walked toward the door of the
apartment, but paused before he had reached its
threshold.

"Such women as you are," he said, "have no
real sex. If I were as bad as you paint me, I
might remember this fact to your bodily harm."

"If you struck me," replied Mrs. Romilly, "I
should not be at all surprised. I think such men
as you are have often, before now, struck women.
And I suppose they have always made some
excuse."

A silence followed. Tremaine, with averted
face, scanned the carpet. Suddenly he turned
toward Mrs. Romilly, and said, in considerably
changed tones: "I want my wife to live with me
again. I have my reasons for wanting her to do
so. You and I hate each other. Agreed. A certain promise is required of me. Suppose I make
that promise?"

"If you make it, your wife will return to you.
If you keep it, she will live with you. But these
are the sole conditions. And I do not hate you.
I hate no one."

He tossed his head. There appeared to be scorn in his concession while he gave it. "Very well," he said; "I'm willing to make such a promise."

"To Leah herself?"

"To Leah herself."

Mrs. Romilly at once withdrew. Leah presently appeared in her stead.

XII.

A LL publicity of scandal was for the time avoided. By a week or two later, Leah and her husband were occupying their former New York residence. For several weeks afterward Tremaine conducted himself with a scrupulous observance of reputable usage. There had been no formal reconciliation. Perhaps both shrank from this, as from a needless hypocrisy. Tremaine was admirably courteous, however. He had a faultless set of manners; they were like a perfectly-equipped dressing-case, in which nothing is wanting, from the ivory-backed hair-brush to the little silver box for holding soap. Leah would sometimes watch him in secret consternation. She wondered if any hard, voluptuous and narrow spirit ever clad itself in softer and more tasteful guise. That was the sole meaning of Tremaine — he had good taste. It ruled him as a creed, and covered him like a garment. His cruel comments regarding others, his choice of reading, his selection of apparel, his mode of dining, his bow, his smile, his favorite phrase, were all set in one key of good taste. The vice which had begun to victimize him, stealing in by the path of selfishness, was wholly irrelevant to this dainty nicety. He was the last man in the world, you might have said, who would have taken to drink. But intemperance is very often the Nemesis of a man's own callous inhumanity. A life wed to idleness and swayed solely by personal concern will sometimes hoard unawares a store of venom, through which may come to it, in slow but certain way, the death of the viper that has stung its own flesh.

Leah and her husband now rarely appeared in society together. It would have been fortunate at this period if a child had been given her. She would have lavished upon it untold affection and derived infinite comfort from the protective duties of motherhood. She had flung away husks, and hungered for true nourishment. Suffering had drawn a veil from her eyes; she looked at the world as a place in which thousands were daily feeling worse pangs than hers, and where the vast common ills of her race could be fought with no weapon save a resolute charity. Many noble sayings of her mother shone as if in golden letters through the clearing mists of memory. And her love for that mother, always profound though often so erratic in its display, now became a steadfast tribute, more fond than the one which Lawrence Rainsford had long paid, and yet quite as reverential.

Rainsford and she now often met at her mother's dwelling. It never occurred to Leah that his old wound had not healed. Seeing all things in a new light, she saw herself as a kind of maimed failure. She could not have brought herself to believe that he regarded her in any wise except with a generous pity.

"Why has Rainsford never married?" she said to her mother, one day. "There must be so many good women who would most gladly join their future with his. It would be like setting out to sea in a stanch ship that wreck has no terrors for."

Mrs. Romilly gave a smile of involuntary sadness.

"In one of your talks together," she replied, "you might ask him. Perhaps he would tell you."

But Leah did not ask. These talks to which Mrs. Romilly referred were sometimes held in her sitting-room during a brief absence of her own.

"You grow more famous every year," Leah once said to him. "The critics all have a kind word for you, too. That means a great deal."

It was a mild afternoon, and the room where they sat was full of declining yet still vivid sunlight. Leah looked very lovely. She wore a dark bonnet that brought into richer relief her golden hair, above the pure, exquisitely refined face. Her hands, in their long gloves, were crossed upon her lap. To the artistic eye of Rainsford no lissom trait of her figure, in its sombre-hued, clinging draperies, had been lost. She leaned a little toward him as she spoke these last words, and he could not but feel how changed she was, while yet, in all graces of physical enticement, so winningly her former self.

"I often think it may mean very little," he said, "when all the critics have a kind word for you."

"No, no," objected Leah. "I believe that the best critics set the fashion for the inferior ones. The last are mere copyists, I should say. And when there is a war of opinion, it is because the best follow different models — that is, the few who know of what they write are insecure and disturbed in their judgments."

"But real greatness always disturbs the real critics," said Rainsford, smiling with interest. "At least in the beginning."

"Not always," responded Leah. "This age is

so keen-sighted and live a one that I think the fine critics are apt to agree about the fine painters, poets, musicians, or actors nearly as soon as the world sees their work. I question if Keats would be neglected to-day. I think Shakespeare would be idolized."

" I did not know you had such great faith in your century," said Rainsford.

" I have immense faith in it ! " exclaimed Leah. " Mamma will tell you that ! We have had some memorable talks together lately — memorable, I mean, for myself. I hold it to be the grandest age that history has yet recorded. Think of the problems solved, the educational progress made, the mighty push of science, the splendid achievements of art ! " . . . She paused for a moment and gave a faint sigh, not so faint that he failed distinctly to catch its sound. " Ah," she presently went on, looking straight at him with a melting sympathy in her brown eyes: " How happy are they who really *belong* to the age — who represent it by stable accomplishment and by sincere purpose ! "

" Do you speak with envy of such ? " he questioned, quite off his guard. " You ? "

The color slowly flushed Leah's face. " I, at least, have the right to *envy* them," she answered.

"But you used to think so differently," he began. And then her hand, lifted with a soft impatience, interrupted him.

"Pray do not refer to what I used to think, or
what I used to be!" she gently cried.

"I will not, if it displeases you," he said.

"It does not displease me — it pains and shames
me. I had no excuse for my contracted views of
things. You know what a mother was mine. I
was reared under the shadow of her wisdom and
strength, yet I gained nothing from either. I let
the merest superficialities deceive me. I shut my
ears to the large music of life; I deliberately listened only to the sounding brass and the tinkling
cymbals." . . . She sighed again, bowing her beautiful head.

Rainsford watched her in silence for several
seconds. Compassion deeply stirred him. Perhaps if he had not let a slight interval succeed
her last words his own would have been less firm
and secure of utterance.

"I think that I understand you very clearly,"
he said. "You misvalued the exterior meaning
of society. What is bright and felicitous in a certain part of it misled you, at a first view, into supposing that no hollowness lay below."

Leah lifted her eyes to his. They were full of

eager meaning. She raised both hands and waved them slightly while she spoke.

"I was charmed by external glitter — nothing more. I thought that perfect manners meant perfect morals. I have seen my wretched mistake. For this reason it is not strange that I have clung to certain people. The Marksley sisters, for example; with all their frivolity I find that they somehow ring true. And Mrs. Chichester . . . with all her belief in gentility and keeping up a perpetual heaped altar before it, I have seen in that woman a certain cleanly self-respect which leads me to feel as if she were of the stuff that what is best in antique aristocracies must have been made of. She is at least loyal to her own traditions; she is stagnant in her conservatisms, but the stagnancy has nothing foul about it. And then there is little Mrs. Forbes, too, with her pending divorce, which I am sure she will get — a woman whom great wrongs have not yet soured, and whose laugh is still as merry as her heart is good, while she stands up bravely against a husband who would have literally ground her under his heel. These people all love what I have latterly got to hate — the senseless whirl of fashionable pleasures. Yet there is a bond between us; in their different ways they assure me that the faith to which I was once so zealous a convert has not all its members cut after the same valueless pattern. They save me from too sweeping a disapproval; they prevent me from being an extremist in my condemnation."

Rainsford shook his head. " I fear your conversion is yet too partial," he replied. " Best if it were absolute. I think that as your outlook widens it will become so. These exclusionists, who base their assumptions of superiority on the shadow they call birth or the substance they call wealth, deserve an unqualified censure. They are the curse of our republic; in a manner they threaten its advancement and its prosperity. They are a taint in its rich young blood, and they mean a chronic malady whose development must work incalculable harm." His voice loudened as he continued to speak, and his demeanor changed its habitual repose for an indignant ardor. "Aristocracy has no right of existence within this land. The frauds and corruptions in our politics are not one-half so perilous as this other rapidly-increasing ill. Our dishonest state-craft has sprung, after all, from democracy itself; democracy, who is responsible for it, may one day cure it with her own medicines. But this aping of what had its rise long ago in the dark feudal ages of Europe — this subservience to a vicious and degrading vanity — this open and cruel sneer at the very laws by which our country must either shape her destiny or perish — ah! that is quite another matter! The great social inequalities of our uncompleted civilization are lamentable enough; but education is always waging her war against these, and it is not a millennial dream to trust that she may one day vastly modify if she does not wholly annul them. But when pretentious braggarts have succeeded in making new social inequalities, feeding the bigotry which applauds them upon their own hoarded capital, what shall prevent the national spirit itself from sinking to a level with this disastrous change? Our government will lapse into monarchism — that poisonous nourishment on which the patrician idea has in all times most malignantly thriven. There is not a very wide step between the monopolist of millions who drives a pompous drag up Fifth Avenue and the miscalled 'nobleman' who has received from his king the preposterous hereditary right of making a country's laws. To my own ears there is an ominous mutter of revolutionary bloodshed at this very hour in our land. I sometimes almost wish that such calamity might fall upon us quickly, if any vital good were to follow. Yet revolutions too often accomplish nothing save ruin. Meanwhile the luxuriously selfish class yearly grows larger. American society, as it is called, is no longer provincial; the day for declaring it so is past. People come to us from European courts and marvel at the scale of splendor on which our revelries are conducted. We are foreign and imitative only in our snobbery — and, perhaps I might add, our immorality."

There was no touch of cynicism about Rainsford's final sentence. He spoke it with lowered tones and an accent of unquestionable regret.

"If you hold these opinions," said Leah, after a slight silence, — "and I scarcely dissent from any of them — then you seem to me all the more enviable, because, while so near a movement in which you scorn to participate, you can absorb yourself with worthy and durable occupation." She looked very helpless for a moment, lifting her brows and letting her eyes wander transiently past Rainsford rather than meet his own. "I think of it so often," she murmured. "I mean the need of a purpose, a pursuit. I have no real talent. The women who paint pottery and disfigure mantels with abnormal sunflowers, don't spur me into any rivalry. I am just beginning to feel what a hard doom it is, this being forced to sit with idle hands in a century that is so busy, so creative, so energetic!"

"I think that no one is forced to sit with idle hands, unless ill health compels it."

She looked at him with a great directness. "Tell me what I can do," she said. "I think you can tell me quite as well as mamma could; and I hate to let mamma see that I am unhappy or even *distraite.*"

"Did it ever strike you," slowly answered Rainsford, "what an active woman your mother is? how she concerns herself with many silent, unostentatious charities? how she visits the sick, personally inquires into the needs of the poor, advising, consoling, encouraging both? I have watched your mother's life well for years past. It seems to me more finely correspondent to the best essential meaning of Christian precepts than any other which my experience has record of."

Leah mused for a little while, her eyes brightening in a meditative, convinced way.

"How strange!" she presently broke forth. "Mamma's goodness has become a commonplace to me. I have taken it for granted since my early girlhood, as though it were the charming hazel of her eyes or the unblemished whiteness of her hands. . . . If I could only join her in those modest and patient deeds of help! If I could get her to let me sit at her feet and learn how to

be of use in the world ! . . . Ah ! I talk as if it
were difficult!" Leah's voice faltered now, and
she passed a fleet hand over either eye, in that
way which has but one import. "I shall use
some of my old tyranny," she went on, giving
a little laugh replete with sadness. "I shall be
rebellious, as I so often was in the past. She
will accede then; she is so used to my defiant
moods." .

Leah's voice lingered over these ending words.
They were invested, for Rainsford, with a supreme
melancholy. Their wistful irony literally pierced
him by its pathos. What a transformation they
revealed, and what a piteous remorse !

Leah's conquest of her mother was an easy one.
It was, in truth, no conquest, but a surprised and
glad acquiescence on Mrs. Romilly's part. Still, a
strong tinge of sorrow colored her joy. Leah had
bought this new aspiration at a dear price. She
had gained the higher path and she was willing to
tread it; but had she not gained it with bleeding
feet and a weary heart ?

She showed a quiet enthusiasm regarding the
fresh motive that now filled her days. She accompanied her mother on various missions of relief,
and watched, often with tear-dimmed eyes, those
resolute, practical benignities which had long ago

become the outward though unheralded proof of a most sincere philanthropy.

" I never really knew till now, mamma, just how glorious a creature you are," she would say, kissing her. " I suppose it's on the same principle as when people have lived for years within a few miles of Niagara and never been there. . . . Well, I've made my visit at last," she would add, with a touch of her former gayety; " I've been across to the Canada side and gone under the Falls. It's all a great deal more wonderful than I expected; it is certainly an amazing natural curiosity."

Leah now had her daily routine of benevolence. She constantly witnessed the most painful sights. She grew familiar with the worst rigors of poverty; she saw the awful results of that one regnant vice, drink — how its fangs are buried in the heart of so many homes, and its coils tightened round so many struggling lives; she watched the malign despotism of inherited disease, wreaking its harms upon the new-born infant, sending the youth and maiden to untimely graves; she noted the sluggish lethargy with which ignorance enthralls countless minds, and the stubborn downward push that it gives its victims into deeds for which the law takes fearful toll. She realized the immense anguish of humanity, and how feeble a

minority of it has crept from night into light.
Perhaps the sturdy philosophy of her mother alone
guarded her now against the dangers of a bitter
pessimism; perhaps it kept her from that rash indignation which judges all evil with no relenting
palliative — from the futile reasoning which de-
clares sin a fixed necessity — from the cold intel-
lectualism which cramps all morality within utilita-
rian fetters — or from the too mawkish compassion
which deplores crime with over-facile tears.   Leah
soon felt her mother's truly sublime tolerance in-
fused into soul and intellect.   She found herself
forgetting to rail at the ill in fighting for the
good.   Meanwhile she met a few other women,
full of heroism and sacrifice, who had long loved
her mother and served under her lofty leadership.
Two or three of these Leah had met in past times.
She remembered, now, that she had once thought
them dowdy and dull — and a pang of conscience
always went with such recollections.   It was true,
she told herself, with her old turn for satire showing even in her present repentance, that very few
of these courageous workers had taken the leisure
to see Newport in the season, and that none of
them would look presentable at one of Mrs. Chichester's glittering dinner-parties; but they had
their trivial duties to perform, nevertheless, even

though these were not chronicled among the society-notes in the morning journals.

Leah's new friends were of various religious creeds. But it was silently understood among the little body of which she had been made a member that all diversities of belief were welded into one common and satisfying faith — the beneficence of steadfast humanitarian diligence. Here they all assembled, so to speak, as in a temple, of which Mrs. Romilly herself was the calm and pure high-priestess.

"I see that we are asked to three dinners next week," said Tremaine to his wife one morning at breakfast. "Do you mean to accept all the dinners this season ? "

"No," she answered; "I have quite given up all that."

He stared at her in his mild way for a moment. "Do you expect me to go without you ? " he said.

"If you choose — certainly."

A note of impatience stirred his reply.

"It is not good form. I suppose you know that. I wish to' accept at all three places. I like the houses, and the people whom one meets there. Am I to be kept at home because it is your whim to keep me ? "

"It is not my whim to keep you at home," she answered. "But it is my sincere desire to keep myself at home."

He gave a nervous, annoyed gesture, and began to stir his coffee somewhat briskly. His old, graceful languor had in a great measure left him of late; he was thinner, and at times actually haggard. Leah was not at a loss to account for this change. When they met at breakfast (which was not often) his hand would sometimes be tremulous and his eyes bloodshot. She rarely saw him after dinner, and frequently he would dine away from home. She had a certainty that he seldom returned at night before a very late hour. She never inquired of him concerning his goings and comings.

This morning, however, he looked better than usual — that is, than on the occasions when they breakfasted together. She plainly saw that she had irritated him, and knew that he would presently make this evident.

She was not mistaken here. He fixed his eyes upon her face very soon after she had spoken, and addressed her in these words:

"I think you must see the absurdity of our pulling against each other in this fashion. I can't dine out unless I do so with *you*, and because you have taken to prowling among the highways and hedges, and permitting yourself to be fooled by lazy paupers, who no doubt chuckle over your credulous inexperience, I don't see that this is any reason why I should be kept from the natural and proper enjoyment consequent upon the position to which I was born."

This was the first suggestion he had ever given her that he had cognizance of her altered aims. She had hardly doubted that he must have seen them, and yet he had never spoken regarding them. Her mind worked fleetly as she reflected, without a pulse of effrontery, upon his recent speech. While he waited her answer he expected argument if not dissent; but neither came. Leah simply said: "I do not see that I am privileged to disagree with you. I will accept the invitations in both our names." . . .

"You think I did right, mamma?", she afterward said to her mother.

"Unquestionably, my dear. He is your husband. His demand is not unjust. I wish that he had always done nothing more blamable than to make it."

Leah gave a great sigh. "These assemblages are simply odious to me now," she said. "It is not that I have ceased to like the glow and grace of them. But all the people think and talk such trivialities! They live so utterly out of their time! It makes me think of the palace of the Sleeping Beauty, with the inmates wakened after a hundred years of slumber. The world has gone rolling on, and they have known nothing about it." . . . She dropped her voice almost to a whisper, and spoke as though some harsh disaster were threatening her. "I see my proper course, perfectly, mamma. I have married that man, I dwell under the same roof with him. I must yield my preferences to his so long as mine are unconventional, militant against those ideas and forms to which I knew him wedded when I became his wife. I put on the yoke as if it were a necklace of jewels, and I must wear it, though it prove a collar of iron!"

"Leah, I hate to hear you speak like this!"

"But you assent to my theory. While he preserves the decencies I must live with him. And while I live with him I must shield from outward notice and comment the hollow falsity that our marriage has grown. You will agree with me there." Leah paused for a brief space. "Lawrence Rainsford would agree with me, too."

Mrs. Romilly gave a visible start. "Why do you mention Rainsford?" she quickly asked.

A moment after the question was spoken she regretted it.

"Why?" murmured Leah. She laughed in an abrupt, tired way. "I — I don't know," she answered, avoiding her mother's look. She seemed to scan the carpet while she went on: "I suppose it is because he is so sure a judge between right and wrong — and so richly endowed with the noblest qualities of manhood as well."

"If you had only thought that not so very long ago!" passed through Mrs. Romilly's mind. But she was far enough from openly expressing the wish — one that had to do with a profound and unassuaged regret.

Leah went again into gay circles. It occurred to her that she was very little of a success, in popular phrase. She tried not to be bored, yet she was secretly by no means bored. She had still enough youth left to feel the buoyancy of aimless merriment and festivity. Her laugh was blither than she knew. It was possibly her exquisite beauty that still made her a favorite, though people declared her to be changed, and deplored the change as a consequence of her husband's reputed misdoings. Her mental brilliancy and native wit remained the same. She pleased in spite of herself. The Marksleys, and perhaps Mrs. Forbes as well, had circulated the story of her novel departure from received formulas of allegiance. But she never aired her late opinions. This second advent was enforced; she would not have made it but for her husband's desire. And yet she made it with a commendable good sense. Tremaine was covertly pleased; he saw her shine, and in a manner reign. It tickled his egotism to find her still admired and courted.

But her devotion to the new career continued absolute. She attended few large entertainments excepting afternoon receptions, and never permitted these or any similar festivity to interfere with the fulfilment of her gracious offices. It is possible that her condemnation of all worldliness now seemed to her unduly sweeping; her converted state had lacked the needful equilibrium, and had presently righted itself; she had swung from one extreme to another, and recognized this fact; society did not strike her as quite so hollow, after all, as she had pronounced it, nor quite so black as she had painted it. She now accepted it as a requirement, where before she had sought it as a delicious diversion. By a good deal that occurred there she was emphatically amused. Lawrence Rainsford's denunciations would occasionally haunt her memory, not seldom with doubts as to its full justice, and yet often with complete endorsement of its asperity.

Autumn had meanwhile lapsed into winter. Tremaine still hid his excesses from his wife, though she continually perceived their results. He managed never to appear before her in wine; she would have resented such an indignity by a prompt withdrawal from the room if he had ever inflicted it; she had prepared herself just how to act in the event of its occurrence.

She had formed no intimacy with any of his relations, though visits of ceremony were punctiliously exchanged between herself and not a few of his kinswomen. She did not at all object to this turn of affairs. It would have stung her pride if these aunts and cousins had all failed to pay her the simple courtesy of admitting the place that she held and the name that she bore. As for Tremaine's mother, that lady had thus far shrouded herself in a silence and seclusion which Leah felt convinced would indefinitely continue. It was widely known that she and her mother-in-law were " not on terms." But neither her husband nor any of his clan had made the least reference to this estrangement since her marriage. Indeed, it could hardly be called by that name; Leah had never seen the elder Mrs. Tremaine, and had no desire to see her. Not that Elizabeth Romilly's daughter cherished any anger. This had long ago become

indifference; she had fallen, at last, into the habit
of regarding Mrs. Tremaine's behavior rather with
pity than resentment. And she had taken it for
granted that her husband's condemnation of the
words then used, and the attitude then assumed,
remained quite unaltered.

But one day her eyes were opened to a wholly
different perception of this latter point. She discovered that Tremaine was in sympathy with his
mother's extraordinary conduct. The discovery
was a sharp blow.

He entered her room at about four o'clock, one
afternoon. She had passed the morning in a hospital with her mother, and had soothed the last
hours of a woman dying with great physical
agony, and half-crazed by the conviction that she
would soon pass among eternal torments. Leah's
nerves had been severely shaken, but a slight
sleep had relieved her distress; she rose from a
lounge as Tremaine's knock sounded at her door,
and afterward received him with excellent composure. He had ostensibly sought her for the
purpose of discussing an over-charge made with
respect to certain household repairs during the
previous summer; but he soon deserted this
topic, and almost before Leah knew it, he had
said:

"By the way, did it ever strike you that my mother and you ought to be friends?"

"Of course it would have been better," she answered, somewhat confusedly.

"Better? It would have been the proper thing." He gave a slight shrug of the shoulders, a moment afterward, and turned away from the window through which he had been gazing down into the adjacent street. "However," he went on, with a blunt brevity that of late had got saliently into his manner, "I'm afraid you don't care about the proper thing any more."

Leah ignored this thrust; she felt that she could afford to do so; it was such a mere pin-prick. She was silent for a little while, and then she said, measuring each word: "Why have you spoken of your mother?"

"Why?" he repeated, starting irritably. "Because, as you very well know, family quarrels are in shocking taste."

"There has been no quarrel."

He laughed harshly. "I don't know what you call it."

"Then I can tell you very easily," Leah replied. "I call it a one-sided attack, in which blows were given but not returned. They were warded off, if you please, in self-defence, but nothing more. . . . I

am not prepared to hear that you approve your
mother's course. I shall be terribly sorry, however, to learn that you do."

He stood watching her for a moment, with his
changed eyes, that had got a reddened, fatigued
look about the lids and a curve of darkness below,
toward either cheek. " Oh, pshaw ! " he suddenly
said, in a kind of mutter, and with another movement of the shoulders while walking to the door ;
" there 's no use of hoping for common-sense from
you nowadays. I give you up in despair."

Leah wondered, now and then during the next
fortnight, what motive might have lain behind
those allusions to her mother-in-law. But at
length she had ample cause for understanding.
Her luncheon-hour was usually one o'clock; when
at home, she would descend by this time into the
dining-room, and eat a cold morsel and drink a
cup of tea. Her husband was never present
at this meal. But one day she was almost
startled to find him standing before the fire-place
in the dining-room, as she entered that apartment.

"Do you want luncheon ? " she said, with an
amazed little laugh, and a glance at the rather
meagre repast spread upon the table. " If so, I
will order something hot to be cooked. I would

have had it prepared beforehand if I had known you would be at home."

"Thanks; I had a bite at the club," Tremaine answered. His face was averted from Leah's; he appeared to be looking straight at the ruddy turmoil of the brisk wood-fire.

"I came at this hour for a special reason," he went on, breaking an interval of silence. "It relates to my mother."

"Your mother?" Leah repeated, in quick interrogation.

"Yes. She is coming to see you." As Tremaine spoke he slowly turned and faced his wife. "She thinks it best."

"Oh, very well," said Leah, in dubious undertone.

"She was to be here a little after one." He took out his watch and glanced at it. "She is due now. And I may as well tell you, Leah, that mother considers she is making a decided concession by coming."

"A concession?"

"Yes. I dare say she will be a little stiff, too. She thinks, you know, that the first advances should have come from you."

"From *me*, Tracy?" said Leah, who had turned pale, and who now rose from her chair.

He slightly frowned, and his tones were peevishly raised, as he answered: "There is no use of echoing every word I say, like that! Yes, from *you!*"

"From *me?*" persisted Leah, touching her bosom with one hand. "From the daughter of the lady whom she insulted?"

Just then a bell-peal sounded in the outer hall. "There she is, now!" exclaimed Tremaine. "I do hope you intend to behave properly."

Leah looked with fixity into her husband's face. "I shall make no concessions," she said. "I am prepared to receive them."

"Bah! what an absurdity! Mother is a woman of sixty. Besides, she is—though you may not grant it—a person of marked importance." (It is not easy to describe the peculiar accent with which he gave this last sentence; they who best knew the Tremaines knew the intonation well when they heard it, and they never heard it except when a Tremaine referred to himself or others of his blood, in the sense of caste and distinction.) "You certainly don't suppose that she is coming to you with anything so nonsensical as an apology."

"I do," said Leah, with great firmness. "I shall receive her on no other terms."

He bit his lips; his eyes had begun to glitter.

"Remember that you are in your own house. On that account, if no other, preserve some respect for yourself."

"I wish always to preserve a great deal of respect for my mother," she answered.

"Your mother and you are two different people."

"In a matter of this sort we are one."

"Her quarrels belong to herself."

"They belong to me as well — whenever she has been wronged."

At this moment the draperies overhanging a doorway which communicated with the near drawing-room were parted, and a servant appeared, bearing Mrs. Tremaine's card. Tremaine himself took it, at once dismissing the servant.

"She is here," he said, speaking with low speed to Leah. "Do I understand rightly that you refuse to see her?"

"Oh, by no means." Leah advanced toward another curtained doorway as she spoke. "Her offence was a serious one, but I shall not consider it beyond pardon."

He went close up to her side. "Pardon!" he sneered. "If you have any such idiotic expectation, you will be finely disappointed!"

"Did your mother send her card to me or to you?" she quietly asked.

"To you — of course."

"Then, of course, I will see her."

He scanned her pale face with a morose acuteness. "A moment ago you said that you would not receive her."

Leah gravely nodded. "I did. But to see and to receive are not, in this case, the same."

"I fail to discover any difference between them."

"You shall be afforded the opportunity, perhaps, if you choose to witness our meeting."

He drew a deep breath. "Don't make me curse the hour that I ever married you!" he muttered, in his throat.

"Shall you enter with me?" asked Leah.

He did not reply. He was observing her with a look of suppressed exasperation. She brushed aside one of the curtains, and passed into the drawing-room.

Mrs. Tremaine rose from a chair as Leah approached. The latter, even if she had received no premonition of who it was, would almost have recognized the high, arched nose, the narrow brow, the white back-rolled hair and the dim, cold eyes, from her mother's past description, added to the fact of a certain resemblance which the lady bore to her finer-featured son.

Leah advanced toward Mrs. Tremaine with a gliding step and an entirely self-possessed mien. She reached a chair not far from that which her visitor had just vacated, paused beside it, and rested both hands upon its back. She had no desire not to be abrupt, but she wished not to be unmannerly. She at once spoke, in a voice so modulated that it seemed sweet as well.

" I am your son's wife," she said.

Mrs. Tremaine gave a little fluttered sigh.

" I know you by sight, my dear," she replied. " I saw you at Newport . . . but you did not see me . . . I was in my own apartment, nearly always, when you passed with Tracy — or else I saw you from my carriage-window — I am such an invalid — I am constantly forced to hide myself from the air — from the open sunshine, you know. But I remember you — I should have known you immediately if we had met elsewhere."

She was silent for a little while; her thin lips trembled, once or twice, as if from indecision what to say next. Suddenly she put forth both her black-gloved hands, which looked as if their encasing kid had never left them since they had waved themselves before her agitated face during her strange talk with Mrs. Romilly more than two years ago, and took several rapid steps toward Leah.

" I hope you will think no more of the past, my dear!" she said. "*I* don't want to think of it. I — I want to be friends with my daughter-in-law!"

Leah gazed for a second at the extended hands, but she did not extend her own. Her countenance was not stern, yet it was exceedingly serious.

" Your daughter-in-law wishes also to be friends with you," she said. " If you place it within her power to be friends with you, Mrs. Tremaine, she will thank you very much."

The reply was at first a look of wonderment; there was not a trace of *hauteur* in it, as the lady put her hands still farther forward.

" I do place it within your power, my dear child," she exclaimed, as though eager to correct some misapprehension.

Leah receded, then, shaking her head. " Pardon me," she objected. " You have not done so yet."

Mrs. Tremaine's hands dropped at her sides. " Why, what do mean?" she asked, in her light, cool, thin voice.

"Merely this," said Leah, with a sadness and tenderness commingled. "At Newport, a little while after my engagement to your son was made public, you addressed language to my dear mother which I must believe, unless you tell me otherwise, that you now regret. They were cruel words, Mrs. Tremaine, and quite unprovoked. But they will be overlooked and forgotten if you are willing to meet my mother and declare to her that you do regret them. I think that I speak from a full knowledge of her large and generous nature when I tell you she will require no elaborate or formal apology, but merely a simple expression of the sorrow it has cost you for having dealt a deep sorrow to her."

Leah had scarcely ended her final sentence before she saw something of the result which was to follow this appeal. Mrs. Tremaine stared at her with back-thrown head now, and a kind of electrified rigidity about the slim, dark-clad figure. The very intensity of her scorn carried with it a majesty. Supreme prejudices, however repellent to contemplate, are always supreme facts. Mighty bigotry may shock us by its perversity, but we cannot effectually deny its might. That remains in bulky, granitic assertion.

Between the brains, the motives, the creeds, the

temperaments of these two women, as they now regarded each other, there lay a distance that might almost be called interplanetary. Or, at least, their meeting was like the dead past brought face to face with the living present. A whole history of human progression stretched between their opposing minds. On both sides the antagonism was sincere enough. The stanchness of their mutual contempt made it doubly important. One clung to her belief in the positive sanctity of birth and name quite as tenaciously as the other clung to a belief in the emptiness of both. It is possible that they recognized one another as natural foes during the brief but pregnant pause that now ensued. In the clear brown eyes of one seemed to burn the strong, active vitality of to-day; in the faded and frosty gaze of the other lay the ember-like dimness of a thousand yesterdays.

"You think that I will degrade myself by apologizing to *her?*" at length sounded Mrs. Tremaine's gasping whisper. "You *dare* to think so?"

Leah's wrath had leaped up into her face. And she meant to give that wrath full freedom, now. She felt that she had no longer the least cause for restraint — no, nor the least excuse for it. It flashed through her that here was one of the rare cases when to be angry is to be right. She was defending what she loved. This woman had tempted punishment. She should be taught a lesson. Yes, one that till her dying hour she should never forget.

XIII

PERHAPS Leah remained silent five or six good seconds. During this interval she was slowly measuring the form of her companion. She began at the dark rim of Mrs. Tremaine's dress, and let her eyes lift themselves with a deliberate scrutiny up along the fragile stature till they met the narrow visage. Then she spoke.

"I shall not answer either of your questions, madam. Their impertinence is too pitiable. But perhaps you would care to know, since you have presumed to suggest that you are my mother's superior, how far below her I rank you. She is the sort of woman who leaves the world better for having lived in it; you are the sort of woman who tries to leave it worse. She has a great intellect and a great heart; you have a little intellect, and no heart at all. She loves her kind, and has dedicated her life to help the sick, the maimed, the poor, the unfortunate; you despise your kind, and never give an hour of thought to them, against the distinct command of that Christ whom you

have the insolence to worship every Sunday of
your selfish, unprofitable life. When my mother
dies there will be hundreds who will weep for
her; when you die you will be taken to your
grave without a tear. Who are you, pray, that
you should disparage such a grand and stainless
life as hers? An aristocrat? Why, even that
flimsy claim will not serve you. You come of a
respectable family — nothing more. You have no
long descent, no line of ancestry, no illustrious
name. In Europe your absurd pretension would
be laughed at, as you well know. . . . Come, then,
what is your self-valuation based upon? Is it
education? Why, my dear madam, you cannot
even spell your own language. A note of yours
once fell into my hands. It was carelessly given
me by your son, to whom you had written concerning a certain scandal at Newport, where you
remained later in the autumn than usual — I think
because of his abominated wedding. The brief
paragraph which I read barely missed being illiter-
ate. But my mother can not only spell English
correctly; four other languages are as familiar to
her as her own. Few of the world's immortal
writers and thinkers have escaped her knowledge;
she is as intimate with them as you are doubtless
ignorant of them. . . . Whence, then, comes your

audacious reason, not only to scorn a being so immeasurably above you, but to mingle that scorn with personal abuse? What last excuse remains to you?—or indeed, what last miserable makeshift of excuse? Do you excel her in her manners? Why, there is hardly an unlettered pauper among all those whom her lovely charities daily befriend, who would not shame to attack a fellow-creature with the coarsely arrogant sentiments which you then delivered. That my mother should even be willing to accept an apology from you is but evidence of her surprising generosity. That you, after so atrocious a transgression, should defend your behavior, merely stamps you as incapable to appreciate a spirit that you are miserably far from resembling!"

All rebukes, however just, may be spoiled in their effect from an overplus of passion. But Leah, angry as she was, kept the flame of her ire from out-soaring the bounds of dignity. Her impetuosity was leavened by moderation; her sentences came fleet and warm, yet each one was tellingly trenchant. She hinted, in voice, in mien, in expression, of a reproachful power yet held in reserve.

Once or twice, during her speech, Mrs. Tremaine visibly shivered; once or twice she lifted her hands imprecatingly; once or twice she uttered a low, horrified moan. But at length, as Leah ended, she cried out with querulous sharpness:

"Why did I ever enter this house? I might have known what to expect!"

"Surely you *did* know," sped Leah. "Then why *did* you come?" .

Mrs. Tremaine strove to moisten her thin, blanched lips. She was very agitated; she even appeared like a person in straits for breath.

"You are as brazen as your mother!" she exclaimed with husky difficulty. "No, you are even worse than she is!"

"Ah! you don't know what a compliment you are paying me!" said Leah, with freezing satire.

"I — I shall never forget this hour!"

"It was my intention to fix it in your memory."

"I — I don't know how to deal with such people as you are! I — I have been educated to — to always avoid you!"

"Pardon me. You have not been educated at all. I made that very clear a moment ago."

"You — you should at least have the decency to remember that I am the mother of your husband."

"That is just the point. You have had the indecency to ignore it."

" Of course you excel me in — in *brains !* But that is all — *all !* "

" By no means.   You forget breeding."

Mrs. Tremaine clenched her gloved hands together, at this point, looking the picture of impotent distress.   Her suffering was quite real — even more real than it had been during her encounter with Mrs. Romilly.   She esteemed herself the victim of a most frightful outrage.

" Breeding ! " she repeated, with the disdain of a weak thing that will sting till its weakness has been wholly crushed.   And then she gave a little dry, sour, feeble laugh.   " As if an adventuress like you could teach me that ! "

" No one could teach it to you," said Leah, feeling an actual pang of compassion as she watched the frail, perturbed shape from which this last malicious protest had burst.   " You are beyond all power of learning it ! "

She turned, and was about to leave the drawing-room.   Contempt had prevailed against wrath.   A weary unconcern possessed her.   It passed through her mind — " How much wiser mamma was to disdain it all !   I was mistaken ; to be angry is always to be wrong."

Suddenly Leah's eyes fell upon her husband.   He was advancing from the farther room.   Some-

thing in his white, twitched face made her instantly
indignant again. Then, as he plainly scowled at
her while passing her, she felt her mood regain all
its former fire.

He went straight to his mother, and put one arm
about the lady's waist. Mrs. Tremaine had seen
him some seconds ago. She now clung to him, and
wailed with hysterical violence :

" Oh, Tracy — my son — I have been so terribly
treated — did you hear it ? — this is what has resulted from my coming here — take me at once to
my carriage, Tracy — I shall be ill for weeks after
this."

" Remain, if you choose, mother," he said.

" I forbid her remaining," said Leah.

" You hear ! " cried Mrs. Tremaine putting one
arm within her son's, and speaking with the tri-
umphantly childish accent that conscious defeat
will employ when it has abruptly found an ally.
" *She* forbids me to remain ! I — I don't wish to
remain. I — I was very wrong to come. But
still, my son, you hear ! *She* forbids me ! "

Tremaine looked at his wife. He spoke to her
as we address a rebellious servant.

" I believe I am master in my own house," he
said.

" Certainly," Leah answered. " And I am also
mistress here."

" Come, Tracy — come," said his mother, pulling at the arm she had grasped. " I — I have made a fearful error. I — I am justly punished."

" That is perfectly true," said Leah, as mother and son gained the threshold of the doorway which gave upon the outer hall.

Tremaine now turned and once more looked at his wife.

" You have behaved like a tigress," he said in an undertone.

" Then I have only played the part," she answered, " which my sweet and noble mother was once too human to play. Even a tigress will always defend her young. . . ."

She felt wretchedly tired and sickened after they had gone. Repeatedly she asked herself what view her mother would take of her conduct, and at last she firmly concluded to tell her mother nothing of the whole deplored occurrence. She thought with portentous concern of her husband's future action. For several hours she paced the floor of her chamber, and strove to set a line of conduct which should be followed with skill and tact. But incessantly there rose before her mind the probability of his unqualified blame. How could she endure that? Would she merit either his open arraignment or his covert innuendo? When they met at dinner how should she treat him? It was like surveying the region of a masked battery, and wondering from what special quarter the first dogged bullet would dart.

But Tremaine did not appear at dinner. Leah ate the meal alone, or rather almost failed to eat it. She retired at a comparatively early hour, but could not sleep. Her memory naturally drifted toward that hateful event which had succeeded their last quarrel at Newport. She knew that any plea, however paltry, would serve him now for drinking immoderately. A hundred recent signs in him told her that his vice had strengthened.

"If the least vestige of love remained," she mused, "it would all be so different! I could pardon so much! As it is, I have to reflect just what it will be proper to pardon, and just what will mark the boundary line of all possible indulgence."

Waiting in her bed for some sound below that would apprise her of his return, Leah questioned her own thoughts respecting her reason for keeping this whole late affair from her mother. Was it not as much because of Lawrence Rainsford as it was through regard for the loved one's mental peace? True, Rainsford knew of her dreary matrimonial mistake. But why let him know these

final bitter facts? In some unguarded moment
her mother might tell him all; they were such con-
fidential friends. No; it was enough that Rainsford should understand the complete failure of her
marriage. Let pride guard from him any further
humiliating details.

But Tremaine did not return that night. When
Leah saw her mother on the succeeding day, he
had not returned. Still, she kept entirely silent
regarding all that had passed. Another night
went by, and yet he gave no sign. But on the
following morning a written order to pack certain
articles of apparel and leave them at a well-known
hotel, was brought her by the man-servant who had
received it.

" This was sent to you, Thomas ? " she said, in
cool, matter-of-fact tones, after she had read the
message.

" Yes, Mrs. Tremaine," was the man's reply.

Leah raised her brows, and looked with chill
composure at the speaker.

" Well? Why do you bring it to *me ?* If Mr.
Tremaine gives this order you have nothing to do
but carry it out."

At the same time she was secretly relieved to
learn the intended course of her husband. He
chose not to return home. He had decided on a

plan of temporary absence from the household. He had taken up his abode at a hotel. But this precipitate change could not continue long. They must soon meet, if for nothing else than the arrangement of a permanent separation.

Still, Leah said nothing to her mother. When two more days had elapsed she began to feel not only the biting discomfort of suspense, but the mortification of confronting her servants, and of fancying that she read either sympathy or curiosity in every new shade of expression that crossed their disciplined countenances.

On the afternoon of the third day she determined to seek her mother and declare just how matters stood. With this intent she left the house at about three o'clock. The walk was not a long one; there had been a snowfall on the previous day, and as Leah passed along Madison Avenue, breathing the brisk wintry air, an occasional merry, jingling sleigh sped by her. The pavements had little flecks of snow upon them; the sky, seen only in those niggard strips which the close-built city affords, was of a lucent yet milky azure. But Leah's mood was not in accord with the bracing weather. The blithe sleigh-bells found no echo in her dulled spirits. She was thinking, as she moved onward, of the public exposure that

might be waiting her, with all its consequent hurts
and torments.   Yet she would play no part of hostile assertiveness.   If the worst came — if her husband were unwilling to live with her longer, she
would accept his decision, but never goad him into
any rash clinching of it.   As far as she knew, or
had the right to doubt, he had preserved a certain
promise.   That promise once broken, she would
be justified in annulling their marriage-relations.
But until then she would be willing, even glad, to
remain his wife before the eyes of the world.

Strangely enough, fate itself seemed to answer,
a few moments afterward, these latter reflections.
She had gained a certain corner at which was situ-
ated a very handsome and imposing mansion of
red brick, with fanciful and unique stone copings,
and a wide vestibule, where you saw doors of
brilliant stained glass in Gothic design above an
interspace of quaintly tessellated flooring.   Leah
had often noticed this dwelling before; she knew
that it was the residence of Mrs. Fortescue; it
seemed to her a model of all reposeful elegance
and dignity in metropolitan architecture; there
had been a time, and not very long ago, when she
had envied the easy fortunes of its proprietress.
Now, perhaps, she would not have given this per-
sonage a thought if it had not been that a glossy

coupé, drawn by two alert and stylish bays, dashed up to the curb only a few yards in front of her, and then suddenly halted. The next moment a gentleman alighted from the carriage; he at once assisted a lady to alight. Leah was meanwhile advancing toward them both. A great tingling thrill of consternation and shame swept through her as she recognized her husband and Mrs. Fortescue.

XIV.

LEAH briefly hesitated as the truth rushed upon her; she was only a few yards away from the pair; the recognition on either side was no less complete than abrupt; they both palpably started as they perceived who she was. While passing onward, with steps that she tried to make as firm and even as before, she wondered if they had observed the hot, red blood dye her cheeks. "He has broken his promise," she was telling herself, a little later, while her heart beat wildly, and her face burned like fire in the chill afternoon air. "It was the one contemptible thing left him to do, and he has done it. Now my action is plain to me."

She did not go to her mother's house. By a different course she retraced her steps homeward. Soon after the return she wrote and dispatched a note to her mother, mentioning Mrs. Tremaine's visit of three days ago, yet not giving any of its details, and ending with an account of what she had so recently witnessed. "I shall be busy for at least two hours," the note then ran, "in making preparations for a permanent departure. I will never sleep under the same roof with him again. Will you not come for me a little before dusk, if you receive this in time? I will wait for you till after dark; then, if you are not here, I will go to you. I am terribly in earnest now, as I know you will understand. . . ."

Dusk came, but it did not bring Mrs. Romilly. When dinner was announced, Leah descended from her own apartment into the dining-room. She even seated herself at the table, while feeling that she had neither wish nor will to eat a morsel. But she had both wish and will to preserve appearances; her retreat should be a dignified one. Tremaine's empty place opposite her own addressed her through its vacuum, as if with a positive presence. A very short while after she had seated herself, she heard a peal sound at the outer hall-door.

She supposed that it might, most probably, mean the arrival of her mother, and after hearing the door opened she rose, about to enter the hall. But just then a quick, approaching step, which she more than half recognized, made her pause. Almost immediately afterward her husband entered the room.

"Go," he said to the servant, who stood near by. "Don't come back till you are called."

The servant obeyed this peremptory dismissal. If it had not been given, Leah might still have remained ignorant regarding the condition of him who gave it. But there was no mistaking that thick, reckless utterance; and as she looked more closely into her husband's face, she saw that its unusual pallor was mingled with an unusual harshness — even savagery of expression. He had kept his eyes fixedly upon her since his entrance, except during the moment of pronouncing his recent command. A timid woman might have felt fear; but Leah felt none. She returned his gaze without a tremor until he spoke.

"Well, I'm back again."

The roughness of his tones had a dogged bravado. They were as unlike his wonted suavity as it was possible to imagine. The change in him had scarcely been more radical on that hated bacchanal night; then he had been incapable; now, however, he looked very capable — and in a strongly sinister sense.

"I'm back again," he repeated, with a high, brief laugh. "Well, what have you to say to me?"

"Nothing," she replied.

His step was heavy and a little unsteady as he

walked toward an easy-chair and dropped into it. The heat of the room had begun to tell upon him already; the air outside had sharpened still more with the winter nightfall.

"Oh, come," he said, moving his head from right to left against the tufted back of the chair. "I know very well you've got a lot of talk prepared for me. I'd like to get it over as soon as possible."

Leah walked quietly to one of the doors. She had seen quite plainly by that last sentence that his mind was so clouded with drink as to leave scarcely a trace of his ordinary personality.

"I told you that I had nothing to say," she responded, and with a direct, bold frankness. She knew that any assumption of dignity, of reproach, or of regret would all equally be lost upon his blunted perceptions.

She was on the verge of quitting the room when he rose with precipitation. "Stop!" he exclaimed, "You saw me this afternoon. What do you mean to do? I know you're not going to pass it over."

"Then you know what I am going to do."

"I do *not* know!" he contradicted, with a frown. "Tell me."

"I told you before."

"Before? When?"

"A little time previous to your giving me a certain promise — a promise which you have since broken."

He smiled. The smile was not precisely a leer, and yet it resembled one. "Oh, yes, I recollect; you said you would 't live with me any longer."

"I said so. I meant it. And I mean it still."

His dulled eyes each caught a sudden sparkle. If he had been his sober self he might have tried satire, but he would have seen the absurdity of anger. As it was, the mere animal rage that drink so often rouses for slight cause now broke leash, for what seemed to him a potent, impelling grievance.

"You mean it, do you?" he muttered, his voice sombre with threat. "Go, then, if you please! Do you think I care whether you go or stay? Do you think I want to live with a woman who refuses to know my own mother? And who are you, that you *should* refuse? When I married you, I made you somebody — I took you out of the common ranks — I gave you my name. Yes, my name! You don't think that was anything! Oh, no; of course you don't. What business have *you* with pride? You *might* have some pride that I made you a Tremaine; but you've no cause for any other."

Leah looked full at him now. She was white as death, and she had curled her lip.

"You are right," said she. "I have no cause for pride now. I had once, when I thought that I was married to a gentleman."

He literally sprang toward her, then. If she had not been greatly angered, she might have felt a timid throe; she might have drawn away from him. As it was, she held her ground; she did not withdraw an inch, but met his near eyes, bloodshot and kindled, with her own clear and calm ones.

"How dare you say that I am not a gentleman?" he again muttered. His look swept her figure from head to foot. "Ah! mother was right. A man should never marry beneath him. *I* married that way; I see it very plainly at last!"

"It took you some time to make the discovery," flashed Leah, forgetting how foolish she was to bandy either word or wit with one whom drink had pushed into insensate passion. "You did not make it until you had disgraced yourself in two ways — by drunkenness and by falsehood!"

He caught one of her arms, just above the wrist. His clasp was so tense that it pained her.

He peered so closely into her face that she smelt the wine-taint in his breath.

"Let me go," she said, trying to recede. ·

His hand tightened instead of relaxing. "I will take no more insolence from you!" shot his next words. "You've called me nearly everything that's bad. I'll show you that I can still be worse."

"You cannot frighten me," said Leah, without a quiver in her voice. Her straight glance did not quail, either. "What that is worse *can* you show me, except that you are a miserable coward?"

He dropped her arm. As he did so she turned to fly from him. They were both quite near one of the draped doors. At this moment he struck her. The blow was given with his clenched hand. It fell upon her head just above one temple. She reeled for a moment; then, as she was sinking to the floor, dazed and stunned, she felt that she was in some one's arms, and that these arms had kept her still erect, though she drooped feebly against a supporting form. Was it her mother's voice that she now heard? It seemed so far off . . . it seemed like a voice in a dream. . . .

"If you strike again, strike *me!*"

What other voice did she now hear? Was it

her husband's? . . . But it was so different — so changed. . . .

"Mrs. Romilly — I was mad — I despise myself — Oh, my God! — I did not mean to do it — I . . ."

Leah heard no more, after that. The blank that followed seemed a very long one when she awoke from it. She found herself in a dim apartment, whose details gradually resolved themselves into those of her own drawing-room. . . . Her mother was bending over her. . . . Then it all suddenly became clear.

"Mamma," she murmured, "I — I am to be with you to-night?"

"Yes, Leah ; yes, my darling."

"This — this is *my* house, is n't it, mamma?"

"Yes, Leah."

"Can't we go? . . . Can't we go together?"

"Yes, my child. The carriage that I came in is outside. I was at the hospital till quite late; I ordered a carriage and came to you as soon as I got your note. I reached here — "

"Yes, I know. . . . It was you who caught me when he . . . "

"Yes, Leah, it was I."

"Where is he now?"

"He is upstairs. I told him you were better, and

he went away. You *have* been better, Leah, though you did not know it. You have been talking foolishly, but that was nothing. I knew it was merely hysteria. . . . I have seen so much sickness, of so many kinds, that I have grown quite a doctor, my child. . . . He is worse than you — far worse ; he is half crazed by what he did."

" But I — I am not to stay here, mamma. You don't mean that ? "

" No, no, my darling. You are to go home with me — to *my* home. The carriage is waiting. . . . There — see — you are able to stand very nicely. . . . And you can walk well, too. It will only be a step. Here, let me put on your bonnet ; I had it brought down ; I knew you would presently be better. . . . That is perfect. . . . Now hold fast of my arm. We only have to get down the stoop, you know. Why, you are almost as strong as I am. . . . Leah, don't stop ; use a little real nerve ; you have so much of it, darling. I sent all the servants away ; they think you are still on the sofa ; and *he,* as I told you, is upstairs. He will not know we have gone until we are actually away. . . . Hold fast of my arm. We are on the stoop now, Leah. The carriage is just below. . . . Why, you are walking splendidly. . . . Be careful of the steps. . . . There, you have got down in ex-

cellent style. . . . Now, here is the carriage. . . .
Raise your foot a little — that is the way my
love."

Leah sank back on the cushions of the carriage.
Presently she had a sense of motion, and of lips
pressed against her cheek. Then a kind of fierce
strength came to her. She put both arms about
her mother's neck. The wild mood, of whose real
vehemence she had no memory, still lingered in
brain and nerves.

" Oh, mamma," she cried, " how right you were
long ago? Tinkling cymbals. . . . that is all it
ever was! . . . Tinkling cymbals! . . . And I
thought it such fine, lovely music ! . . . I could
not hear the discord — I thought it all so sweet
—I was so wayward, so bad, so foolish! . . ."

A little later her mind wandered in a way that
keenly alarmed her mother, whose neck her arms
still clasped.

" Who put that tract into your book, mamma?
Was it Tracy Tremaine? Let us leave this house ;
I don't like that woman with the pale face and
white hair. The Marksleys say that she's *his*
mother. But I can't believe it. . . . No, I can't
believe that *he* would strike Lucy Forbes. Poor
Lucy ! She has had a hard time of it. She says
that her head shows a mark where her husband

struck her. Look, and see. Tracy Tremaine did
not strike her. . . . It was her own husband. . . .
Tracy is a gentleman. . . . The Tremaine family,
you know, is the oldest in the country. . . They
date hundreds of years back, to an old, thin,
queer woman who once insulted me — no, not me,
mamma — *you!* I wouldn't have minded if it had
been I. But she said such dreadful things of you.
She prayed for you, and got a little woman with a
little horrid dog, whose name was Mrs. Dickerson,
to set the dog upon you. . . . Don't you recollect
it all?" . . . And then Leah laughed a loud, dis-
traught laugh. . . .

She never remembered entering her mother's
apartment. And for many days afterward her
memory was lost in the fiery whirl of fever.

Her illness was at no time dangerous. Her delirium now and then took a woful form, but the
physician who attended her constantly declared
that although the brain was inflamed and the pulse
at a rapid stroke, her physical strength still gave
no sign of that fatal downward collapse which,
in so many cases of fever, is the prelude of
death.

His prophecy proved correct. Leah's recovery
was as rapid as her seizure had been. " Yesterday
you were convalescent," her mother cheerfully

said to her, one morning, "and to-day you are nearly well."

A little later she saw Lawrence Rainsford, who had known every least detail of her illness, though Leah herself had no idea of his solicitude. Mrs. Romilly insisted that the interview should be a brief one, and at its end Leah surprised her by saying:

" Mamma, why did Rainsford start when he first saw me to-day ? "

" Did he start, Leah ? "

" Yes. Am I changed at all ? "

" Oh, not much my dear."

" You have always dressed me. You have never let me see a glass. There is no glass in this room. There used to be one. Why has it been taken away ? "

Mrs. Romilly clasped one of Leah's hands in both her own and pressed it softly against her lips. Then she spoke several sentences to which her daughter listened with keenest attention, drawing a long sigh at their end.

"Very well, mamma," she soon said. " Let me look at myself, any way. Bring me a hand-glass."

The hand-glass was brought, and Leah looked into its tell-tale depths. She saw that her golden hair was very deeply streaked with gray. She burst into a flood of tears; the glass almost fell from her hand.

"I am an old woman!" she exclaimed. "Lawrence Rainsford must have thought so. That is why he started when he saw me. . . ."

In a fortnight longer she was able to leave the house. The weather was now verging upon early spring. With her mother she would take walks of slowly increasing length. Thus far she had made no reference whatever to her husband. One day, during a walk of this sort, she questioned her mother concerning him.

"I hear that he is very ill, Leah," was the answer.

"Who told you?"

"Rainsford. He has heard."

"Do you mean dangerously ill?"

"Yes. And from dissipation. But, perhaps, I am wrong to say that. The truth is, Lawrence knows his attending physician; they chanced to be old friends. Dr. Holcroft says that his patient had passed through a terrible period of self-indulgence; he had disappeared from the society of all his acquaintances; for a long time no one could find him. But at last he was discovered, and in a most wretched state. Dr. Holcroft was summoned. An attack of delirium tremens soon afterward ensued, from which the unhappy man gradually recovered. But on the verge of recovery a malarial fever set in, due, no doubt, to the reduced condition of his system. No fear was entertained for several days. Then the fever changed to one of typhoidal nature, with a complication of pneumonia besides. In this condition he still lingers."

A long silence followed Mrs. Romilly's announcement. Leah at length looked at her mother.

"I am his wife, after all," she said. "I ought to go to him."

"You, Leah! You, who are yourself just recovering from a severe sickness!"

Again Leah was silent. Then with a certain tender timidity, her eyes once more sought those of her mother.

"Oh, mamma," she murmured, "you are so fine, so noble! He insulted you, but still, after all, he *is* my husband! . . . And you have always found it so easy to forgive. . . . What if *you* should go to his bedside now? Do I ask too much of you when I ask you to go in my place?"

"I went four days ago, Leah," said Mrs. Romilly, quietly. "I went, and offered my services. A domestic came and told me that they were not needed. There was no other answer."

Leah felt a thrill pass through her as she listened to these simple yet significant words. She saw her mother's beautiful soul in a new light, as we see a sunbeam strike the peak of a sublime mountain-top in a new way.

"You are a saint!" she exclaimed. "Nobody but a real saint could have acted like that!"

Mrs. Romilly answered with one of her peaceful smiles.

The next day the tidings came that Tracy Tremaine was dead.

XV.

LEAH felt no grief. The old love had long been dead in her heart. Still, this miserable end of so young a life, once treasured past all price, could not but shock and sadden her. She thought how wild her grief would have been if death had dealt him its blow in those happy vanished days. Perhaps this reflection increased the melancholy of her mood. In the black garb which she at once assumed, with her golden, gray-streaked hair and her face which now, after her sickness, would always look a little faded, though still most interestingly and refinedly beautiful, she made a picture that only a very careless eye could dwell upon without afterward remembering.

"I will do just as you tell me," she said to her mother. "It seems to me that I should forget everything now."

"Yes, Leah, that is right; but you must not go there alone. I fear to have you do so. I have heard from Rainsford"—

"What have you heard from Rainsford?" she eagerly broke in.

"That the Tremaine clan has massed itself together in displeased congress; that very bitter things are said of you and very compassionating things of your dead husband; that your claim to inherit as his widow is held a matter for legal dispute, on the ground of deliberate desertion. I suppose we are to be two against a great many. But we must make a firm stand. We must not permit this overbearing race to drive us to the wall."

Leah went to where her mother sat. She put both hands about one of Mrs. Romilly's, and held it thus while she spoke.

"You shall find me strong and resolute, mamma. . . . But I only wish that he had given some sign of regret before the last. That would have taken from what we are about to do the atmosphere of mere worldly policy which now surrounds it, and have touched our action with a color of real sentiment. I don't mean as regards the opinion or judgment of society; I mean, rather, the new impulse which would be born of pardon and pity for the dead. We should both feel it, mamma. I find that it is hard not to forgive the dead, simply because they have passed away, whatever were their misdeeds. But if they have wounded or wronged us in life, and yet leave some souvenir of repentance to reach its appeal out of the final silence, why, then I should fancy that it was a very easy thing to let our thought of them grow as tender as the grass-blades that the next Spring will draw from the cold earth above their graves! . . . Oh, I should so like to believe, mamma, that Tracy Tremaine does not side with his people *now*, wherever and whatever he may be! And if I only had some proof of this — some proof besides those remorseful words which you said he spoke on that wretched evening — I should gain twice the courage that I mean presently to show, and feel myself possessed of twice the reason for showing it."

The unshed tears stood in Mrs. Romilly's eyes as she looked up at Leah and said:

" My darling, it cannot be! No voice can come to us from the dead! But your place is now at your husband's side; they must not push you away; they must not be let to push you. It is something that we need not argue about; it is something that we may merely understand and accept. As for *his* justification of our course, I am confident that amid the immortality in whose existence I have never through all my life lost faith, he must now (spiritually cleansed of faults that have cost us both so much pain) approve and sanction our behavior!"

Only an hour or so after this Leah received a letter written by her dead husband. It seemed like a direct answer to her eager yearning. It was dated a month previous to his death. Tremaine had never been a scribe; the style of the whole communication was weak enough, and some of its sentences not only lacked grace but coherence as well. And yet the spirit of the document breathed a sincere contrition. Its writer appeared to anticipate his approaching end. He expressed himself unworthy of ever again receiving his wife's notice; still, he had yielded to a mood of intense remorse, and had determined that she should one day learn of the bitter self-contempt from which he suffered. That day would doubtless be when he was no more. He had no hope of her pardon, and therefore he would arrange that she should not read these lines until after he was dead.

Such a letter was precisely what Leah had wished.

"It arms us both," she said to her mother, just before they started for the house in which Tremaine lay. "The dead man is on our side; we know it now. Let this haughty family deny our claim; he authorizes it."

Leah passed the threshold of her residence with a steady step and a collected mien. She inquired of the servant who admitted herself and her mother where Mr. Tremaine's body had been placed. On hearing the desired tidings she went quietly upstairs to the room indicated, followed by her faithful and devoted mother.

The room was empty when they entered it. They looked together at the face of the dead; it was fearfully altered. Scarcely a vestige of its old beauty remained. Excess and disease had wrought miserable wreck upon it. A little later Mrs. Tremaine entered the room, accompanied by two ladies, both her near kinswomen.

All three of the new-comers directed looks of mournful horror upon Leah and her mother. One was a Mrs. Amsterdam, who had been a Miss Tremaine; she was the sister of the dead man's mother; she was stouter than Mrs. Tremaine, but had the same light-tinted eyes and arching nose. The other was a Mrs. Van Corlear, who had also been a Miss Tremaine, though her relationship was more distant. She had a handsome, swarthy, black-eyed face, and a very queenly carriage; she was a great leader in society, and noted for her strong patrician tendencies. Both Mrs. Amsterdam and Mrs. Van Corlear had met and known Leah; they had, indeed, been present at her wedding, and extended their full, gracious recognition of the alliance.

But they both regarded her now as though she were some impertinent intruder. Leah quickly saw their plain and positive hostility. She began coolly to untie her bonnet-strings. At the same time, in a low voice, she said to her mother:

"I want you to remain here with me to-night, mamma. You will, will you not?"

"Certainly, Leah."

The three ladies exchanged shocked looks. Then Mrs. Van Corlear spoke, addressing Leah:

"You cannot possibly mean what you have just said."

"Why should I not mean it?" Leah asked calmly.

"Oh, do not attempt to argue with her here," murmured Mrs. Tremaine, in a sort of frozen whisper, to Mrs. Van Corlear. "They — they would not scruple, you know, Katharine, to speak loudly, to — to say dreadful things. . . . And we — we are quite in their power; we must submit, you know."

"True," said Mrs. Amsterdam, very faintly, with the edges of her lips. "Anything would be better than the least disturbance."

Leah gave her mother a despairing glance. Immediately afterward Mrs. Romilly said, with her sweet voice so modulated that it seemed a portion of the hush which filled this chamber of death:

"Ladies, there is nothing that could induce either my daughter or myself to cause a shadow of disturbance. Pray be certain of that. Leah to-day received a letter written by the dead. In that letter Tracy Tremaine implores her forgiveness. I am sure that she had already forgiven him, and" —

"Forgiven him!" broke forth Mrs. Tremaine, bursting into tears. "Oh, Katharine, Susan, did I not tell you they had come here to insult us? . . . What shall we do? It is so hard to act in a case of this terrible sort!"

The next moment Mrs. Tremaine was clasped in the arms of her sister, who endeavored to soothe the trembling lady with certain very low words.

But Mrs. Van Corlear had meanwhile fixed her fine black eyes upon Leah.

"Do you really intend to remain in this house?" she asked, with chilling superciliousness.

"It is my house," Leah answered.

"You left it. You deserted *him.*"

"Ah," said Leah, very placidly, and with a sad

smile, "you must not presume to address such words to me. If so, I shall have but one course left."

"What course?"

"I shall insist upon your immediate departure."

Mrs. Van Corlear's large frame visibly quivered. She was a sort of social despot, in her way; it seemed to her that this was the very acme of daring insolence.

"You have no right to be here — none whatever," she said. "You are a faithless and culpable wife. Your conduct has horrified us all. We come of a family that support each other. We will not have one of our race injured and insulted without resenting it. We have all gathered about poor Tracy now, and you cannot drive us away. We are of the same blood with him; we are Tremaines. Of course you do not understand what it is to be a Tremaine. We showed you the greatest tolerance and forbearance until you proved *that* to us. We acknowledged you. No Tremaine had ever married like this before; but we acknowledged you. In place of gratitude you have exhibited the worst sort of thanklessness. You cannot assert any wifely dignity now; it is too late. You cannot drive us away; we will not go."

"Not a word, Leah," said Mrs. Romilly. She saw her daughter's face pale and twitch; she put an arm about Leah's waist, and a hand within hers as well. "Remember *where we are*," she went on. "Say nothing. Bear this, and more, in silence. Silence is far best."

"You are right, mamma," Leah said. "Let us go into another room. We remain here to-night — both of us." She loudened her voice a little as she continued: "And to-morrow, at the funeral, I shall know where my place is, and keep it. Come."

They left the room together. They remained in the house that night. They saw no one until the following day, except two of the servants. But a great family-conclave had assembled. Steps passed their closed door, and low voices were heard in halls and in neighboring apartments until quite a late hour. Then, at last, all was still. Neither Leah nor her mother got much sleep that night.

"Oh, what would I have done without you?" Leah said, while her arms clasped her mother's neck. "How could I have gone through it all? You are my staff. If I had not you to lean upon, the arrogance of this strange, implacable family would have overwhelmed me. I should have sunk down; I should have had no nerve, no spirit to bear up against them. Trouble and sickness have tamed me so, mamma, darling! I am so changed from that wilful Leah of other days!"

"Changed! yes!" said Mrs. Romilly, kissing her; "but changed for the better, my child. I think that I love you even more now than I did then!"

"No — no," said Leah. "You have always loved me the same! Yours was the perfection of a mother's love — from the very first! All the fault, all the shortcoming, all the error, lay in myself!"

The funeral took place at ten o'clock the next morning. Leah and her mother went below stairs at half-past nine. The drawing-room was filled with her husband's kindred; they had mustered in full force. Leah clung to her mother's arm. Together they moved toward the coffin. Leah's face was draped with a heavy widow's veil. Mrs. Romilly guided her daughter to the head of the coffin. Mrs. Tremaine sat there, surrounded by several dark-robed ladies. The husband of Mrs. Van Corlear, a tall man, with bushy gray whiskers and gold eye-glasses crowning an austere nose, stood solemnly at the side of Mrs. Tremaine.

No chair was near at hand, and this gentleman offered none.

Mrs. Romilly looked at him with a stately mildness.

"A chair for my daughter, please," she said.

Her words were hardly above a whisper, but they carried command.

Mr. Van Corlear, with an august gravity, went and got two chairs. He placed them at the foot of the coffin. Mrs. Romilly bowed her thanks, and then, with her own hands, moved both chairs to within a few inches of where Mrs. Tremaine sat. A flutter passed through the little sombre-clad group. A shivering sob was heard from Tremaine's mother, as she buried her face in her black-bordered handkerchief. Mrs. Romilly pointed to one of the vacant chairs. Leah sank into it. She then seated herself at Leah's side.

The funeral was to occur at a church in the lower portion of Second Avenue, whose contiguous graveyard had long held the Tremaine family-vault. Carriages were in waiting outside. When the coffin had been borne to the hearse, and the relatives rose to follow it, Leah slipped her hand within her mother's arm, and so passed out through the hall and down the stoop. Mr. Van Corlear had given his arm to Mrs. Tremaine.

They were directly in front of Mrs. Romilly and Leah; the former, with watchful promptitude, had contrived to make this intervening distance as slight as possible. But when all four had reached the sidewalk, and Mr. Van Corlear, having opened the door of the first carriage, was about to assist his companion inside of it, Mrs. Romilly, with Leah's hand close-pressed round her arm, glided in front of them.

"My daughter will take this carriage," she said, very softly.

The gentleman's grasp was upon the door-knob of the vehicle. For just an appreciable instant he opposed what Mrs. Romilly sought to do. Then their eyes met. His were full of gloom, bewilderment, and even decorous indignation as well. Hers were clear, peaceful, determined.

"His mother!" broke from Mr. Van Corlear, as if those two words, however faintly uttered, could exert a paralyzing force.

"His wife!" said Mrs. Romilly, indicating Leah with a decisive yet thoroughly courteous motion of the head. And then she composedly pushed her child toward the open doorway of the carriage. A loud, distracted sigh sounded from behind Mrs. Tremaine's heavy veil. But the dark little drama had ended. Mrs. Romilly had gained her point, and at least twenty eyes had seen her gain it. She closed the carriage door with her own hand after they were both seated. Then she pulled down the curtain at either window, and kissed Leah, who had begun to tremble.

"There, my child," she said, "I think it is all over now. They will give you your fitting place, after this. They see that I will not let them take it from you. You shall be nearest him at the church, nearest him at the grave. . . . But I am almost sure that there will be no further trouble."

She was right. They had seen the last of this dreadful, untimely antagonism. Whatever form, in the future, the offended pride of the Tremaines meant to take, it had resolved upon at least a present course of concession and surrender.

XVI

BUT Leah, in the months of seclusion that followed her husband's death, gradually found that no further torments of hostility were to be inflicted upon her. She received the full amount of her inheritance, paid over in polite solemnity by Tremaine's executors, who had both been near of kin to him. But the whole family dropped her acquaintance forever. This was their majestic revenge for having presumed to let one of their race stain his own name by wronging her. If she had been notably to blame — if they could have surrounded the decease of their kinsman with any romantic perfume of melancholy martyrdom — if they could have persuaded themselves that he had not injured the sanctity of that precious affair which they called "his position," and that Leah had not come forth from the unhappy episode with a provoking accompaniment of innocence and misfortune, they might have extended to her no small amount of lenient indulgence. But that certain real and disgraceful facts had transpired, and that both sympathy and pity had been given the young widow to the detriment of her dead husband's past repute as a gentleman, these high-strung relations found flagrantly offensive.

Malicious reports reached Leah, but she hardly heeded them. She had grown quite careless of the world whence they sprung. She now reoccupied with her mother their former residence. When her term of conventional mourning had ceased, she took pleasure in entertainments of a purely social and yet moderate-toned description; gatherings at which there would be some one, perhaps, who could produce charming music, or some one who could read with skill and feeling from the poets, or some one famed for rare gifts of conversation. She would sometimes reflect on the milder yet richer enjoyment which evenings like these afforded, and contrast it with the feverish rush, the garish glitter, the excited whirl of other hours.

"What a vain pomp that all was!" she more than once said to her mother. "And to think that it all goes on just the same! — that the cymbals are still tinkling, and the vanities still flaunting themselves with the same old peacock strut!"

"And yet you are not socially satisfied, Leah,"

her mother once said, with a look at Rainsford, who now often dropped in during an evening. "We have both noticed it; have we not, Lawrence?"

"I am afraid that we have," agreed Rainsford, with a latent touch of humor stirring his native gravity.

Leah gave a soft laugh. All her tones and movements were softened, nowadays. Her dark robes suited this change; they brought out the poetry in her thinned, faded face, with the gray-streaked hair above its pathetic delicacy of outline. She still had beauty, and of a most uniquely interesting sort; only, she did not dream that the least remnant of it had been left; she would look into the glass and openly call herself an old woman. Perhaps it was because of this complete unconsciousness with respect to a single personal charm, this entire absence of the remotest coquetry, this pretty and yet thoroughly sincere demureness, that now invested her with a novel and original fascination.

"Have you both found me out in my culpable discontent?" she asked. "Well, I will make you both a confession; I have picked and chosen the members of my little *salon* with great care; I have gone very devoutly and diligently to work. But I feel that it is quite a failure, after all."

"And why?" asked Mrs. Romilly, though she suspected what answer would come.

"Why?" echoed Leah. "My people are so few of them enough in earnest. There is the main trouble. My first danger was in founding an asylum for disappointed fashionables. But that danger I foresaw and avoided in time. There is nothing so abhorrent to me as the woman (yes, she is usually a woman) who, because she has not the proper amount of money or beauty or caste to shine beside such bright butterflies as Mrs. Chichester, would cultivate what she calls 'an intellectual taste.' She must nurture that dainty sort of hypocrisy in some other drawing-room than mine. I could instance several distinct cases where I have found her in several distinct shapes, and headed off her intentions with adroit strategy. Then my second danger was in falling upon the mere scholars. If there is anything at once both delightful and dreary it is scholarship. I have not the least objection to all of my guests acquiring Sanskrit; but they must not be professional with it; they must not simply know books, they must have a feeling for them. Learning unleavened by imagination produces the pedagogue;

and the place for the pedagogue is not the parlor,
it is the schoolroom." Here Leah paused, laughing. "Do I bore you?" she asked, looking at
both Rainsford and her mother equally. "Do
you find my confession tiresome, or do you want
to hear what was my third danger?"

"By all means we want to hear," said Rainsford. "In giving us the details of your struggle
you can make us perceive more clearly your unat-
tained ideal."

She laughed again at his sober satire; the notes
of her laughter were still young and sweet. "My
third danger," she re-commenced, "was the Bohemians. . . . Oh, you need neither of you look
incredulous! Of course, I don't mean the gentlemen with soiled collars and shiny coat-sleeves, nor
the ladies with drooping ringlets and skirts that
barely touch the floor. There are plenty of Bohemians who respect their milliners and tailors, I
find. But they are Bohemians, all the same; they
think with an incessant laxity; they never read
anything, but always skim it; they regard science
as a fairy-tale, philosophy as a fantasy, literature
as a trifle; they are strikingly clever, and nothing
more; everything about them is filigree and embellishment, and they possess so much that it's a
mystery how they can thus attach it to nullity.

They always pass for persons of great mental culture, but they are really the most hollow of shams. Their minds are stocked with the names and the substance of many things, but they have reached the spirit of nothing. . . . Well, these (and perhaps a few others whom I will not mention) were the dangers I wished to shun. But now I discover that my little sifted and sorted community doesn't satisfy me, after all. There is such a small amount of genuine talent about it. I want to secure people who will not be mere lookers-on in my Vienna; I want them to be more individual and operative, less unassertive and sympathizing."

"Such assemblages are not possible in this new land of ours," said Rainsford, very seriously. "We need at least a century to make them so — if we live a century longer as the republic we have aimed to be. Brilliant men and women will meanwhile rise among us; not a few such have already risen. But a wide diffusion of just that special humanity to which you refer is yet a future gain. Our universities must throw a broader academic shadow; then, like the sturdy ivy of other climates, that kind of growth will thrive there. . . ."

But if Leah was truly disappointed by what she

chose to term her failure, the pleasant buoyancy
of her spirits gave slight evidence of this fact.
She had been more than three years a widow when
her mother said to her, one day:

"Leah, if I should die how lonely you would
be!"

"Mamma!" she cried, "how can you speak like
that!"

Mrs. Romilly gave a very cheerful smile. "Oh,
I can't live forever, darling; and there is a good
difference between our ages."

Leah was close at her mother's side now. She
was looking very intently into the sweet hazel
eyes that she knew so well.

"Tell me," she murmured, with great earnestness, "have you fancied anything, mamma? Have
you had any premonition of illness?—any. . . ."

"My dear," broke in Mrs. Romilly, very fondly
stroking the young widow's gray-gold hair, "I
never was better in my life."

Leah watched her wonderingly. "Then why
did you try to frighten me?"

"Not at all, darling. I did not try. Is it like
me to try?"

"No, said Leah, kissing her a little dubiously.

"I only meant," Mrs. Romilly continued, "that
you would be quite alone if I had to go. And of

course the chances of your outliving me by a good many years, child, are very strong."

"Oh, but I don't want to think of them."

"Is it not best to think of them?"

Leah gave a sudden start. "What do you mean?" she questioned, in quite an altered voice.

"Suppose you married, my love?" said her mother, with great tenderness. "Very happily, I mean, *this time.*" She laid strong accent upon the last two low-spoken words.

Leah broke into a nervous laugh. "Married?" she exclaimed, incredulously. "I? At my age?" Then she laughed again. "Oh, no, of course I am not old — that is, not in *years*. But look at my hair — it's grayer than yours!" Here her face took a comic sadness. "I can't dream what has put this idea into your wise, cool head. Because you are in love with me you must n't think anyone else is. Why, who would ask me to marry him?"

"I know one who would, Leah."

She watched her mother with a trembling lip for several seconds, after this. Her face had grown quite pale.

"Yes!" she exclaimed, with a mournful bitterness. "I understand! He might ask it if he thought you wanted it. He might ask it out of *pity!* Hush, mamma, . . . he is a great painter, now; he is still young; men grow old so much more slowly than women. It is dreadful for me even to fancy his making such a sacrifice, when he might. . . . Oh, no; let us never speak of this again! Never, now! Promise me."

"But, Leah," came the gently persistent words, "if it were not a sacrifice? If—"

"But it *is!* I know better than you! Promise me that this shall be the last of the subject between us!"

"I promise, then," said Mrs. Romilly.

That same evening Rainsford came to the house. Leah sat in the drawing-room alone, letting her fingers wander listlessly over the keys of the piano. She had not heard the outer bell ring. But it had last rung some time ago. Mrs. Romilly had contrived to meet Rainsford in the hall, and to hold a conversation of some length with him in an adjacent room. He was forced to louden his step a little as he now approached the piano. Then she turned and saw him.

"Pray do n't rise," he said. "I will sit just there, at your side. You can go on playing, if you wish. You know how I like Schumann."

Leah played on for a little while.

"But it is so absurb," she presently said, paus-

ing. "I have no touch—no style—no expression. There is so much music in me, and yet I
never could bring it out, somehow."

"You play much better than you did," he said,
with a critical directness which might have struck
her as brusque in anyone else. But she had long
ago grown used to his grave candor.

"Do you really think that?" she asked, inter-
estedly.

"I am sure of it."

"How long is it since you have noticed the
change?"

"Oh, a long time."

"A long time?" she repeated, in surprise. "Do
you mean a year ago?"

A very rich smile filled his rugged, thoughtful
face. "No," he answered; "longer than a year
ago. Three years. . . . Since the time when you
began to see everything so differently—to be the
high-minded, large-souled woman that you are
now."

Her head had slightly drooped. But she gave a
faint laugh. "When I began to get old," she said.

"You have never been old."

She stole a sad glance at him. "Don't tell me
that gray hair is n't an accompaniment of age," she
said, "or I shall accuse you of paying me a wan-

ton compliment. And how funny that would be
from you!"

"I can't help what you think of it. The change
has only made you more beautiful in my eyes. It
tells me of the other change."

She looked at him wistfully, eagerly, then, while
he bent nearer toward her. Her voice had a
tremor as she said: "Ah! you mean that it
makes you sorry for me!"

"Sorry? It tells me that you have suffered,
surely."

The tears glistened in her gaze, but they did
not fall.

"I — I don't want to be pitied," she said, with a
pathetic, faltering wilfulness, that was like a dreamy
memory of other long-past rebellious days. "It
makes me pity myself more. And it is not well
to do that. It turns one's heart away from all the
many sorrows in the world which one can help."

"That you *do* help so often! That you conse-
crate your life to helping!"

She had drooped her head again; both her
hands lay folded in her lap.

"I was very wayward and selfish once," she
said. "I have a great deal to make up for."

"So you think, now, of the sorrows of others
for this reason?"

" I try to think of them."

" I wonder if you have thought much of one special sorrow." .

" Whose ? " she said, still not raising her look.

" Mine," he responded.

" Yours ? "

" Yes, mine. The sorrow that you gave me . . . well, not so very long ago. It has never died. I think it has even gained in strength since it was first dealt me. To see you grow more lovely, more womanly, more worthy of a man's complete devotion, has made it heavier and keener."

She looked up at him then. Her eyes were burning through their mists of tears.

" I thought all that was past ! " she said.

" No," he answered; " it can never pass except in one of two ways. Death must end my pain, Leah, or love — your love — must end it ! If you cannot give me your love, tell me so to-night. Then I will wait — as bravely and as patiently as I can — for the other colder cure."

She slowly rose, looking almost saintly in her sweetness; then, standing beside him, with her dark robes and her pale, pure face, she reached out for one of his hands while he still remained seated. She took it between both her own, and slowly raised it to her lips. As she did so he knew that her tears were falling upon it. But her voice was now quite clear, though very soft, as she murmured:

"You need not wait for death. I give you love instead. . . . I give you a love that will last, I think, even beyond death!"